Suddenly he heard a strangled cry coming from the shower

Without thinking, Mac threw back the curtain.

"What is it...Grace? What's wrong?"

Stark naked, she stared at him with wide eyes. Her mouth formed a perfect little O.

Even as he tried to reassure her that she was okay, he couldn't help but absorb the details of her body.

An unexpected heat of desire knocked him on his heels. Good to know past betrayals hadn't killed every impulse in his body, but talk about poor timing. He tried to turn away, but Grace ran shaky hands across her flat tummy.

And then he finally understood her distress.

Across her belly, vertical lines, so faint they were all but invisible.

The lines a woman's abdomen acquires as her body stretches to accommodate a pregnancy.

She was somebody's mother.

Dear Harlequin Intrigue Reader,

As we ring in a new year, we have another great month of mystery and suspense coupled with steamy passion.

Here are some juicy highlights from our six-book lineup:

- Julie Miller launches a new series, THE PRECINCT, beginning with *Partner-Protector*. These books revolve around the rugged Fourth Precinct lawmen of Kansas City whom you first fell in love with in the TAYLOR CLAN series!

- *Rocky Mountain Mystery* marks the beginning of Cassie Miles's riveting new trilogy, COLORADO CRIME CONSULTANTS, about a network of private citizens who volunteer their expertise in solving criminal investigations.

- Those popular TOP SECRET BABIES return to our lineup for the next *four* months!

- Gothic-inspired tales continue in our spine-tingling ECLIPSE promotion.

And don't forget to look for Debra Webb's special Signature Spotlight title this month: *Dying To Play*.

Hopefully we've whetted your appetite for January's thrilling lineup. And be sure to check back every month to satisfy your craving for outstanding suspense reading.

Enjoy!

Denise O'Sullivan
Senior Editor
Harlequin Intrigue

UNDERCOVER BABIES

ALICE SHARPE

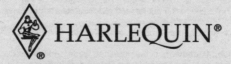

HARLEQUIN®

TORONTO • NEW YORK • LONDON
AMSTERDAM • PARIS • SYDNEY • HAMBURG
STOCKHOLM • ATHENS • TOKYO • MILAN • MADRID
PRAGUE • WARSAW • BUDAPEST • AUCKLAND

This book is dedicated, with love, to my son,
Officer Joseph Sharpe.

ISBN 0-373-22823-6

UNDERCOVER BABIES

Copyright © 2005 by Alice Sharpe

www.eHarlequin.com

Printed in U.S.A.

ABOUT THE AUTHOR

Alice Sharpe met her husband-to-be on a cold, foggy beach in Northern California. One year later they were married. Their union has survived the rearing of two children, a handful of earthquakes registering over 6.5, numerous cats and a few special dogs, the latest of which is a yellow Lab named Annie Rose. Alice and her husband now live in a small rural town in Oregon, where she devotes the majority of her time to pursuing her second love, writing.

Alice loves to hear from readers. You can write her at P.O. Box 755, Brownsville, OR 97327. SASE for reply is appreciated.

Books by Alice Sharpe

CAST OF CHARACTERS

Grace—She wakes up in an alley, dressed in rags, with no idea who she is or where she belongs. Only an overpowering anxiety and the marks on her body that signify she has given birth keep her going.

Travis "Mac" MacBeth—The former whistle-blowing cop, now a private detective, was abandoned early in his life by his mother. He makes it his mission to reunite Grace with the baby she can't remember.

Police Chief Barry—For political reasons, he's mounting a vendetta against Mac that will keep him from reclaiming the career he loves. Is there nothing Barry won't do to discredit Mac?

Beatrice Dally—Mac's elderly aunt. She senses immediately that Grace isn't a homeless addict and helps Mac recognize the first clue to her identity.

Elvis—Who is this flamboyant Elvis impersonator, and why does he keep showing up at the most opportune of times?

Casey Bellows—How does this terrifying killer always seem to stay one step ahead?

Doctor Daniel Priestly—The doctor of Boward Key, Florida. Has this arrogant, autocratic man set in motion the disaster that befalls Grace, or is it Grace's past catching up with her as he insists?

Paula Priestly—Though she always has and still does support her husband without reservation, she's also been a friend to Grace when she needed one.

Officer Neville Dryer—This lawman makes it clear he believes Grace's unsavory past is responsible for her current problems.

Chapter One

The minute she opened her eyes, she knew everything was wrong.

The coarse pavement on which she half sat, half lay. The iron stairs disappearing up the side of the cinder block building above. The row of padlocked doors, each with no number, no window. The Dumpster she leaned against. The crumpled cardboard boxes. The dark crevices. The pervading stink of rot and abandoned hope. All wrong.

And the rain. Half sleet. Cold. Icy. Miserable.

Wrong.

She tried sitting straighter and felt a sharp pain in her left shoulder. She rubbed it with numb fingers. The tattered sleeve of her red-and-black plaid coat alarmed her. She checked out the rest of her clothing. No hat. That explained the rain dripping off the end of her nose. Grungy gray pants, no socks, brown boots that looked and felt as though they belonged to someone else, a man, maybe.

She got to her feet, her bare toes rubbing against the wet leather. She ached, head to toe.

What was she doing dressed this way? What was she doing in this alley?

Another question knocked her back against the Dumpster. *Who was she?*

Panic pushed the air out of her lungs, left her gasping. She racked the recesses of her memory, pleading with the synapses to wake up. *Give me a name, a purpose, a home, something…anything,* she begged. Moments passed and she found herself still lost in a fog as murky and unfathomable as the gray puddles at her feet.

Lost, inside and out.

She looked up and down the gloomy alley. No answers, but one end looked brighter than the other and the light drew her. Within a few halting steps, an uneven edge of worn pavement caught the toe of her boot and sent her plummeting to the ground. She landed in a heap, one cheek imbedded in gravel, the other pelted by biting rain. For a while, she lacked the drive, the energy, the will to move. Eventually, survival instincts kicked in and she struggled back to her feet.

Gray mud dripped off the front of her coat. A new tear in her pants rubbed against a matching slash in her knee as she staggered forward. Reaching the light at the end of the alley became a goal of tantamount importance. Salvation lay in the light.

The sound of footsteps from behind startled her and she stumbled to one side of the alley, cowering near a short flight of cement steps all but obscured by soggy drifts of wet newspaper. The approaching figure evolved into a man with a stride so menacing she couldn't look away though she yearned to do so. Her heart thundered in her chest as he came abreast.

Rain hammered the brim of his hat, the shoulders of his black mackintosh. Pausing, he stared straight at her, eyes as dark and flat as the shadows from which he'd materialized. If she'd harbored even a glimmer of hope that she could turn to this man for aid, it died in that instant.

And then he moved off toward the coveted light at the end of the alley. Shivering as rivulets of freezing water found their way between her shoulder blades, she fled in the other direction, toward the dark end of the alley, toward an obscurity as far-reaching as the vacuum inside her head.

TRAVIS H. MACBETH, known to everyone but his favorite aunt as Mac, was sick of the rain. The fact that the new year had just begun and the bulk of winter lay ahead didn't help. Welcome to Billington, Indiana, January-style.

He should be home tallying up nice, dry numbers and sipping something hot and fortifying instead of slogging through the wet, cold evening.

It had all started out so straightforward. Help an old friend's father collect data in his bid for the next mayoral race. Maybe do some good, maybe shake up the status quo, maybe, if he was really lucky, help give the boot to both the current mayor and Police Chief Barry.

What Mac hadn't figured on were his own compulsions.

At thirty-seven, a private detective with at least two careers behind him, shouldn't he be wise enough to avoid situations like this one?

As he sloshed through the sludge, the answer was clear— apparently not.

Of course, he didn't *need* to make the rounds of Billington's less desirable localities. No one made him walk this dusk patrol and, in fact, he'd been warned by his former partner on the police force that his presence down here annoyed the hell out of the reigning powers that be. Of course, he already knew this. He had the citations for breaking laws no one else even knew existed to prove it.

As for the street people he encountered? Night after night, the same weary faces regarded him with the same indifference. His presence here warmed no one's heart, least of all his own.

He knew it, he just couldn't seem to stop himself.

As he approached the alley right before Broadhurst, he slowed his pace. Inside a soggy paper sack, he carried a giant roast beef and Swiss cheese hoagie. He wondered if Jake would be waiting for his sandwich in such horrible weather. On the other hand, where else did the old man have to go? Jake wasn't a homeless shelter kind of guy.

So every night on his walk, Mac made it a point to mosey this direction and bring the old boozer a sandwich, one packed with as much protein and as many calories as possible. Jake seemed to appreciate the gesture, so there went Mac's earlier speculation that no one cared if he patrolled these back streets.

Jake cared. Well, probably.

A man had to settle for what he could get.

From his peripheral vision, Mac saw a dark shape charge from the mouth of the heavily shadowed alley. He braced himself for an attempted mugging, then he recognized Jake's coat, a red-and-black hunters plaid that always looked out of place buried in the city. He relaxed. Big mistake. The old man plowed into him so hard it rocked Mac on his feet.

"Damn it, Jake, what in the hell's going on?" Mac growled as he grabbed bony shoulders and twisted the slight figure away from him. The deli sack bounced against the old man's chest as Jake wrapped a muscular arm around his attacker's throat, tight enough to stop further aggression, not so tight as to hurt him. "Since when do you assault people? And jeez, man, what in the world did you tangle with? No offense, but you stink."

As he spoke, he moved the two of them into the weak light of a street lamp and was surprised to see how dark the top of Jake's gray head looked. From the front it had always appeared so gray.

Jake went slack.

"That's better," Mac said. If turned loose, would Jake attack the next passerby? Mac looked up and down the abandoned street and admitted there likely wouldn't be a next passerby, not on this wild winter night.

Old Jake suddenly grumbled a half dozen words in a voice that shook Mac down to his shoes.

"Jake? Is that my name? Jake?"

Mac withdrew his arm as he backed away. That wasn't Jake's alcohol-soaked slur.

He found himself staring into the dazed eyes of a young woman in her early twenties. Short black hair lay plastered against her head. Large blue eyes dominated her face though high cheekbones and a surprisingly sensual mouth demanded their share of attention, as well. She seemed half child, half woman, a rather beguiling combination marred only by blue-tinged lips and the aura of fear mingled with shock that hovered around her like the wavering halo around a winter moon.

She was also wearing Jake's coat and what looked like his boots.

"Who are you?" he demanded.

She blinked. She looked confused and miserable, and he wished he had an umbrella to offer her.

"Is Jake my name?" she repeated.

"You don't know your name?"

As she shook her head, his heart sank. She had to be homeless, penniless, adrift in a fog of drugs or booze or mental illness. She had to be someone's daughter, someone's lover, a beauty faded before it blossomed with such a shocked look in her eyes that it brought to mind a small animal trapped by a larger one.

Eyes like his mother's eyes, so many years ago.

He resisted the urge to turn away from her but it was there, growing more pronounced by the moment—the desire to turn away, to shield himself from her raw pain and the subsequent feeling of helplessness it engendered in his soul.

She rubbed her throat where he'd manhandled her.

"Sorry about that," he said and, as an act of penance, took off his favorite gray felt hat and pushed it down on her head.

Engulfed by the hat, she stared at him still, her eyes glittering slits beneath the brim. "Do you know me?" she insisted.

He shook his head. "No."

Her voice turned to a pathetic squeak as she mumbled, "I'm not Jake?"

"No, but you seem to be wearing his clothes. Where is he?"

She managed to look even more bewildered and he knew she didn't have an answer. He also knew he couldn't leave her like this, nor could he call the cops and risk their sometimes heavy-handed treatment with the down and out, not when it was so obvious she struggled just to stay on her feet. It also wouldn't help her win hearts if the cops found her with him. There was a shelter within walking distance, one run by two ex-nuns with medical training. He'd take her there.

But first, he'd make sure she hadn't clubbed old Jake and stolen his clothes. "Come with me," he demanded, moving toward the alley.

She stood her ground, if that teetering sway could be called standing.

Opening the sack, he produced the hoagie. "Hungry?"

She stared at the sandwich for a moment before nodding.

"Then come with me. You can eat while we take a short-cut through this alley."

Still, she hesitated though her gaze never left the tightly wrapped hoagie he offered as bait.

"Listen," he said, suddenly impatient. It was cold and his head was wet, thanks to the impetuous gift of his hat. He was worried about Jake. He'd testified in court that day and thus wore a suit under his raincoat, which meant he also wore his good shoes that might never recover from standing around in this torrential downpour. The day had been long and arduous, and he still had paperwork to do.

Taking a couple of powerful steps toward her, wincing as his approach caused her to shrink inside her pilfered clothes, he said, "If I'd wanted to hurt you, I'd have already pulled you into the alley. I wouldn't have waited around risking pneumonia and I wouldn't have offered you a perfectly good sandwich. Come with me or stay here, it's your call."

"Don't leave me," she pleaded, suddenly straightening her slender body and, for a moment, transcending her environment. She wiped the rain from her face and extended a hand. "Please," she added.

He handed her the sandwich and turned away, aware when she fell into step behind him, pleased that she had at least enough street smarts to give herself a little running room in case he turned into an ogre. After all, who knew if she'd stay at the shelter or leave as soon as they fed her properly? If she wound up back on the street, she'd need to be wary if she planned on surviving.

Wary, like his mom.

The girl stayed in the middle of the alley, eating her sandwich with a determination that surpassed mere hunger and spoke of elemental need. As she ate, her gaze darted this way and that, as if she expected a ghost—or worse—to materialize at any moment.

Mac moved aside boxes and shined a small flashlight into dark corners, into Dumpsters, under stairs and in old doorways. The girl stayed close by, moving forward as he did, quiet but watchful. When he upset a nest of empty bottles, the clatter made her jump.

"Your old stash?" he said with an oblique look.

She shook her head, thought about it a moment and then shrugged. "I don't know," she said softly. "Maybe. I...I don't recall...er...drinking."

She smelled as though she did, not only her clothes, but her hair. He didn't know if Jake smelled like booze. Jake had never allowed Mac close enough to get more than a cursory whiff. Jake was little more than a darting hand, an occasional grunted thanks, a turned back. For that matter, Jake wasn't really Jake. Mac had pinned that moniker on him.

They reached the far end of the alley without finding a single sign of Jake. This was the first time Mac had actually entered this particular alley, so there was no way for him to tell if things were the same as usual. After this brief but thorough tour, however, he doubted Jake actually slept there. Not enough cover, not enough privacy. He probably just dropped by at dusk on his way to panhandling drinking money on a busier street, waiting for Mac and his nightly hand-delivered sandwich for fortification.

Mac could think of nothing else to do but get rid of the girl and take himself home. "I know where you can sleep," he told her.

She looked suspicious so he added, "Would you rather stay here in the alley?"

Her answer was immediate and delivered as she glanced back over her shoulder. "No. Please, don't leave me here."

"Then come with me. I know of a shelter run by a couple of fine women. They'll give you a bed for the night and maybe allow you the soul-satisfying pleasure of earning your keep by mopping a floor tomorrow morning. You'll like them."

She wadded up the paper that had surrounded the late, great sandwich and stuck it in her pocket. *Jake's pocket...*

"I'll be happy to earn my keep," she said softly. She punctuated this statement with a yawn that she covered with wet fingers.

She looked so damn pitiful that Mac wanted to fold her in a hug and protect her from the rain, from her confusion, from herself. Instead, he walked away quickly, checking every now and then to make sure she followed, not sure what he'd do if she stopped. What could he do? Who knew better than he that you couldn't help someone who didn't want help?

Her trust in him would have been heartwarming if it wasn't so obvious she was lost enough to follow anyone who offered a ray of hope. It was a big responsibility, being trusted in this way, one that made him antsy lest he fail her. He didn't want to make her significant problems worse, but he wasn't equipped to save her, either. It had taken him most of his life just to save himself and, come to think of it, he hadn't been terribly successful at that chore. If he had, Jessica wouldn't have left him, right?

Thinking about his ex-wife wasn't Mac's idea of a good time, and he approached the shelter with a sigh of relief.

The door to the place stood wide open. Sister Theresa stood framed in the open doorway, talking to a man wearing a long, old-fashioned-looking raincoat. The man carried a compact black bag.

A doctor? If Mac paid the guy for his trouble, would he examine the girl and help her out?

Sister Theresa called to him. "Mac? Is that you? Come in out of the rain. Have a hot cup of coffee or some cocoa. And bring your friend. Everyone's welcome here."

He felt a tug on the back of his coat and turned swiftly. The girl was shaking her head, trembling from the cold or a bad case of nerves, or maybe something less obvious.

"You're going to be fine," he said, putting his hands on her shoulders, trying to reassure her.

She peered around his side, then back at him. My, she had pretty blue eyes. "Is that the woman you mentioned? The *kind* one?"

He furrowed his brows. The quaint phrasing of the question sounded odd, especially coming from this drowned rat of a woman whose sodden clothes probably outweighed her.

"That's Sister Theresa, though you'd never know it by the way she dresses. As you can see, the good sister doesn't go in for the traditional habit. Seems it's your lucky day. Her visitor looks like a doctor—"

He stopped talking because the girl had wrenched herself free and was now walking away from him as fast as she could, which wasn't all that fast but was decidedly determined. He called out to Sister Theresa that he'd be back and trotted after his waif, calling for her to wait up. She pulled the hat down farther on her head and kept walking.

He caught up with her easily and even as he seized her arm, he wondered why he bothered. Reasonable or not, she was a grown woman with the right to make any decision she so desired. No cop would arrest her for changing her mind about a shelter. So far as he knew, she'd done nothing wrong and hurt no one, not even herself. But he couldn't ignore the vulnerable slump of her shoulders or the way her gaze faltered when their eyes met.

She was afraid. If not of Sister Theresa, then of what? Or whom?

"What's the matter?" he asked.

She cast a wary look toward the still lighted doorway and the two figures who had turned back to their conversation. She shook her head as though unable to put this new fear into words.

"Is it the doctor? Do you know him?"

Again she shook her head.

"Then let him examine you." He touched her hand. "Come on—"

Again, he was talking to thin air as she'd managed to dart away. Instead of walking, she'd broken into a run. He'd seen a flash of terror in her eyes before she turned and that flash now yanked him after her.

"Wait," he called, but she only ran faster. The clomping of her boots echoed on the wet sidewalk. A gang of five or six boys parted like the Red Sea as she plowed heedlessly through their midst. He heard them heckle her. Wearing that plaid coat and a man's hat, they probably mistook her for Jake. He doubted she heard a single word.

Then he was among the kids, a few of whom he recognized from the dozens of times he'd seen them roaming the streets. They ignored him, he ignored them. Determined not to lose the girl, he kept up the pace.

It was inevitable that sooner or later the icy sidewalk would claim her and it did as she rounded a corner. He saw her feet slip out from under her and heard her cry as she hit the concrete.

He was there in a second but she was already scrambling to her feet, driven it seemed by panic, more powerful than any drug.

But of what? Of a doctor she'd never met? Of a nun?

She fell again, on hands and knees this time. Another sob, another mad scramble to her feet. He grabbed her shoulders and pulled her toward him. She came kicking and screaming, out of control. She kept crying, "No, No. Please, no."

He wrapped her tightly against him. "It's okay, honey," he said. "Calm down."

"I don't want—"

"I know, I can see that. I'm not going to make you do anything. Tell me what you want me to do."

She collapsed against his chest.

Another group of teenagers—apparently the only people willing to brave the elements—passed on the other side of the street. Mac could see more people peering from sheltered doorways.

He couldn't abandon the quivering mass of flesh and bones who clung to him for support. He just couldn't—not here, not like this.

"Try to walk," he told her. "Let's get out of here."

With his arm around her, he helped her along, but not back toward the unknown terror of the doctor or the Catholic nun.

But where?

The shelter seemed to be out of the question. Making a snap decision, he said, "I'm taking you to my place for the night. You'll be safe there. Tomorrow, we'll think of what we should do."

Even as these words left his lips, he recognized the foolishness of this decision. He was promising this extremely needy young woman a haven for the night and help the next day; he would keep his word, but the motivation for his offer had as many facets as an octopus has arms.

Oh, well.

Where before she'd followed, now she leaned on him heavily, her slight weight no problem, but her sudden emotional withdrawal unnerving. He tried asking her questions, but she ignored him and seemed to put all her energy into the act of walking. She must have hurt her knee when she fell; he noticed she'd developed a slight limp and a whimper when she stepped hard on her right leg.

Eventually, he got her back to his car. By now, he was as wet and smelly as she was. On the way around to the driver's door, he found a spanking new parking ticket tucked under his windshield wiper. Jeez, did these guys follow him around and wait for a meter to run out? The citation went into the glove box with all the others. If the cops didn't knock off all these tickets, he was going to have to go to the D.A. and complain.

It took several minutes to navigate his way across town. During the drive, he tried not to inhale deeply. The two of them smelled like old rubbish stewed in street grime and booze. He'd probably have to fumigate his car.

The girl rubbed her left shoulder and said nothing.

For once, there was a parking spot within a block of his apartment. If anything, the rain had grown icier and more vicious, and, heads down, they made their way to his place. A short flight of stairs seemed like more of a challenge than she was up to; without hesitation, he swept her into his arms and carried her up the stairs.

By the time he unlocked the door, she seemed more zombie than human. He didn't want her clothes, or his outerwear, either, for that matter, inside the apartment proper. He wasn't sure how to tell her she had to strip.

Thankfully, the entry floor was tile, as they both dripped a river of rainwater. An opposing door that locked on its own led to the apartment itself, providing a nice barrier for cold winters. Now, it gave him a staging area for getting his guest ready to come inside. He carefully locked the door to the outside, wondering when the girl would realize she was trapped, tense because he knew he was taking a chance and unsure why he'd put himself in this position.

Wouldn't Chief Barry just love to have him investigated for kidnapping or assault….

Taking off his own coat and hanging it on a hook, he found his testify-in-court suit still relatively dry and clean. His shoes were hopeless. "Take off your clothes down to your underwear," he told her softly. "I'll get you a robe."

She stared down at her clothes as though she'd never seen them before.

"Okay, then," he said, and unlocked the second door. Turning on all the lights as he went, he made his way quickly to his bedroom, the carpeted floor a welcome cushion under his sock-clad feet. He grabbed the raw silk robe his aunt had brought him back from Hong Kong a decade before and hurried back to the entry.

She was still standing where he'd left her. Her eyes were

closed and she looked as if she'd fall down if he blew on her. His first thought was to call a doctor. He quickly dismissed that and comforted himself with the thought that she'd rally after a hot shower and a good night's sleep.

"I'll help you," he told her.

That seemed to rouse her a little. A least she opened her eyes. In the bright light, her irises looked as blue as a summer sky and as guileless as a picnic. Again, he felt a surge of protective ardor that was totally out of place.

He unbuttoned her coat. Jake's coat. Where did she get this awful garment? Under what circumstances did a burned-out boozehound give up his coat on an icy winter day? For money? This girl didn't look like she had two coins to rub together. Out of some kind of loyalty or caring? Did Jake know this woman?

He removed his ruined hat from her head, peeled the wet coat from her body and deposited it on the tile floor. She stood facing him in a flannel shirt so dirty it was hard to tell its original color. Her pants were way too big and tied around her waist with a length of rope. The boots on her feet suddenly looked huge, like clown shoes. He knelt down and untied them, but it really wasn't necessary. They slipped off in his hands and he found she was barefoot underneath. Her tanned feet were damn near frozen to the touch.

"You might want to take the rest of these wet things off," he said, raising the robe between them as a privacy shield.

He heard nothing and ventured a peek. She stood there, swaying.

"All-righty then," he said, and biting the figurative bullet, hoped a sense of modesty didn't pay her a belated visit. Talking all the while about the virtue of hot water and soap, he unbuttoned her shirt and stripped the wet cloth away. He tried to do this without looking, but that proved impossible, especially after he caught a glimpse of what lay hidden under the shirt.

Black silk. A tiny glittering sea horse sewn on to a wisp of black lace.

It was like peeling an egg and finding a diamond instead of a yolk.

Though he tried not to notice, he was a man, after all, and he couldn't help but take heed of the size and shape of her breasts. Not as large as Jessica's, but firm looking and beautifully rounded, this woman's breasts filled the cups of her bra with what appeared to be damn near perfection.

"Pretty underwear," he said, hoping the comment might startle her into speech. More likely, it would earn him a slap across the face, a slap he deserved if his increasingly wayward thoughts were to be considered. She didn't move.

That's when he noticed her staring at the inside of her left arm. He followed her gaze and saw what so mesmerized her were several needle marks and surrounding bruises.

Damn.

Here he'd just about decided she wasn't a druggie and, *pow,* proof. Would she start climbing the walls when her latest hit wore off? "Are you okay?" he demanded. "Talk to me."

She stared at him and shook her head. Had she gone into some kind of shock induced by cold and stress?

"Say something," he demanded.

"I'm…I'm cold," she stammered, hugging herself. Her left shoulder was black and blue.

And then she began plucking at the snarl around her waist, trying to untie the rope, having no luck. She cast him a helpless look and so he tried to come to her aid, but in the end, it proved necessary to take out his pocket knife. Bypassing the knot, he hacked through the rope. The pants immediately slid over her slender hips, puddling on the floor at her feet.

Her panties matched her bra—bedecked with a dazzling sea horse, feminine, expensive, out of place. They, too, covered lovely mounds of flesh, as well as a trim stomach. Both her knees were red, but the right one sported a two-inch gash that looked relatively superficial. Additional bruises marred her thighs and legs.

As she held his hands for support and stepped out of her pants, he wondered again. Who was she? A coed gone astray? A working girl whose favorite john indulged his fantasies by dressing her in fancy lingerie and then pummeling her?

Awkwardly, he pulled the robe over her arms and tied the sash around her waist, studiously trying to ignore the feel of her cold but petal-soft skin. The ripe smell of the alley helped squash amorous thoughts. Supporting half her weight, they shuffled inside the apartment. He closed and locked the door behind them, still babbling like a demented man, covering his own apprehension with the sound of his voice.

"I can't keep thinking of you as 'the girl,'" he said. "It's politically incorrect and after our recent familiarity, a little silly."

No rise from her. No flicker of an eyebrow or curl of a lip. No indignant sneer, no anger. Nothing.

"How about I call you Grace?"

She stared at him, wrinkling her brow as though trying to think.

"Is that name okay with you?" he said, trying his best to force her to speak, concerned that she still could.

She mumbled something that sounded like yes and he let it be. Within minutes, he had her in the shower, underwear and all. He could almost see the hot spray coax her back to life. When she grabbed the soap from his hand, he knew it was time to step away and leave her alone.

"There's shampoo on the shelf in there," he told her.

She answered by handing him her underwear, which she'd wrung out.

As he dropped it in the sink, he heard a strangled cry coming from the shower, then another. Without thinking, he threw back the curtain.

"What is it…Grace? What's wrong?"

Stark naked, she stared at him with wide eyes. Her mouth formed a perfect little *O*.

Even as he tried to reassure her that she was okay, that he'd leave the room or call for help, whatever she wanted, he couldn't help but absorb the details of her body. And wow, what a body she had. Nipples like pink rose buds. Curvaceous waist and hips. Long, shapely legs. Lots of tanned skin, discreet areas of lily white.

The unexpected heat of desire knocked him on his heels. Good to know his ex-wife's betrayal hadn't killed every impulse in his body, but talk about poor timing. He tried to turn away, but the woman—Grace—ran shaky hands across her flat tummy and a new fear crystallized in his head. Was she going to throw up?

And then he finally understood her distress.

Across her belly, vertical lines, so faint they were all but invisible.

The lines a woman's abdomen acquires as her body stretches to accommodate a pregnancy.

His gaze met hers. Tears streamed down her face.

She was somebody's mother.

Chapter Two

Grace managed to gather enough wits to wash her hair and towel dry herself. The man didn't leave the room, though she could feel his intense desire to do so. If he stayed, it must be because she looked as awful as she felt.

A pregnancy. She had a child.

She wiped the tears from her face with shaky fingers.

A baby.

Or not. Maybe the pregnancy hadn't ended well. Maybe that was the tragedy that had propelled her into a lifestyle that ultimately led her to find herself in a stranger's bathroom, needle marks on her arm, covered with bruises, her mind little more than a foggy cliff edged with perilous drops into nothingness.

The man handed her a tissue which she took gratefully and blew her nose.

Competing for attention with an exhaustion so acute it ate away at her joints was a growing sense of anxiety. There was someplace she needed to be, someone she needed to see, something she needed to do.

But what?

"Here, put this on," the man said.

She stared at the blue garment and realized she'd been standing there with the towel clutched to her chest, the rest of her body stark naked. She knew what he offered was a robe, she knew he wanted her to put it on, to cover herself. She even knew, in some remote part of her mind, that he felt disconcerted by her nudity. She reached for the robe, but everything seemed to happen in slow motion. At last, she got it around her. She could feel the man's relief.

What kind of woman is so unconcerned about a strange man seeing her naked?

She didn't even want to contemplate the possibilities. She was too tired to ponder such a troubling question.

"Thank you," she mumbled.

He shrugged broad shoulders still encased in a gray suit jacket now stained with shower water. As she watched, he took off his jacket and draped it over a towel bar, then rolled up the sleeves of a white shirt. He had nice forearms, strong looking, dusted with fine, dark hair.

But what she'd noticed first about him still dominated his looks and those were his eyes. They were green or maybe blue, it was hard to tell, and framed with dark lashes and brows. All sorts of things seemed to swirl in them: compassion, challenge, distaste, self-awareness, humor, trouble, danger. She'd seen all those things and while some had dismayed her, others had warmed her and given her courage.

She stared at the rest of him as he dug in a wall cabinet. He was tall and powerfully built. When he'd carried her up the outside stairs, she'd felt like a feather floating on the wind, like no burden at all. He had a habit of rubbing the back of his head, ruffling the short brown hair, stretching as though there was so much going on inside his head that it put a strain on his neck.

She suspected that she herself was the cause of his current tension.

He produced a box of Band-Aids and a tube of ointment. "Sit down on the edge of the tub," he told her, and she did as he said. Was she always this wishy-washy, this easy to control?

No. She knew she wasn't.

Kneeling in front of her, he treated and bandaged her knee. She made herself rally to ask him a few questions. First, his name.

"Travis MacBeth," he said, gazing up at her. "People call me Mac."

The nun at the shelter had called him Mac. Now she remembered. The next question was harder. "Who is Jake?"

"An acquaintance." When she stared, he added, "A homeless boozer."

"And my clothes…they're his?"

"I assume so. Seems kind of unlikely there are two identical coats running around the back streets of Billington. Plus, this is the first night in two months that Jake wasn't waiting for me at the mouth of that alley and the first night you were." He paused for a second and added, "Grace? Why did you run out of that alley the way you did?"

She wasn't sure what he was talking about.

"Were you running from something or someone?" he persisted.

She was running. Toward the light? Away from the light. Away from Jake?

Maybe her face reflected the unease the hazy memory of that alley engendered because Mac patted her arm and said, "Don't worry about it."

"Do you think…do you suppose…I hurt Jake? To get his coat, I mean. Was that why I was running?"

He stared at her and then smiled. Was it the first time he'd done that or had he smiled before and she'd forgotten? At any rate, he had a good smile, the kind a person could find themselves working to see again. The kind that took years and cares off a man's face and gave a glimpse of what lay hidden in his heart. He said, "No. I don't think so. We looked for Jake, remember?"

They'd walked through the alley. She could recall the clanging of empty bottles and the look of disgust in Mac's eyes as he asked if they were hers. "How old do you think I am?" she asked.

Again he stared at her. "Early twenties, maybe."

"And I've had a baby."

"You've apparently had a pregnancy. And a husband."

That jolted her. "A husband?"

He touched the ring finger on her left hand. "There's a tan line here. There are tan lines on your body, as well."

Sure enough, there was a discernible white line on her finger. She stared at it until her eyes burned. It didn't help. No memory of a loving husband surfaced. No memory of an awful husband surfaced, either. She felt a new spurt of anxiety and wondered if it was related to the husband whose ring she'd apparently forsaken.

Or hocked. Or lost.

Or to a baby she held in her arms, nursed at her breast, and now couldn't remember.

It was all too much.

"Which brings to mind all sorts of questions," Mac said.

She gazed at him and waited, but when he finally spoke,

she found she couldn't comprehend what he said. She just couldn't. His words stretched out and away and began to seem like musical notes in some bizarre song.

Could she sing along?

What were the words?

She felt his hands on her shoulders and realized her eyes had drifted closed. When she opened them, she found Mac supporting her, his gaze filled with alarm. He lifted her off the edge of the tub and she melted against his solid chest, circling his neck with grateful arms and closing her eyes again. Wrapped in his arms, she felt safer than she had since this ordeal began.

And then she felt a creepy sensation steal over her body. Flat black eyes stared at her behind a glistening silver curtain. Red hot hands grabbed her.

Screaming, she pushed her attacker away. The jolt when she hit the floor forced another scream from her throat.

"Grace, Grace, it's okay," Mac said.

She was on the floor. Mac bent over her. Gathering her in his arms, he held her for a moment while the fear subsided and the tears died in her throat. He helped her to her feet and onto the bed. She looked around for her assailant. No one else was in the room.

Somewhere in her head, she knew there never had been.

Mac tucked her between snow-white sheets. She caught his hand and held it for a moment, loath to give up the connection. She wanted to thank him for helping her, but the words were swallowed by fatigue and she drifted off to oblivion…or death.

What was the difference?

MAC SAT at his desk. He downed a stiff drink in two swallows.

The desk had been his father's. Mac had grown up doing

his homework on its polished surface, shoving aside the blotter and suffering his father's wrath when the older man caught him doing it. Mac now ran his finger over the myriad of shallow indentations that still existed, ghosts of long-ago essays and algebra equations.

He stared down the hall at the bedroom door that he'd left slightly ajar and wondered what he was going to do with this woman come morning. He reviewed the impulses that had led him to bringing her into his home. Her confusion. Her distress. Her minor injury. Her robotic behavior.

Her vulnerability.

Her fragile beauty.

The memory of his mother…

That's how she'd gotten here.

Now he was confronted with the realization that she was, or had been, married. She'd been pregnant, possibly still had a living child waiting for her return. Had she run away from her husband and her child?

Like his mother had.

Tempted to pour himself another drink, he stayed seated instead.

She was an addict. Drugs, liquor…something. If the marks on her arm weren't witness enough, that fit she'd had while he carried her to bed was. She'd gone berserk, sleeping like an angel one moment and screaming like a banshee the next. He would spend the night in this chair to keep an eye on her, and then the next morning, he would take her to Sister Theresa's or back to her alley, whichever she wanted.

And what about her child?

Burying his head in his hands, he found it almost impossible not to feel that child's loss. He understood all too well the ache for a mother who has vanished, the ache that never goes away.

But what could he do?

Find him or her?

Find Grace's husband?

How did someone do any of that when the person he was helping didn't seem to have the slightest clue as to who they were?

Swearing at all the ambiguities, he opened the drawer and took out a dozen pages of facts and figures. Maybe he could lose himself in his work.

Once upon a time, way back when, Mac had had a best friend named Rob Confit, an army buddy who died as a result of injuries suffered in a helicopter crash. Since Rob's death, Mac had become close to Rob's father, and now the elder Confit was challenging the current mayor in next fall's mayoral race.

It was Bill Confit's contention that the city government's mishandling of homelessness within Billington had resulted in skyrocketing inner-city crime. Appointing a privately funded task force to investigate this situation, Confit had asked Mac to act as chairman. Who better, he'd asked, than a former cop who'd risked his career to unveil corruption within the police force?

There was no way in the world Mac would think of denying Confit's request. At first, he'd approached it readily, able to put his own past in perspective. But gradually, he'd come to see his mother's face superimposed on every derelict he came across and the old wounds resurfaced.

Hence the need he felt to get out on the streets and see how the people who had next to nothing managed to survive. Did they prey on one another and the public at large? Were they responsible for rising crime rates and dying inner cities, or were they the victims of apathy and budget crunches?

Mac didn't know the answers yet, but he was becoming increasingly determined to make sure that the homeless and the defenseless didn't take the brunt of the censure unless they deserved it.

So far, he didn't think most of them did.

The current mayor disagreed.

The police disagreed.

Most of the committee disagreed.

And to top it off, Mac couldn't swear his own agenda didn't sway his conclusions. Most people thought facts and figures were foolproof, that there was only one way to translate dry, hard data. As an ex-cop, Mac knew nothing could be further from the truth. There was always room for interpretation.

But tonight he couldn't make his eyes focus on the papers. He kept seeing flashes of the woman he'd dubbed Grace. Naked in the shower, her skin and features breathtaking; crying; dripping wet in the alley, looking at him from under the brim of his hat. Her tan lines suggesting recent sunbathing, marriage and happy times.

Her image seemed to fill his mind and even a little corner of his heart. He knew it was foolish and he knew it was dangerous. Not only for him, but for her. He just didn't know what to do about it.

Rubbing his forehead, he shuffled the papers back into the drawer and thought to walk down the hall to check on Grace. He had every intention of doing this.

Sometime later, he awoke with a start. For a second, he felt confused, wondering why he'd fallen asleep at his desk, his head on his arms.

And then he sat up. The noise that had awakened him finally registered, and he tore off down the hall toward his bedroom.

Breaking glass. That's what he'd heard. His guest had woken up, panicked and tried to escape. She'd hurt herself if she tried jumping to the sidewalk....

Light from the hall flooded the bedroom as he threw open the door. It twinkled off the shards of glass that littered the floor beneath the only window in the room, one that opened onto the street half a floor up from the sidewalk. A jagged brick lay amid the glass.

Grace had apparently slept right through the mayhem. Sidestepping the worst of the mess, he peered out the window. Sometime during the night, the rain had turned to snow, but not the greeting card variety. Instead of making the city glow, this snow just colored the world in shades of gray.

With a lingering look at Grace's peaceful form cuddled beneath his down comforter, Mac grabbed a heavy wool sweater from his closet and a flashlight from his bedside drawer. The entryway was as he'd left it, filled with soggy, smelly clothes and puddles of water. He hurried down the steps and along the sidewalk until he was under the window that glowed faintly above his head.

Examining the snow proved pointless. It was sludge at best. There was no hope of discerning a footprint and peering up and down the street, he could see no moving form at all. Mac stared at the distance between himself and the window and gauged how hard it would be for someone to toss a brick through the window. Not that hard.

But why? Without wings or a ladder, no one could use the

broken window to get inside. Once again, he scanned the street. Zip.

That left intimidation as a motive and it didn't take much of an intuitive leap to figure out who might want to intimidate him.

So far, the police harassment had been relatively minor. Parking tickets. Speeding tickets. Hang-up calls. Citations for breaking archaic laws like the size of lettering on his office sign and the potted plant he'd left on a step. But today, he'd testified in court on behalf of a bum accused of shoplifting. Mac knew the poor guy was innocent; he'd been in the store, he'd seen the rich kid who originally took the camera in question and then shoved it into the bum's hands when it appeared he was going to be caught. It was Mac's testimony that had swayed the jury to dismiss the charges.

This time, his testimony had counted. A year before, he'd been the only cop to speak out against three officers whose use of excessive force had led to the unnecessary death of an addict.

Bottom line: If not to intimidate, what was the purpose of breaking the window?

It couldn't have anything to do with Grace. It was just co-incidence that she was sleeping in that room. If it wasn't co-incidence, then that would mean someone who knew something about her knew she was here. And *cared* that she was here.

He walked back inside and down the hall. He found Grace sitting on the side of the bed, staring at the shattered glass, shivering in her robe thanks to the cold air now streaming through the broken window. The thought that the broken window had anything to do with her seemed ludicrous.

"What happened?" she said.

"Nothing to worry about," he snapped, guessing she wouldn't question anything too closely and, sure enough, he was right. She rubbed her eyes and closed them again.

"We need to get you back to bed," he said, his voice brusque to cover the tender feeling he could sense stealing over his heart.

She nodded without opening her eyes.

Stepping around the glass, he leaned down and hoisted her over his shoulder.

She screeched, "Put me down!"

In that heated demand, the woman whose rounded bottom currently rested atop his shoulder and whose head was now upside down facing his back, had packed more passion than he'd so far heard from her and it reassured him. "Can't have you cutting your feet," he said as he carried her out of the room and deposited her on the sofa.

She tugged on the robe, the first sign of modesty he'd witnessed, and that, too, reassured him. As she grumbled, he found pillows and blankets in the hall closet. By the time he had made her a new bed and tucked her into it, she was asleep again.

For a while, he stood in the open bedroom doorway, ignoring the ice cold air. He stared at the brick. Should he report the incident to the police? Wouldn't the jerk who threw it love that! There was no way the brick sported fingerprints. Better to swallow the cost of replacing the window himself than give Chief Barry the satisfaction of knowing he'd rattled Mac's cage.

This was proof, however, that as the months passed and the election neared, the stakes would grow higher.

It was also proof that the only job he'd ever wanted—to be a cop, to make a difference—was lost to him.

The only niggling worry was Grace. If someone had tracked her to his apartment, then she was being watched.

Was she in some kind of danger?

Impossible to speculate on that when he possessed so little information. Reason said no one wanted her, no one had tracked her.

He swept up the mess, closed the bedroom door and sat back down at the desk. Behind him, on the sofa, Grace slept soundly.

SHE AWOKE when the phone rang. She could hear the rumble of a man's voice. For one blissful moment, she snuggled in the cocoon of warm blankets and thought to herself how nice it was to be warm when the world all around was cold.

Cold?

Grace sat up abruptly. Mac appeared in the kitchen doorway, two coffee mugs gripped in his hands.

"Morning," he said, handing her one. "How do you feel?"

She'd noticed how big he was the night before. This morning, she added attractive to her observation. He'd changed into jeans and a black cotton shirt, which he wore like a second skin. His dark hair, damp from the shower, fell boyishly over his forehead. The expression in his eyes was cautious. He probably wondered if she was going to flake out on him again, if she needed a hit of some illegal substance or a drink.

The only thing she craved was the caffeine she'd just introduced into her bloodstream via the excellent coffee. She said, "I feel okay."

"Did you remember anything about yourself?" His face now reflected how anxious he was to hear the right response. Unfortunately, she couldn't give it to him and she shook her head. The enormity of her situation flooded back. She still had no idea who she was.

For a while there, she'd thought that at least she would be able to think clearly today; the veil of exhaustion seemed to have lifted with the coming of the morning sun. But now, the old confusion was back and she felt tears welling in her eyes. She bent her head to hide them.

Mac moved away as though to give her space. "My wife was about your size," he said, gesturing at the desktop where he'd placed a modest stack of clothes.

"Won't she mind—"

"She's in New Jersey and she isn't my wife anymore, so no, she won't mind if you use her castoffs. I'll go scramble some eggs while you use the bathroom."

"Wait."

He paused for a second while she fought to find the right words. It was no use; she hadn't the slightest idea what they might be. A plea for him not to abandon her even though she could sense he was dying to get her out of his hair? What argument could she make? The logical place for her would be a hospital but the thought of going to see a doctor terrified her. *Why?*

She said, "Who was on the phone?" fully aware that it wasn't any of her business.

"Sister Theresa," he said curtly. "Before that, a friend of mine. Before that, the building super who wanted to know why one of my windows is broken. Now go get dressed. We'll talk after breakfast."

Balancing the clothes and the coffee mug, she made her way down the hall into the bathroom. She could feel a draft of cold air blowing from beneath the closed bedroom door as she passed, and the night's adventure came back to her.

A broken window. Made a person wonder exactly what Mac did for a living that someone should break his bedroom window.

The first thing she did in the bathroom was look at herself in the mirror. She found a twenty-something woman with extreme black hair cut painfully short. Blue eyes, full lips. Tanned skin. An abrasion on one cheek.

The face belonged to a stranger.

The next thing that caught her eye was the bruise on her shoulder, the bruises cascading down her left side, the needle marks on her arm, scraped knees, one of them bandaged, and, most distressing of all, the faint stretch marks on her stomach.

No memories of any of it, but the unease she'd felt the night before, the pressing urgency of a task undone, of somewhere she needed to be, someone she needed to be with, came rushing back. She put her hand on the doorknob, ready to march right out and demand—what?

Maybe she'd dress first…

She found her fancy black underwear still draped over the towel bar where Mac had hung it to dry the night before. Where did she come by such exquisite lingerie?

Mac had provided black wool-lined slacks that felt snug through the rear and a light blue sweater too tight in the chest. His ex-wife must have been a trim little woman, she thought as she pulled on socks and slipped her feet into the woman's designer loafers, which fit a lot better than Jake's boots had.

The clothes were warm and more or less comfortable, boring and predictable, but good quality. Still, she entered the kitchen awkwardly, feeling insignificant in Mac's presence, wondering if he would look at her decked out like this and think of his ex-wife.

"Everything fit?" he asked as he buttered toast.

"It's all fine. Listen, I have to go."

His eyebrows lifted in surprise. "That's great. Then you've remembered who you are and where you live?"

"Well, no—"

His expression reflected a disappointment almost as vast as her own. He said, "You can leave any time you want, but why not eat breakfast first?" As he said this, he handed her a plate dominated by a cheese omelet and toast.

"I can't eat—" she began but he cast her a stern look so she shut up and sat down at the table. Her stomach was too twisted to handle food. She began to regret drinking the coffee. Mac, not knowing this, of course, refilled her mug before sliding his own omelet onto his plate. He took the seat opposite her at the small, round table.

"I have to go to work," he said after taking a few hearty bites. "I'll drop you off wherever you want—"

"The alley," she said, putting down her fork and dropping all pretenses of being interested in food. For something to do with her trembling hands, she picked up the mug and was grateful for its warmth.

He repeated her destination in a wooden voice. "The alley."

"It's where this all started. I have to find out what's going on. I have to know…there's someone I need to go to…somewhere I need to be. Time is passing. I'm wasting time…"

Her voice trailed off as she heard her words. They sounded desperate, grasping. She'd walked down that alley with Mac the night before and there had been nothing there but a pile of empty bottles. And though the sense of urgency wouldn't go away, how did she act on it when she had no idea who in the hell she was?

"I think you should go to a hospital and be examined. Maybe you suffered a head injury or—"

"Absolutely not," she said emphatically. Her head pounded with the effort of staying focused and she rubbed her temples with one hand. "I'll just stay here until my mind clears—"

"You can't stay here alone."

"Why not?"

One corner of his mouth lifted in a parody of a smile. "Well, beyond the fact that I don't know you and am not in the habit of leaving strangers alone in my house, there's the fact that someone broke the window of the room you were sleeping in last night."

"I don't understand," she said. "Why would anyone care where I sleep?"

"Good question. Maybe no one cares. I don't have enough information to tell."

"Couldn't the brick have been intended for you? Do you have any enemies?"

"A few. But my enemies would aim for my head. Unless it was a cop."

"A cop?" As sketchy as her memory was, she knew enough to be surprised that a man who was obviously intelligent, lived in a nice apartment and dressed well had an antagonistic relationship with the police. "The cops are your enemies?"

"Not all of them. In fact, I was a cop myself until a year ago. I talked to my former partner early this morning. He confirmed that tensions are high around the precinct, but he doesn't think anyone would stoop to a sophomoric trick like tossing a brick through a window. Maybe he can help you—"

"No police!" she said. She slammed the mug down too

hard on the table. "No police!" she repeated, not sure why she felt so strongly but knowing she did.

Did she subconsciously know she'd done something wrong, broken a law, was wanted by the authorities?

"Okay, no police," he said calmly, ignoring the puddle of coffee spreading across the table top.

She nodded, swallowed and dabbed at the coffee with a paper napkin. She felt tears burning her nose. Her stomach was a tight knot. She said, "What did Sister Theresa want?"

"She warned me that I should be careful, that you might have needs I can't fill, that I might hurt you by trying to help you."

"Or that I might hurt you," Grace whispered.

"I'm invincible, so don't worry about that. Listen, you can't stay here and you won't go to a shelter or a hospital. Where do you want to go?"

The response came without thought. "Home," she said softly. "I just want to go home."

Chapter Three

Of course, he couldn't take her home, because her only "home" was the Broadhurst alley. While he intended on paying the place a visit, he didn't want Grace anywhere near it when he did.

For one thing, he wanted to catch Jake unawares and coax him into telling his story. He wanted to know if Grace had cajoled him out of his coat or if she'd had an accomplice. He wanted to pinpoint the beginning of her amnesia without her presence serving as a distraction. Was Jake up to discerning things like that? He'd see.

Plus, he had other errands to run that were best run alone. In the end, Mac had realized there was only one place to take Grace for a few hours. What had been difficult was getting her to agree to his plan.

His aunt, Beatrice Dally, lived on Blade Street in three stories of stately elegance. To help look after the place, she employed two servants, the Coopers, a husband-and-wife team of the old school. The wife, Maddie, was an incurable gossip with a big heart. She cooked the meals and took care of various housecleaning chores, though a service came in twice a week to do the hard stuff.

Maddie's husband, a man everyone called by his last name, answered doors, drove the car and clipped the hedge once a year. He also ironed—a chore he claimed to enjoy as it gave him an opportunity to watch the afternoon soap operas without the Mrs. calling him a lazy bum. Mac thought they were both pushing seventy, which was still a good decade younger than his aunt.

Aunt Beatrice herself was a grand-looking woman with a ramrod-straight back and the will to match. She'd always been kind to a fault, but she was no one's fool. Married to a wealthy older man when she was all of eighteen, she'd been widowed now for fifty years.

Beatrice Dally had never married again and had no children of her own. She said she didn't need a child, she had Mac. Mac adored the old woman, as much for her independent will and strong convictions as for her indulgent love of him.

Cooper opened the door on the first ring of the bell and showed Mac and Grace into the checkerboard-tiled entry. Mac was too frequent a visitor to be treated formally, though he could see Cooper trying to figure out the relationship between himself and Grace.

"Hey, Cooper. Tell my aunt I need to see her, will you?" Mac said.

He got a raised pair of bushy eyebrows and a nod of a snowy white head. "Very well, sir."

Mac was very aware of Grace standing close beside him. He'd tucked her into one of his coats and it hung on her. Worse, though she'd started the day with a show of determination, it had all but abandoned her and now she seemed lethargic again. She wasn't even grumbling about being "parked" in an out-of-the-way location anymore.

"Let me take your coat," he said, shrugging off his own and then helping her disentangle herself from the folds of wool that all but enveloped her. He draped them both over the back of a chair. It was a bit unnerving to see Grace dressed in Jessica's old clothes, even though she carried off the casual country club look easily. Only that garish black hair sounded a false note and it dawned on him suddenly that her hair was dyed, that she was probably a blonde or maybe a light brunette by nature.

Her nude image flashed across his mind.

"Why are you staring at me?" she asked, her voice little more than a whisper.

He thought of the other hair on her lithe body, all of it light-colored. "I don't think you were born with black hair," he said.

She touched her jagged locks.

His aunt came down the stairs with a vigor that defied her years. She was almost as tall as Mac, with steel-gray hair waved away from an aristocratic face. Mac introduced his aunt to Grace, who produced a wan smile.

Aunt Beatrice took one look at Grace and turned to Cooper. "Tell Maddie to come here. No, tell her to make tea first and then come here." She dismissed Cooper with an imperative wave of her hand and took Grace's arm.

"Come with me, child," she said, leading Grace into the living room. Grace went willingly, sinking into the huge white chair his aunt offered.

"Maddie will bring you tea. Eventually, anyway. She doesn't move as fast as she used to. Then again, who does around here? Would you like to close your eyes for a few minutes?"

Grace blinked, then nodded as she apparently deciphered his aunt's rapid-fire comments and got to the one that suggested what it was so obvious she wanted, *needed,* to do: sleep. Mac slipped a sofa cushion behind her head as Grace murmured her thanks and leaned back.

"Leave her be," Aunt Beatrice commanded and Mac, caught staring at Grace's exquisite profile, felt his cheeks grow warm, just the way they had when his aunt caught him doing something slightly illicit when he was a teenager.

Like coveting something he wasn't supposed to want, let alone have.

Aunt Beatrice herded Mac into the connecting den, where he took a seat in his favorite chair and she faced him from across her antique desk. Through the door, he could see Grace's recumbent form.

His aunt cleared her throat.

Tearing his gaze away from Grace, he said, "It's a long story."

"And no doubt an interesting one."

He filled her in on the highlights, how he'd met Grace, how she was dressed, her fear of the doctor, her lethargy, but his aunt stopped him when he got to the part about Grace's fancy undergarments.

"And how did it come about that you saw that girl's underwear?" Aunt Beatrice demanded.

"Someone had to help her get out of those horrible clothes," he said, hoping he didn't look as embarrassed as he suddenly felt.

His aunt, looking scandalized, said, "And you couldn't find a willing female friend to come help?"

"Trust me, Aunt Beatrice, Grace didn't mind. There was nothing…titillating…about it."

His remark was greeted with arched eyebrows.

"Anyway, like I was saying, her things are obviously quite pricey. There's a little sea horse with what I swear is a diamond eye sewn right onto the—"

Here he paused, not only because his aunt appeared to be close to swooning, but also because he was at a loss for words to describe that area of a bra that occupies the space between a woman's breasts. He finally tapped his own chest in the appropriate spot and continued. "Right here."

"L'Hippocampe," his aunt said with an impeccable French accent. "That's the brand. It's French for sea horse."

"I looked, there was no label."

"Of course not. It's very exclusive. No labels, not ever. How odd that a girl like that would be wearing such things."

"What I need from you, Aunt Beatrice, is a baby-sitter. I can't leave Grace alone and I don't know where else to take her."

"She seems drugged to me. Are you sure she didn't have something stashed away in a pocket that she might have taken when you weren't looking?"

"Positive."

"How could you be positive?"

"I checked her pockets," he said, hoping his aunt would let the matter drop and he wouldn't be forced to explain the intimacy of seeing Grace nude. "Maybe some substance from the night before is still in her bloodstream," he added. "She's got needle marks on her arm, bruises up and down her body. Don't leave her alone with your liquor cabinet or your good silver."

"I'll have Maddie keep an eye on her."

"Maddie will talk her head off."

"Tsk. Anyway, even if she does ramble on a bit, perhaps it will be good for the girl. Where are you headed?"

"I've got an appointment with Bill Confit. I've finished my report and I'm anxious to hand it to him and get out of this committee. Then I thought I'd stop by and see my old partner on the force. After that I'll figure out what to do about Grace. I'll be back by evening."

"Travis, if the child doesn't remember who she is, how do you know her name is Grace?"

"I don't," he said as he stood. "I gave her that name last night."

"And you're sure she's for real?"

That comment stopped him. "What do you mean?"

"I mean, dear boy, that you have half of this city's finest upset with you because of your association with the mayor's rival. The other half thinks you're a traitor because of that mess last year."

"I know," Mac said.

"What I'm saying is that you have your fair share of powerful enemies. A win for your friend Confit will mean disaster for not only the current mayor, but for Chief Barry, as well. Everyone knows you've taken to bringing that old drunk a sandwich every night. Isn't it odd that your Grace should show up right there at *that* alley, wearing *your* bum's clothes? Maybe she's just waiting to get you into a compromising situation that would discredit you and, ultimately, Bill Confit."

"Aunt Beatrice," he said, putting an arm around her slender shoulders, "I think you've been watching way too much television."

"I beg your pardon," she replied haughtily. "I do not watch television."

"Then reading too many mystery books."

A moment of silence was followed by a soft chuckle. "*That's* a possibility."

They both regarded the snoozing figure in the white chair and Mac said, "She doesn't look much like a spy, does she?"

"No, she doesn't. She's very young. And very attractive." This last comment was accompanied by a lift of her eyebrows and sounded more like a question than an observation.

He shrugged as though he hadn't noticed.

"And you can't keep your eyes off her."

"That's nuts," he grumbled.

"It's true."

He shrugged again. He knew from long experience there was no lying to his aunt. He added, "Well, there's something about her, that's all."

More arched eyebrows and a smug tilt of her head let him know she thought she knew exactly what he was getting at. He wondered if she'd care to explain it to him, because he wasn't sure what was fueling this obsession of his.

Aunt Beatrice, however, didn't say another word, so Mac tiptoed around Grace. For a moment, he paused and stared at her, at the pretty set of her mouth, the sweep of lashes against her lightly tanned cheeks, her spiky black hair.

Was there a husband nearby praying for her return? A child crying himself to sleep at night, aching for Mommy?

Or had she burned her bridges, left no one behind to care, no one to love her or worry about her, to help her find her identity and reclaim her life?

Or…did she really want to reclaim her life? Had she put herself into the homeless scenario before she lost her memory? If and when her memory came back, would she find herself still lost and disconnected?

Looking at her, it was difficult to believe that could be the case, but beauty is no protection against illness, no protection against self-destruction or heartlessness.

He moved away from her chair before she opened her eyes, knowing if she pinned him with her blue gaze it would be harder than ever to keep thinking of her as a problem to be resolved and forgotten and not as…Grace.

THIS TIME WHEN Grace woke up, she felt clearheaded. True, she still didn't know who she was, but just the fact that recent events weren't lost in a hazy mire was a huge relief.

She got to her feet and stretched. Just like that, as though she'd pulled a cord in her body when she raised her arms above her head, that inner swell of anxiety returned.

Pressing her fingers against her forehead, she searched her mind.

Who needed her? She was letting someone down and the thought that it might be a child—her child—well, the very idea made her heart hurt.

Or a husband.

She looked at her left hand and tried to envision a diamond, a gold band…anything.

Oh, where was Mac? Why had he brought her to his aunt's house and then abandoned her?

Restless past enduring, she searched the bookcase, looking for a title that might divert her attention from things she couldn't control. Aunt Beatrice's tastes seemed to revolve around books printed before the turn of the century, however. A deck of cards sitting atop a beautifully inlaid cribbage board caught her attention, and she slipped them out of the pack.

The backs were all printed with the same royal blue and gold fleur-de-lis pattern. She shuffled them in her hands, absently enjoying the silky feel of the cards sliding through her fingers.

Looking through the mullioned window, she saw that the rain had stopped. Mac was out there somewhere. She assumed he'd return for her, but then what? If she couldn't remember who she was, if she couldn't go home, then she at least wanted to be with him. But why in the world would he want to be with her?

She turned away from the window and paced the elegant room, coming to a stop in front of a row of photos hung against a wall, all black-and-white and artfully suspended in gilded frames.

She bypassed the ones that looked old and moved on down to the more recent photos. There was Mac with an older man who looked enough like him to be his father. Mac looked to be about twenty. Another photo showed Mac in fatigues, standing with his arm around another young man, both of them grinning, a helicopter serving as backdrop.

The next picture showed Mac accepting a plaque of some kind. This time he was in a policeman's uniform, surrounded by others wearing the same thing, all of them in front of furled flags and a large insignia affixed to a wooden partition. There was no grin on Mac's handsome face in this photo. Resignation had replaced the enthusiastic flush of youth. The picture looked like it could have been taken the day before.

"Grace, dear, you're awake."

Still gazing at the last picture, Grace said, "Tell me about these photos, Aunt Beatrice. Tell me about Mac."

Aunt Beatrice had advanced far enough into the room to touch her arm. "I'll tell you anything you want to know, but not right now," she said softly. "We have a guest."

Grace whirled. A middle-aged man with a bald dome stood just inside the doorway. His eyes were thoughtful, but kind.

"This is my accountant, George," Aunt Beatrice said.

George closed the gap between himself and Grace, his hand extended, his grasp firm and friendly. "I'm very pleased to meet you," he said.

"George is having lunch with us," Aunt Beatrice added. "You are hungry, I hope," she added.

"As a matter of fact, I'm ravenous," Grace said.

George wasn't as big as Mac, nor as intimidating. Of course, he also wasn't as attractive or engaging, but she was willing to forgo those qualities for the moment, preferring the sense of comfort the accountant exuded. He reminded her, with just the warm pressure of his hand and the gentle sound of his voice, of a father. For the first time, Grace wondered where her own parents were. Were they looking for her?

"I'm ravenous, too," George said, patting her hand, "and it's not very often I share lunch with two young ladies."

Aunt Beatrice giggled like a schoolgirl.

"You'll have to tell me all about yourself," George said as they adjourned to the dining room.

Grace smiled wistfully. That wouldn't take long.

HEAD BENT against the rain, Mac thought about Grace's tan, which was neither dark enough nor uniform enough to have come from a tanning salon or a misting machine. That meant she'd recently spent at least a few weeks in a sunny climate, which eliminated Billington and anywhere else within easy driving distance.

Of course, she could have gotten it on a recent vacation. The most provocative element of that tan was the whitish line on her wedding ring finger which indicated that at the time she'd been sunning herself, she'd been married. So why wasn't her husband looking for her?

After he'd met with Confit and turned over the report, he'd gone to precinct headquarters and, ignoring baleful glares, cornered his ex-partner, Lou Gerald. Without revealing much about Grace and the circumstances under which he'd met her, he'd coerced Lou to check missing person reports, not only for Billington, but for all over the country. No one seemed to be missing a woman matching Grace's description.

How could that be?

How did she get to Billington? Why had she stripped down to her fancy underwear and donned Jake's clothes? Where were her jewelry and her identification? Why had she lost her memory? And where was Jake?

He slowed down near Broadhurst and approached Jake's alley, hoping to find the old guy waiting as usual. With any luck, Jake would have a story to be told and Mac was prepared to pay to hear it. He came armed with loose bills and pastrami on rye.

It was early, so Mac wasn't surprised when Jake didn't materialize out of the gloom. He turned down the alley. Maybe Jake would be sitting under some kind of protection, waiting for his sandwich.

The alley was just as oppressive as it had been the night before, but this time Mac also felt a sinister presence, as though the shadows held more than the debris of life, as though they also concealed calculating eyes. He was just about at the far end when he saw a leg and a shoe protruding from under a big flap of cardboard tucked up against an overflowing Dumpster.

Mac made some general noise to warn whomever was hiding under there that he was about to tear away his protection, but the foot didn't twitch. He hauled away the soggy cardboard and found a man staring up at him.

Jake!

A whoop of pleasure at finally finding the old guy died in Mac's throat and he perched on his heels with a growing sense of dread. He felt the wrinkled throat out of habit, praying he'd detect even a thread of pulse but knowing it was too late.

"Aw, man, what happened to you?" he whispered.

For a second, as the rain hit Jake's grayish face and ran in rivulets down his crumpled chin, Mac saw another face, a softer face. *His mother's face...*

Was she still alive or had she, too, died alone in an alley? Would he ever know?

He forced her image from his mind. It had been ten years since he'd seen his mother and he really didn't expect he would ever see her again. He made himself come back to the alley and deal with the present.

Jake was wearing a pair of blue jeans so new they looked stiff. A yellow shirt had a price tag stapled to the collar as though it came from a thrift store. He also wore waterproof boots and a green overcoat that had been dry before Mac moved the cardboard and exposed it. Large wet splotches now darkened the coat. Jake's longish gray hair was covered with a dark blue watch cap, the kind seafaring men wear. One hand clutched the neck of a bottle of relatively pricey gin.

Jake had either pulled the cardboard over his head and upper body or it had been done for him during the dry part of the day around mid-morning or early afternoon. He'd been relatively warm and dry when he died and, judging from the missing contents of the gin bottle, feeling no pain.

Mac got to his feet and replaced the cardboard carefully, doing his best to protect what might be a crime scene. He pulled out his phone and paged Lou, knowing as he did so that he wouldn't mention Grace, that he'd protect her from questions he knew she couldn't answer. He figuratively crossed his fingers, hoping that Jake had finally succeeded in drinking himself to death and that no one connected with Grace had helped him along.

But he couldn't shake the feeling that it was all just too much of a coincidence. He couldn't shake the feeling Grace was in danger.

THEY'D BEEN closeted away in the den for over an hour and Grace *knew* they were talking about her. At first, she'd been patient, assuming she'd be summoned, and played endless games of solitaire. But now she was antsy and annoyed.

She'd been waiting all day for Mac to come back, but the minute he'd hit his aunt's house, he'd snapped at her to stay in the living room with Cooper and marched his aunt into the den, firmly closing the door without so much as looking at her.

Who did he think he was?

Officious, bossy…

She turned to complain to poor old Cooper and found him dozing. With a little smile, she abandoned her game of solitaire and gathered the cards into a stack. So much for waiting like a good girl.

As she flung open the door, Mac and his aunt stood like a couple of thieves near the bookcase, caught in mid argument. Aunt Beatrice startled at the intrusion, but the second Mac saw her, he strode across the room and gripped her upper arms. "What's wrong?" he demanded, staring into her eyes. "Where's Cooper?"

This wasn't the reaction Grace had expected from Mac. For that matter, the racing of her heart wasn't the reaction she'd expected from herself. But the strength and heat of his hands, coupled with the intensity of his gaze, struck her like a bolt of lightning.

"Where's Cooper?" he repeated.

She gestured behind her and watched Mac's face relax as he caught sight of the slumbering butler.

"I'll be with you in a moment," he told Grace, meeting her eyes with a troubled gaze of his own. "Just stay there with Cooper and don't answer the front door—"

Wrenching herself from his grasp, she felt anger burning the edges of anxiety. "You're treating me like a child," she said, "Now just a moment—"

"She doesn't know what's going on," Aunt Beatrice said calmly. "Just explain it to her."

Mac took a deep breath. "You might as well come in," he said.

"Gee, thanks," she said and sidled past him, suddenly aware of him as a man in a way she hadn't been until a few moments before. It was disconcerting, to say the least. To cover her uneasiness, she barked, "Just what's going on? Am I right in assuming that I'm the topic of conversation?"

"More or less," Mac said, throwing himself into a chair facing his aunt's desk. The older woman gestured at a matching chair but Grace declined with a shake of her head, pretty sure she'd explode if she tried to sit.

Pacing the plush carpet, Grace said, "I know I'm a...problem...for you both and I've been thinking. I don't believe I'm an addict. I don't crave anything and my head has been clear for hours. Also, how do you explain things like my fingernails? I may not have a manicure, but my cuticles are trimmed. My feet are soft, no calluses like I assume there'd be if I'd been walking around a lot, nor am I undernourished. I think I've had a recent pedicure. Does that sound homeless to you, because it sure doesn't to me."

Aunt Beatrice said, "I think—"

But Grace interrupted again. "I don't know why the thought of seeing a doctor makes me feel queasy, but okay, I'll go see a doctor. Maybe that would help. I have to do something. I have to get back where I belong. I'm…needed. I have to hurry."

"You've already seen a doctor," Mac said.

"What?"

"The man I introduced as my accountant is actually my physician," Aunt Beatrice explained as she took a seat. "And Travis here is annoyed with me."

"I didn't know she was going to sneak a doctor in to see you. I guess it did no harm."

"Now listen here, you two," Grace said through gritted teeth. "I admit I haven't been in my best form, whatever that might be, but I will no longer tolerate being left in the dark." She knew her next question might undermine her declaration, but she had to ask it. "What did George say about me?"

"Just what I knew by taking one good look at you," Aunt Beatrice said. "You're no more a homeless addict than I am. I can't believe Mac ever thought you were."

"You're the one who thought she was a spy," Mac snarled.

"I never—"

"Wait!" Grace had to raise her voice. "A spy?"

"It doesn't matter," Aunt Beatrice insisted. "The point is, the doctor thinks you were drugged. He wants to take a blood sample and run some tests."

"And Aunt Beatrice was trying to think of a devious way to get you to part with a vial or two," Mac said, which earned him a dirty look from his aunt. "However, that's not the immediate concern—"

"It is for me," Grace interrupted. "The doctor can have his blood and run all the tests he wants, but no more secrets, no more tricks. Listen, I know you're an ex-cop. Your aunt told me you're now a private eye. How about I hire you to help me find out who I am."

He stared at her. "I don't know—"

"Of course he'll take your case," Aunt Beatrice said. "It's what he does. Ever since his sense of decency got him kicked off the police force—"

"Don't start with that," Mac said.

"You know it's true. You were the only one who didn't participate in that cover-up."

"What cover-up?" Grace asked Mac. As he wouldn't meet her gaze, she glanced at Aunt Bea and repeated, "What cover-up?"

"It was after things went wrong on that drug unit you were part of," she said.

"I got myself kicked off of that, too," Mac said bitterly.

Aunt Bea nodded. "That's right, you did. Whoever said honesty is the best policy never tried being a police officer in Billington."

"That's not entirely fair," Mac said. "Most of the guys are great. Besides, Grace isn't interested in all this."

"Sure I am," Grace said. "Go on, Aunt Bea."

"Where was I? Oh, yes. First, he was part of this elite drug response unit until his protests about their illegal search-and-seizure procedures got him demoted back to patrol officer. Things were going okay for a while and then there was that incident last year when five policemen responded to a call from a fellow officer who said he was under attack."

"I was too late to do much more than watch," Mac said. "It was down near the freeway overpass. A wino had attacked an officer. By the time I got there, another officer was pulling the wino off the cop. One thing led to another, and before anyone knew what had happened, the officer had used too much force and the wino was dead. Another officer planted a knife on the dead guy. When Internal Affairs investigated, all of the other guys said the wino had had the knife all along, that it was a case of kill or be killed. There I was, hanging out in the wind by myself, telling the truth, but of course, I already had a reputation as a troublemaker and my voice carried little weight."

"And that's when he quit," Aunt Bea said, "and got his private license."

"And made the decision to pick my own cases," Mac added firmly.

"Of course," Aunt Beatrice said.

"Then help me," Grace pleaded.

"How exactly would you pay me?"

Grace bit her lip. How did she know she could afford to hire a private detective? But what if she went to the police and they found out she was some kind of criminal or on the run from a questionable situation? Wouldn't it be better to have someone like Mac on her side, someone obligated to stay loyal, someone she could control?

She glanced at Mac's face. Did she for one second think

she could control Travis MacBeth? No. But he wouldn't be bound by the same rules as the police. With him, she could consider whatever he found out about her and decide if she wanted to reenter her life or not. All she knew was what her instincts told her: she needed to find out where she belonged as soon as possible. Someone important needed her.

And Mac looked like her best bet.

She said, "I'll find the money."

Aunt Beatrice said, "Nonsense. I have plenty of money. Travis will get almost everything I have when I pass on, so why not get some of it now through you?"

Grace's eyes spontaneously filled with tears. She hadn't expected this kindness, especially as her behavior since entering this room had been surly.

"Not so fast," Mac said. "The fact is, I've already checked missing persons from all over the country. There are no recent reports that match you."

"Maybe Jake knows something."

"Jake's dead," Mac said, his eyes suddenly hard.

Grace felt her lungs empty. "How did he die?"

"Someone stuck a knife in his back," Mac said. The anger blazing in his eyes momentarily scared her and she made a mental note not to get on his bad side. "The police are investigating."

"Will they want to question me?"

"They don't know about you."

"You checked missing person reports, but you didn't mention me?"

He studied his hands.

"I know you must have," she said, popping to her feet. The need to leave this house was tremendous. Where could she go? She wanted to get away from these people and yet she was terrified at the thought of being alone out in the rain in a city so foreign it was hard to believe she'd ever felt comfortable in it, ever called it home. Why wasn't someone looking for her?

"I talked informally to an old friend of mine. He's willing to take your fingerprints and contact the FBI. Don't get your hopes up. Unless you worked for the government or you're a felon, it's very unlikely your prints are going to help much. Bottom line here is that the police don't know you ever met Jake. I didn't connect you with the alley. They don't know you had anything to do with him."

"But I didn't," she protested.

"You were wearing his clothes," Mac said. "You must have had at least a nodding acquaintance with the man."

"What was Jake wearing when they found him?"

"Clean clothes, like from a thrift store."

"And Travis is the one who found him," Aunt Beatrice added. "After he met with the police and started home, someone followed him back to his car. He lost them—"

"Aunt Beatrice," Mac said sternly, but he was looking at Grace. She felt weak with an unspecified alarm; if she looked as scared as she felt, he must think she was about to faint, bolt or throw up. All three alternatives seemed likely. She sat down instead.

"I lost the tail," Mac said. "But the fact that someone wanted to know where I was headed after discovering a murder victim, combined with our adventure last night is…worrisome."

"You think!" Grace said, shuddering.

"On the other hand, all these things could be unrelated. Poor old homeless bums like Jake sometimes get themselves murdered. Maybe he came into some cash, bought new clothes, abandoned his old ones, which you then adopted.

Maybe he showed a few dollars around and another derelict decided to do him in for his newfound wealth. Maybe the police chief wanted me followed, and tailing me away from the alley was simply the easiest way. I don't know enough to connect all the dots yet."

"I'm frightened," she said.

He stared at her. In fact, his gaze was so focused, she had the feeling of being eaten alive by a benevolent male protector.

She straightened her shoulders. She didn't need protecting. Well, okay, maybe a little, but what she needed was someone to help her, not overshadow her.

She said, "So, are you hired or not?"

His gaze never wavered. He said, "We have nowhere to start."

From behind him, Aunt Beatrice's voice was clear. "Of course we do," she said with a genteel sniff. "There's a perfectly good clue right before your eyes. Well, more or less…"

Chapter Four

"Take off your bra," Mac said calmly, leveling his gaze at Grace.

Grace wrinkled her brow.

Aunt Beatrice scolded him with her eyes.

"That's what you're alluding to, isn't it?" Mac said, staring down his aunt. "Her specially made, fancy underwear? Our one link with her past?"

"Neither piece of my underwear has a label," Grace said. "I checked."

"Forgive my nephew his bluntness," Aunt Beatrice said as she clasped Grace's hand. Her cheeks were highly colored and Mac knew she found discussing a woman's undergarments with a man in the room to be distasteful. However, ever practical, she squared her shoulders and added, "Travis is right. Your unmentionables are the only clues we have. They're a start. So if you wouldn't mind—"

Here she gestured toward a narrow door behind her desk. Mac knew it led to a half bath.

Grace sighed. "If you two think it'll help," she said, and, casting a worried frown at Mac, disappeared inside the small room.

"She's a good sport," Aunt Beatrice said as the door clicked shut.

"She doesn't have much choice," Mac said. He rubbed the back of his head. Images of Jake lying dead in the alley kept getting confused in his thoughts with images of Grace in Jake's clothes and, once in a while, with his mom. He closed his eyes. Too many lost people.

He consciously cleared his head by picturing the night sky. He erased the stars and the moon until there was nothing but a vast blackness. It took effort to keep himself in that sky, immersed in that empty space. Thoughts kept streaking through like blazing meteorites.

Who had trailed him and why?

To find Grace?

Before he'd rescued her, she'd been in the alley. How long? Had Jake seen her, spoken to her? Had someone else bargained with Jake for his clothes and given them to Grace? How could she not remember that?

How could it be a coincidence?

But was Jake's death directly related to Grace?

Were the broken window and the tail today just part of a puerile conspiracy by the police to jerk him around? It seemed unlikely Chief Barry would engage in those kinds of shenanigans.

Mac heard the door and opened his eyes to find Grace emerging from the bathroom, sweater smoothed down over her body, a scrap of black silk in her hands. He made himself glance away from the gentle swell of her wool-clad chest but the image of last night's nudity was so fresh in his memory he would have blushed had he been a blushing kind of man.

His aunt hid her discomfort by crisply demanding, "Hand it to me, dear."

Grace gave her bra to Aunt Beatrice. All three of them

crowded around the wispy garment. The tiny sea horse, its glittering eye twinkling in the light from the desk lamp, stared up at them.

His aunt retrieved a small magnifying glass from her desk drawer and studied the sea horse before announcing in her grand manner, "I'm positive this is a *L'Hippocampe.*"

"What's that mean?" Grace asked.

"It's a brand name," Mac said, straightening.

"It's French for *sea horse,*" Aunt Beatrice added. "The sea horse's eye is a real diamond. I imagine this little thing cost five hundred dollars."

"Five hundred dollars!" Grace gasped.

"Maybe it's a knockoff," Mac said.

"I have a rather snooty friend, Cynthia Sinclair. You might recall her, Travis. Tall woman with red hair that defies the laws of nature? No? Well, she wears only *L'Hippocampe.* Frankly, between us three, she's rather tiresome about it. She's the kind who takes great stock in the exclusivity of an item and tends to go on and on. That's how I came to recognize this from your description."

Mac said, "Call her up. Ask her where she bought it."

"You don't understand," Aunt Beatrice said. "One doesn't go into a store and buy prestigious things like this off a rack. One makes an appointment, chooses material, talks to a designer, is fitted—"

"Just call her up and ask her where she had the appointment," Mac said through gritted teeth. "Please."

"I can't. She's in Europe."

Mac turned on his heel.

"Where are you going?" Grace asked as he strode toward the door.

"Cooper has a computer in his quarters. It's older than dirt, but I'm fairly certain it's connected to the Internet. I'm going to see if these people have a Web site."

"A place like that advertise? Too gauche," his aunt said.

"Everyone is connected these days, Aunt Beatrice. Even upscale enterprises like this one."

"I don't know, Travis. It's true that Cynthia is something of a braggart, but she swears there are only a handful of their boutiques worldwide."

"If they exist, they'll be on the Web," Mac said firmly. "You ladies hang out for a while. Don't answer the door, don't let anyone in. I'll wake up Cooper and go look."

He was aware of both of them staring at him as he shook Cooper awake, but when he turned to toss them a reassuring wave, both heads were bent over the bra, studying the sea horse.

GRACE SET ASIDE the cup of hot tea Cooper's wife, Maddie, had served along with a rambling discourse on the neighbor's new butler.

Now, with Maddie out of the room, Grace felt free to stop pretending to sip the tea. She didn't like the stuff. Unfortunately, Aunt Beatrice seemed to order it at every lull in the conversation.

Mac strode back into the room after being gone little more than thirty minutes. Though she studied his face as he approached her, she couldn't tell a thing from his expression. As a former cop, he was probably pretty good at shielding his emotions.

For a second, he stood over her, staring at the cards she'd set out in neat rows atop the coffee table, red upon black, aces at the top. Then he sat down next to her and took her hands into his.

The pressure of his grip elicited an overwhelming feeling of safety. Shocked by such an outlandish response to such a casual gesture, she pulled her hands from his and clasped them together, steeling herself for what he had to say.

"There are three *L'Hippocampe* boutiques in the continental United States," he began. "One in Canada, a few scattered across Europe. If you bought your underwear in Europe, we're pretty much out of luck.

"The stores here are in Miami, New York City and Washington, D.C. Whether you bought your garments on vacation or whether you live in one of these cities is kind of immaterial. Unless you were overseas, you walked into one of these three stores. Your tan, and the fact that's it's relatively recent, helps narrow the field. New York and D.C. are too cold this time of year. Canada, too, for that matter. That pretty much leaves Miami."

"Your reasoning is full of holes," Aunt Beatrice said as she sipped tea from a porcelain cup.

"Well, I don't have much to work on but assumptions and speculation," Mac said.

"I'm just thinking that after her first fitting, she could have ordered new garments any time she wished. Or perhaps she had half a dozen made at the same time. Although this brassiere looks new, it might in fact be old. Or, she might live somewhere warm and have vacationed somewhere cold where she ordered her underwear. Or, contrarily—"

"Not the point," Mac interrupted. "All we're looking for at this point is a starting place. It really doesn't matter when Grace bought the stuff, as long as we find the where, and then only if someone recognizes her."

"Places like this pride themselves on customer service,"

Aunt Beatrice said. "Their staff is trained to render the personal touch. Grace is a lovely young woman. Someone will recall you, dear."

"I must be very wealthy," Grace said.

"Unless someone bought them for you," Mac said.

Grace touched the faint tan line where it seemed certain a wedding band had recently perched. "Then my husband—"

"Of course," Aunt Beatrice said quickly and, setting aside her cup, rose to her feet.

Mac cleared his throat. "Or a boyfriend," he said softly.

Grace stared into his blue-green eyes. "You mean I might have a…lover? Is that what you're trying to say?"

He shrugged.

Grace felt her face burn. "You're suggesting I cheated on my husband with another man who bought me expensive undies."

"It's a possibility," Mac said softly.

Aunt Beatrice said, "I don't think—"

"Yes, it's a possibility," Grace admitted.

"Bottom line is that it doesn't matter, not now, not when our main thrust is to discover your identity," Mac said.

"And to explain this feeling of anxiety that eats at my gut," Grace added.

"Yes."

"Good," Aunt Beatrice said, obviously glad to move the conversation along. "Now, Travis, you have a place to start. I suggest a nice dinner, a good night's sleep and then you two take off for Florida. I'll have Cooper call the airline and book your flight."

"No flight," Mac said, standing. "Grace has no identification. They won't let her on a plane. We'll have to drive."

"Then, after dinner—"

Looking at Grace, Mac said, "I'm going to leave you here for the night and collect you in the morning. I have things to do before we leave."

He glanced at his aunt and added, "Call your doctor and ask him to come take a blood sample from Grace. He'll have to come here. It's just too dangerous to take her out." With that, his hand briefly grazed Grace's shoulder before he started for the door.

"I need clothes," Grace called after him, annoyed he was abandoning her again.

His gaze pierced her. "There are some more of my ex-wife's things back at the apartment. Will they do?"

"For now," Grace said reluctantly.

He studied her face a moment and added, "We'll pick up whatever else you want once we get out of town."

She nodded.

He kept staring at her and she wondered what he saw. A woman he didn't know decked out in his ex-wife's clothes? A woman who might be responsible in some way for the murder of a harmless old man he'd befriended? A woman who had helped coerce him into driving her to Florida?

She didn't feel like any of these women and yet she was all of them.

She felt alone and anxious, nervous that her only hope—Mac—might walk out that door and rethink his desire to get involved with her. What would keep him from calling his police friends and handing her over? What if his old police training kicked into gear?

She was, after all, connected in some way to Jake. His clothes, his alley. By rights, she should talk to the police; only there wasn't a thing in the world she could tell them.

Did Mac truly believe that? She and his aunt had more or less forced him into helping her; once he was away from this house, would he rethink his position?

How could she blame Mac if he took the easy way out and handed her over to the authorities?

"I'll be back in the morning," Mac said.

Would he?

"Be careful," his aunt whispered, but Mac was already gone.

MAC MADE the tail within three blocks of his aunt's house. Dark, late-model car—the kind undercover cops preferred. Mac found it hard to believe his actions warranted that kind of scrutiny unless Chief Barry was worried Mac might stir up additional trouble.

Or unless the chief was aiming to pin Jake's murder on Mac in the hope that it would get him permanently out of his hair and by association, ruin Bill Confit's chances of a November upset.

It seemed a little over the top, even for Barry. And yet the tail was on *him* and not back at his aunt's house, watching Grace. Unless there were two tails. Mac couldn't see the reason for one, let alone two!

He suddenly realized he'd never gotten any answer from Grace about what had propelled her out of the Broadhurst alley. How did she get there in the first place? Did she remember anything now that her mind seemed clear?

If she'd seen something pertinent, should he turn her over to the police?

No way. Finding Jake's killer was their problem. Protecting Grace was his.

An attempt to get a license plate number failed because the

car didn't seem to have a front plate. In order to shake the guy, Mac made a few tight corners, ignoring the inevitable honks and colorful hand gestures from other drivers. His tail accomplished the same turns until Mac made a hard right at the last moment, all but skidding out of his lane. He watched in satisfaction as the car behind him clipped a row of newspaper machines.

He thought about driving around the corner to check things out from behind. On the other hand, it was a minor accident and he could already see the vehicle backing up. He kept going, making a few more random turns until he was pretty sure he'd lost the guy. Then he pulled into the precinct parking lot.

Mac made his way inside the six-story building he used to think of as a home away from home, ignoring the familiar twinge of sorrow he always felt when coming here. He'd faced the fact long ago that he would never be a cop in Billington again; it was a world that would forever be denied him. He found Lou Gerald at his desk.

"There you are," Lou said, glancing up from a computer terminal. He was older than Mac by a decade, a confirmed family man with four kids and a wife who looked like a swimsuit model.

"We IDed your homeless friend, the guy you called Jake," he said, shuffling through a stack of papers for the right one. "His real name was Michael Wardman, originally from Chicago, but for the last twenty years, from Billington," Lou said as he handed Mac a form. "We hoped his past might point a finger at his killer, but it doesn't look likely."

Mac scanned the paper. "You identified him fast."

"Believe it or not, someone in the morgue recognized him.

Michael Wardman was a doctor back before the bottle got him. His closest living relative is a nephew in Detroit."

A doctor. Grace was terrified of doctors. Did Jake, Michael Wardman, have a connection to Grace beyond the alley and the clothes? Mac said, "How long was the old guy out on the streets?"

Lou shrugged. "Two, maybe three years. And he wasn't that old. Only fifty-eight."

He had looked fifteen years older. The point was, however, that Grace would have been in her late teens when Jake lost himself in booze. Mac didn't know what to make of this information. If Jake being a doctor was directly related to Grace's problems, then the answers to her identity existed in Billington, Indiana, not off in Florida.

He rubbed the back of his head and said, "Did he practice medicine here in Billington?"

"He didn't actually practice medicine. He was in pathology. Worked over at the hospital. That's why the guy in the morgue recognized him. He was in and out of there for years."

Did this mean anything? Seemed unlikely. If the guy had been an OB/GYN, maybe Grace went to him for her pregnancy. But a doctor who studied disease itself? Mac's instincts told him the reason for Jake's murder lay in the present, not in the distant past. Handing Lou the paper he'd perused as he talked, he said, "So, where does the investigation go now?"

"Well, given the climate around here, you won't be surprised to know we're rounding up other derelicts. The mayor will put pressure on the chief and the chief will put pressure on me to solve this case fast."

"Great," Mac said with a sigh.

"It doesn't help matters that the guy in the morgue also

contacted the newspapers. You know how they love a good human interest story and the fact this guy was a fallen MD will give the story legs. Hell, after the stink you raised last year when that derelict under the freeway died, they'll probably want to interview you. I'd say Confit's chances of becoming Billington's next mayor get better every day this case remains unsolved. I'd also say your stock with the chief just took another nosedive."

What's new? Mac thought.

"Can you think of any reason why one of you might tail me after I left the crime scene today?" Mac asked. "Am I wanted for something?" Again he thought of Grace. Had they somehow connected her directly to Jake—Mac couldn't yet think of the man as Michael—and then to him?

"Not that I know of and I'd know, wouldn't I?"

It wasn't a question.

Lou added, "What about that amnesiac girl you were telling me about this morning? Still want me to run her prints?"

It was either an idle question or the beginning of a fishing expedition. Hard to tell which. Mac said, "That won't be necessary after all. I think I've just about located her family."

Lou nodded absently as his gaze roamed back to the keyboard. It must have been an idle question.

Mac knew any investigation engendered massive paperwork and he also knew Lou was a stickler for detail and accuracy. The more thorough the report, the less likely a detective would get himself hauled into court and Lou hated going to court.

Rising, Mac said, "I might be leaving town for a couple of

days. You have my cell number if something else comes up, right?"

"No problem," Lou said, but his fingers were already clicking away.

NEXT, MAC DROVE to his office. He couldn't make a tail this time and he wondered what that meant. He spent a couple of hours dictating notes for his part-time secretary to transcribe next week in case he wasn't back from Florida, or wherever he ended up. He answered calls from worried clients and spent half an hour on the phone with Bill Confit reviewing the report he'd handed over earlier that day.

At home, he found the apartment manager had already replaced the broken window. He packed his duffel bag quickly and then threw the rest of Jessica's old things in a suitcase for Grace. He thought of the way Grace had looked when he'd volunteered his ex-wife's clothing and wondered if it bothered her the clothes were used.

The thought hit him suddenly like one of those bolts of lightning. If someone bought Jake new clothes before they murdered him, might that same someone have donated Grace's old clothes? He found the phone book and searched for a thrift store close to Jake's alley. Sure enough, there was a place just two blocks north of Broadhurst.

His tail picked him up a block from his apartment. Mac did a few fancy turns around town to make sure and then grinned into the rearview mirror. He'd get the license plate number before the night was over and run the plates.

In all, Mac hit three thrift stores. Though he searched through countless garments and found dozens of tags that looked identical to the one stapled to Jake's yellow shirt, he found no piece of clothing that appeared to be of high quality and nothing with French labels. In every store, he was able to talk with the clerk who had worked the night before. Not one of them remembered a man fitting Jake's description buying a yellow shirt, jeans or a green raincoat, nor did anyone recall accepting a high-quality woman's outfit.

As he walked back to his car, he looked across the street, expecting to find the dark sedan that had faithfully followed him from store to store. It was time to stop dithering around with thrift stores and confront whoever was following him.

The only dark car on the block was his own. He watched his rearview mirror as he drove, expecting lights to materialize in his mirror at any moment. The streets were all but empty. He heard on the radio that an ice storm was expected any time. Apparently, the citizenry of Billington had taken heed.

Certain he'd find the dark car lurking outside his apartment, he circled the area several times in ever-narrowing circles.

Nothing. The tail wasn't with him. That left only one place Mac could think of where it might have gone.

Grace.

He took off for his aunt's house.

As Grace snuggled beneath hand-embroidered sheets, she thought sleep would never come. Her mind kept leaping from one thing to another and to top it off, her stomach growled.

Dinner had been a sham. Nerves, tension, Aunt Beatrice and herself both jumping every time they heard a noise…who could eat? It was amazing how many unexplained noises occurred in a big old house like this one on a blustery winter night.

And even worse than the surface tension was the internal anxiety that continued to grow like a cancer gone wild, spreading deadly tentacles throughout her psyche. She needed to *do* something.

But what?

Run?

Run. That's what her heart told her to do. It told her to open the door, defy Mac and his aunt and her own sense of caution, and bolt. It told her she would instinctively know in which direction to flee.

The fact that she so often yearned to run away made her wonder if that was how she usually dealt with problems. If it was, had it contributed to her winding up in Billington, Indiana?

The doctor's after-dinner visit hadn't helped. She'd thrown a hundred questions at him as he took a sample of her blood and examined her bruises and cuts, but he hadn't given her any answers. Just lots of kind pats and consoling murmurs.

At least her fear of doctors seemed to be waning a bit, thanks to him.

So many unknowns. A pregnancy. A baby. A husband. Drug marks on her arm. Old clothes. A murdered man. No memory. Unexplained fears.

Mac!

She wanted Mac. Right here beside her, right here in her bed, his big body hot and consoling. If she was a slut, so be it; bring him on. If she was a married woman who played around on her adoring husband—an adoring husband who apparently hadn't even called the police when she went missing—oh, well.

Warm tears filled her eyes and slid down her cheeks. The hunger was suddenly gone, both for food and for comfort. Fear was back, mangling her innards like a big jungle cat gnawing a fresh kill.

Switching on a bedside lamp, Grace sat up and grabbed the deck of cards. After the doctor's visit, she and Maddie had played a few hands of blackjack. Even Aunt Beatrice had joined in. Both older woman were dismal card players.

In the end, they'd all gone to their bedrooms early, Aunt Beatrice insisting Grace keep the cards for herself.

Grace laid out a game on the bedspread, but solitaire held no allure tonight. Pretty soon, she folded the cards into a pile and turned off the lights.

SHE AWOKE with a jerk that slammed her heart against her ribs.

She lay very still, barely breathing. Searching the dark room with anxious eyes, she found no shadow out of place, nor did she hear anything that would explain what had jolted her from sleep.

Still, something was there.

She knew it.

She considered screaming.

A black shape, man-size, moved across the floor, momentarily blocking the thread of light that rimmed the closed door. Heart hammering, she waited, tensed and poised, until the shape was so close she could hear the sound of controlled breathing. And then she sat up abruptly and swung her fist.

A muffled thud announced she'd connected with someone. So did the stinging in her hand.

Oaths followed.

With alarm, she realized she knew the voice. She said, "Mac?"

"Calm down," he said, switching on the lamp. He held one hand against his cheekbone where she'd slugged him. "It's just me," he said.

"You scared the hell out of me! Why are you sneaking around in the dark? What's wrong?"

The bedsprings creaked as he sat down beside her. He wore a heavy wool coat and she could feel the cold air still trapped within the fibers of the woven material. He looked serious.

"You scared me," she repeated.

"I'm sorry. I didn't mean to startle you."

She felt bad for slugging him. She whispered, "Did I...did I hurt you?"

"You caught me as I was leaning down to wake you," he said as he pulled the comforter up around her shoulders and tucked it around her. She hadn't noticed until then that she was cold.

"Do you need an ice bag?" she asked him.

"No, I'll be all right."

"What are you doing here? What happened? Why are you still in your coat?"

He took both her hands into his. "Grace, listen. Does the name Michael Wardman ring any kind of bell? Doctor Michael Wardman? Think."

She bit her lip and shook her head. "No. Why? Who is he?"

"Michael Wardman was Jake's real name."

"The bum? The bum was a doctor?"

"A pathologist. It probably doesn't mean a thing. Tell me everything you remember before you ran into me last night."

Last night! Had it really been only twenty-four hours since they met? Twenty-four hours since she became the woman she was at this moment?

He prompted, "You flew out of the alley—"

"I don't remember much—"

"Then tell me about the instant you realized you didn't know who you were. There had to be an instant."

She closed her eyes. "I was asleep, like now, and all of a sudden, I woke up."

"Did someone startle you awake like I just did?"

"I don't think so. I just woke up. It was raining and I was cold. I got to my feet." Grace searched her memory, but all she could see was that gray alley, the puddles, the rain. "That's when I realized I didn't have the slightest idea where I was or who I was," she whispered. "I started toward the lighter end of the alley…"

She paused for a second as a black shadow flitted through her mind.

Mac said, "What is it? What are you remembering?"

"A man," Grace said, struggling to keep her voice steady. The truth was that the memory hit her gut like an ice storm. Mac's blue-green gaze focused on her. "He came from the dark end of the alley," she murmured. "I tried to hide. He looked right *through* me. He walked toward the light and I turned around and ran in the other direction—"

"And into me."

"Yes."

"I was walking down 5th. It's a long, straight street. If a man passed you in the alley, he must have come from 5th."

"Was there someone ahead of you on the sidewalk?" Grace said. "Did you see anyone?"

"No. It was raining too hard. I barely looked up. Of course, whoever it was might have already been in the alley, hiding, waiting for you to wake up."

The chill she'd been nursing in her gut tried to claw its way up her spine. Her teeth chattered.

"What did he look like?" Mac asked.

"Tall. He wore a long black coat and a hat. I couldn't see

his face, except for his eyes, but I could *feel* him speculating about me. He terrified me. And then he was gone."

Mac surprised her by pulling her into his arms. His body was solid and real, his coat rough against her cheek. He smelled like rain and the outdoors, healthy and alive. Energy seemed to seep through his embrace and wrap her in its glow.

She pushed him away, gently so it would seem as though she didn't need additional comfort, though the real reason was that she needed and wanted his comfort too much.

"Now what?" she said.

"Get up and get dressed. I want to get you out of Billington."

"Tonight?"

"Right now," he said, standing. "Just put back on the clothes you wore today. Cooper is in the garage transferring our gear to his sedan. Hurry, don't argue, just get dressed. And don't forget your fancy underwear."

Grace all but jumped from beneath the covers. Finally, action!

Mac glanced away quickly and she realized she was stark naked.

Chapter Five

Mac's adrenaline rush fizzled out. In a perfect world, he would pull into a motel and sleep for twelve straight hours. In this world, he kept driving.

By the time they hit highway 65, he was pretty sure he'd lost whatever tail they may have had. Deciding on caution over comfort, he kept driving, determined to put as many miles as possible between Grace and Billington before the sun came up. He'd checked on his computer at work—Miami was a little over a twenty-four hour drive from Billington.

Twenty-four hours.

He couldn't drive for twenty-four straight hours. He didn't know if Grace even knew how to drive. It didn't matter, as she didn't have a license. It was too dangerous to put her behind the wheel. If they got stopped and she had no identification, all sorts of problems they couldn't afford would ensue.

He would have to stop to sleep somewhere.

He'd purposely driven the Coopers' old car because it was nondescript. At the same time they'd left, Cooper and Maddie had taken off in Mac's car with instructions to drive it back to Mac's apartment and bundle themselves inside for the night. And at the same time as that, he'd sent his aunt out in her Mercedes with directions not to stop until she was at her favorite hotel in downtown Billington, where she was supposed to insist the doorman escort her to the desk where she would check in for the night.

He wanted Aunt Beatrice safe.

Just in case.

Hopefully, the tail he hadn't seen since before the last discount store had followed his aunt or the Coopers. Hopefully, by the time the tail figured out he had the wrong car, Mac and Grace would be far away.

Hopefully, his master plan wouldn't backfire when this old car gave up the ghost, stranding them in the middle of nowhere.

He glanced at Grace. The dashboard lights illuminated very little of her face, but he could tell she was asleep, which didn't surprise him. If she'd been drugged, as he suspected she had, the junk would still be working its way through her system. It might take several days before she felt like herself.

Whomever that might be.

He recalled the sight of her standing there nude, all fire and brimstone, ready to go. She was an extremely easy woman to look at and it had taken all his willpower to glance away. What was so blasted sexy about her was the fact that she didn't seem to care a bit about her state of undress.

Her recollection of a man in a dark raincoat with a hat and piercing gaze was almost as troubling as her nudity. And yet the first time they'd met, he must have looked just like that— a tall man in a dark coat wearing a hat. Of course, he hadn't continued walking, but how much faith should he put in her hazy memory?

What he would unequivocally put his faith in was her determination. She wanted to find the truth, he was sure of it. She wasn't working for the mayor or entertaining some other agenda—he'd bet his life on it. Her fear was palatable, her anxiety catching. Even in her sleep, she twitched and murmured as though fighting against her body's need for rest.

Beauty, guts and determination. How was he supposed to keep his dealings with her on a professional level when she presented such an enticing triple threat?

The thought of sharing a motel room with her both alarmed and excited him.

The possibility she had a husband was beginning to concern him less than it should.

And the worry that a man with dark eyes had passed her in that alley had frightened her—well, the possibility of that shadowy figure kept Mac on the road.

"Penny for your thoughts?" Her soft voice jolted him from his musings. He'd had no idea she was awake.

He said, "They're not worth a penny."

"You're tired," she said.

He nodded.

"Let me drive."

He explained about the driver's license. What he didn't add was the fact that he was carrying a concealed weapon in a clip-on holster fitted against the small of his back. He didn't have a license to carry a loaded gun outside the state of Indiana, but that trailing car had convinced him of the necessity of doing so. He didn't need some overzealous highway patrolman finding it.

"We can't afford you getting hauled off to jail," he said, and that was true, as well. "I'll drive."

"But you have to stop sometime."

"I know, just not yet. I thought you were all hot to trot."

"I am," she snapped and he felt instantly bad for questioning her sincerity.

"I know you are. Don't worry. I'm fine. Besides, you're tired, too," he said, doing his best to keep from picturing the two of them alone in a room whose sole attraction was a great big, soft bed.

"Not really. I feel like I've done nothing but sleep since the beginning of time. I guess that's more or less accurate. Since the beginning of my current time, anyway."

"I'm not that tired yet," he said, and passing a road sign, added, "We should be in Louisville by sunrise. One of us might as well be rested. Go ahead and close your eyes."

He was hoping she would settle down and sleep the remainder of the night away. The only thing more alarming than thinking about Grace was talking to her. With a mental slap to his forehead, it all of a sudden occurred to him that as far as he could tell, she had no trace of a Southern accent. If she was from the South, she wasn't a native. Nor was she from New York or Boston. He recognized no accent at all.

Another tiny piece of a puzzle of unknown size.

Grace said, "Did someone follow us out of Billington?"

"I don't think so."

"But you sent your aunt and the Coopers off in different cars at the same time we left. You must have thought someone following us was at least a possibility."

"It was a possibility," he admitted. "I'll be honest with you. I had a tail after I left you and Aunt Beatrice tonight. Keep your eyes peeled for a dark sedan."

"It's night. Every car out here looks like a dark sedan."

"This one won't be whizzing past us going ninety miles an hour," Mac said dryly. "It'll lurk behind."

"Why would anyone want to follow us?"

"If we knew the answer to that—"

"I mean, if there is a tail, it must be on you."

He said, "Everyone who cares about what I do or say is in Billington. They'll all throw a party when they realize I left town. If someone followed us, it's because of you, Grace."

"The only reason someone would follow me is because they know who I am," she said.

"Yes."

"So why don't we trap them and make them tell us what they know?"

"And how do we do that?"

"Trap them or make them talk?"

"Either. Both. Besides, if they're following us now, I can't see them. Chances are good we left whomever it was back in Billington."

She was quiet for quite a while, which was okay with Mac. He had a lot to think about, not the least of which was what he was going to do with Grace if the underwear lead didn't pan out. He supposed he'd have to drive her back to Billington. Hopefully by then, Lou and the rest of the police would have caught the person responsible for killing Jake, er, Michael Wardman. With that loose end tied up, he could take Grace to the police and they could conduct a proper search.

He knew all of this was hogwash even as he comforted himself with it. The police stood no better chance of getting Grace back home than he did. Not as good a chance, for that matter, as their hands were tied in ways that his weren't.

He started thinking about what Grace had said about trapping their tail and making them talk. Maybe it was fatigue doing it to him, but her idea began to make more and more sense. Come to think of it, he should never have left Billington without giving it a try. This kind of caution—the kind that had made it seem imperative to get Grace to safety—was new to him. Normally, he'd stand his ground, but when his ground included her, to say nothing of his elderly aunt and the Coopers, then the stakes were just too high.

Still, he should have stuck them all in a hotel room and tackled the tail back in Billington, back where he knew his way around.

On the other hand, he'd seen no sign of the tail since the last thrift store. Maybe it was some overzealous cop and had nothing to do with Grace.

She said, "What was she like?"

"What was who like?"

"Your wife."

Adroit at dodging uncomfortable questions, he said, "She was like a light beer. Lots of bubbles, not much taste, very little follow-through."

Grace didn't even smile. "What was her name?"

"Jessica."

"What did she look like?"

"Why do you care what she looked like?" he snarled.

For a long time, he thought his annoyed response had put the quietus on Grace's questions. Eventually, however, she said, "Look at all those lights in all those houses." Her voice was soft, dreamy.

He looked out his window and saw the lights and didn't have the slightest idea where she was going with this new line of conversation.

"All those people," she continued. "All those families, all

those lives. All going on behind closed doors, behind blinds and draperies. But all so real."

Now he understood. All those lives, all real, unlike hers. He said nothing.

"Ever since I put on your ex-wife's clothes this morning, I've been trying to picture her," Grace said and he could feel her gaze on him. "I guess you and your aunt and the Coopers are the only people I know right now. My head feels like a great big stadium, one of those monstrosities that seat umpteen thousands of people. Only in my case, just four people showed up for the game. Even the playing field is empty. No game. No spectators. Just this gnawing sense of urgency that won't go away. Can't you drive faster?"

"No, I can't drive faster."

Grace fell silent.

The miles sped by, the old car giving no indication of its age. If a car aged by miles and not years, this car really wasn't that old, Mac thought, as it had spent most of its life in his aunt's garage. The Coopers weren't known for taking long road trips.

He grew alarmed when his eyes drifted closed. If the price for company on this drive was disclosure, then he might as well talk. He said, "Jessica was…pretty. Dark hair, dark eyes, slender. Pretty."

Grace shifted in her seat to stare at him, and he added, "I guess like everyone else, Jessica was just a person looking to get from point A to point B. I was the road she chose to travel. For a while."

"You make her sound like a tourist," Grace said.

"That's a good word for her," he said. "A tourist. I like that."

"How did you meet?"

"A blind date. I'd just gotten out of the army. I was kind of shell-shocked."

"Why?"

He cast her an exasperated glance. Apparently, her vicarious life demanded details. Swallowing hard, he said, "There'd been an…accident. A helicopter crash. My best friend, Rob Confit, died. Anyway, when I got out, Rob's family kind of adopted me. My dad was dead by then, so it was nice for me and they, well, they missed Rob. Eventually, Rob's sister set me up with Jessica."

"Was it love at first sight?" Grace asked wistfully as if she were a little kid and had just read her first fairy tale about a princess and the knight who rescued her from a dragon.

"Kind of. Jessica seemed to hang on my every word. It was very flattering. We were married less than six months after we met."

"So her main attraction was that she seemed to idolize you?"

He spared her another glance. "Hey, don't knock it. Marriages have been built on far less than that."

She shrugged. "So what happened?"

"I let her down," he said, surprised by his choice of words.

"That's hard to imagine," Grace said.

"But it's true," he admitted. "I told people that she got irritated with my preoccupation with work. The drug unit undercover stuff was hard on her."

"You had a career—"

"No. The truth was I wasn't there for her, and one day she got sick of it and found someone else. And in my heart of hearts, I knew I'd been expecting her to leave me since the moment she'd uttered, 'I do.'"

Grace said, "It can't all be your fault, Mac."

"Maybe not," he muttered, unwilling to divulge the ugly details of the nights he'd justified working instead of going home. Her leaving hadn't come as a huge surprise. If he were honest, he'd have to admit that maybe it had even been something of a relief when his marriage was finally over. He added, "But I have to take the lion's share of the blame."

"How long ago did all this happen?" Grace asked.

Another glance at her and he said, "Three years. I was working a homicide. I came home one night and she was gone."

"Just like that?"

"Just like that. Packed up most of her clothes and flew off to New Jersey with a new Mr. Right." Talking about Jessica had always left a bitter taste in Mac's mouth. He noticed the taste wasn't quite as distinct this time. "She left me a note."

Grace cleared her throat. "Is Jessica the reason you looked so angry today?"

"When did I look angry?"

"When we were discussing possible scenarios for my fancy underwear. You implied I might have a lover. I might be as big a floozy as your ex."

"Or maybe you just like nice clothes and have the money to indulge yourself."

"Maybe, maybe," she said wistfully. Then, her voice little more than a whisper, added, "I just hope I'm not a shallow, rich snob."

He laughed. At first, he could feel her stiffen in the passenger seat as though he'd offended her. Eventually, a chuckle escaped her lips and she fell silent again.

WHAT AN ODD thing memory loss was.

Grace knew she didn't like cooked beets and that she did like dogs. She couldn't hold a tune, she didn't like hot tea. She loved beaches.

If she knew so much about herself, then why didn't she know her name? Why couldn't she recall a husband or her pregnancy? How about parents? Childhood? Anything! And why did Billington sound like the wrong place for a home, but Florida sound right?

Right, wrong…all so muddled.

And all so immaterial, because the big issues Mac didn't mention very often were so much more important.

How did she get in that alley? Why had she been drugged? Why wasn't her family looking for her? Did she have anything to do with the death of Dr. Michael Wardman?

"I know your dad died a few years ago and I heard Maddie say I might be just like your mother. What did she mean?" she asked Mac, pressing for the details of something she could understand.

"When did you and Maddie spend so much time together?" Mac growled.

"We played cards. After dinner. She was talkative and I was desperate for something to think about besides these endless questions that have no answers. She whispered the part about your mother to your aunt, however, when she thought I wasn't paying attention."

"Hm—"

"You're avoiding the question. Tell me about your mother."

He rubbed the back of his head with one large hand while gripping the steering wheel with the other. His knuckles on that hand looked white. "There's not much to tell."

"Why would Maddie say I *might* be just like her?"

"Because my mother ran away. I assume Maddie was insinuating that you may have run away, too."

"I don't think I did," Grace said. "I can't imagine I would abandon a child. Oh, Mac, did your mother abandon you?"

"She left home when I was six," he said.

"She left? You mean…for good?"

"For good."

"And you never saw her again?"

"Once. I was twelve. I saw her on a street corner in Los Angeles."

"I don't understand. How did you get to Los Angeles—"

"My father took me," he said curtly. She saw his jaw muscle clench and was half-sorry she'd brought the subject up. Half-sorry. She needed to know more. She needed to know why she might be like his mother.

Mac finally loosened his grip on the wheel.

She said, "Did you talk to her? In L.A. I mean?"

He laughed once—a bark really, no mirth. He glanced at her and then back at the road. Finally, he said, "I don't think my dad intended me to see my mother like that. Homeless. Begging. Wasted away with a drug habit. Eyes dull, hair matted. I learned later he'd been searching for her for years. When a private eye came up with her location, he just grabbed me and off we went."

Grace felt her heart wrench. "That's awful."

"So, no, we didn't have a family chat. No, 'My, how you've grown.' No, 'I missed you, son.' I pretty much stared at her while she tried to hit my dad up for money. I learned later that he had her committed to a drug rehab program. Apparently, she left as soon as he turned his back and that was the end of her."

The end…

"I waited years for her to come find me," he said. In his

voice, Grace thought she detected the remnants of the boy he'd once been and she fought the desire to try to comfort him. She had to sit on her hands to keep them to herself.

"I blamed my father for everything," he added. "I didn't understand that he had tried to take her back home with us, that he'd begged her to let him take care of her, but she'd refused. She didn't care. She didn't care that she had a son or a marriage."

"But your dad cared," Grace murmured.

"Yes. I didn't understand that until years later. I thought he caused her to leave. I didn't know the truth until he was literally on his deathbed and Aunt Beatrice finally spoke up in his defense."

"Why didn't he just tell you himself?"

"He didn't want me to feel rejected by her. He was trying to protect her."

"I think he was trying to protect you, not her."

"Maybe," he said.

"Maybe that's what my husband is doing," Grace said softly. "Maybe I've run away before, maybe he's just waiting for me to come home on my own and that's why he hasn't called me in as a missing person."

Mac cast her a swift, unreadable look. "For what it's worth," he said, "you don't seem like a space cadet to me. You're not an addict. Your instincts are good. You seem rational."

She whispered, "Thank you," but nothing he said really precluded her being as flaky as his mother. So she wasn't an addict—that didn't mean she didn't have a drug habit at times of stress, times that might find her indulging in her all-too-frequent fantasy of running away.

The old car seemed to crawl down the highway. Mac was

yawning a lot and she wondered when he'd admit he was too tired to keep driving. She also wondered how she'd manage to stand eight hours of inactivity when he finally tucked himself into a motel bed. As it was, she had to fight the desire to stick a foot out the door and help the car go faster.

She stole a look at his profile. It was a good one. Strong, competent, a determined-looking chin, an alert gleam in what she could see of his right eye, a nice, straight nose. The kind of man who took on responsibility without hesitation. If he was half as competent as he seemed, she was safe with him; he would see her problem through to its conclusion. He'd proven he could be trusted; he'd not abandoned her—at least, not yet.

But to complicate matters, there was no denying the way her body responded to his. The tingle of awareness that passed between them even now on the big bench seat of the old car. The haven of his arms when she was frightened, the comfort of his voice when she felt alone. Given half a chance, she'd touch his leg or caress his cheek. He was a stranger and yet he was familiar in a way no one else was. And she was lonely to the very core of her being.

What about your husband? What about your child?

A new thought entered her mind. "Mac?" Her voice sounded shrill to her own ears.

He glanced at her. "What is it? What's wrong?"

"What if this urgency I'm feeling is connected to the fact that my husband apparently isn't looking for me? What if at the same time someone drugged me and I lost my memory, he was hurt or kidnapped or something? Maybe we're from Florida, maybe we were vacationing in Billington, maybe I got hit on the head and he got hurt or—something. Maybe he's relying on me to come to his rescue. Maybe our child is with him!"

Mac shrugged one shoulder. "First thing—anyone who can afford underwear like yours can afford somewhere more hospitable than Billington in January for their vacation."

"But I might have family in Billington. Maybe we should have gone to the police and run my picture in the paper."

"You refused to go to the police," he reminded her. "You were quite…adamant."

"I know, but—"

"Grace, I can only drive so fast," he said softly, reaching over with his right hand and grasping her hand. "We can't alert the authorities to look for your husband because we're not sure you have a husband. If you do, we don't know where he might be. We have to start with your identity. That will lead us to your family. If Florida doesn't work out, we'll go back to Indiana and start over, but think of this. If you and your husband and child were visiting family, then surely one of them would have missed you by now and be in contact with the police. I checked. No one was reported missing in the past few days. No one. Not a woman, not a child, not a man. I called the hospitals—no nameless accident victims. My friend on the force will keep his eyes peeled and call if something breaks. Try to stay calm. Try not to think too much."

Try not to think!

What else could she do, trapped in this car with a man she shouldn't be attracted to but was, traveling at a snail's pace, worrying it might be in the wrong direction, worrying that there might never be a right direction or if there was, worried that she wouldn't know it when it presented itself.

Try not to think. Sure. Easy.

She might as well be dead as try not to think.

THE SUN CAME UP as they passed a sign announcing an exit cluttered with gas station and restaurant logos. Chattanooga was on the next sign, but she missed how many miles away it was. It didn't matter.

"We're almost out of gas," Mac said around another yawn. He took the off ramp. The streets glistened with spent rain. The sky promised more to come.

Mac pulled into a station and as Grace looked around, she saw a motel across the street and reluctantly pointed it out. "Maybe we should stop."

He gestured toward a coffee shop on the other corner. "Let's get something to eat. A couple of cups of coffee and I think I can continue driving. If I can hang in there a few more hours, then we can stop for part of the night and roll into Miami tomorrow afternoon. Okay with you?"

She nodded anxiously and watched as he filled the tank, wishing she could do more to help. She found herself staring out all the windows, looking for a dark sedan like the one Mac had mentioned, a car going slowly, perhaps, the driver interested in the pale green car at the gas station. No one cruised by suspiciously, but she couldn't stop watching.

It seemed the farther south they got, the more urgent her worries became. Mac got back into the car and drove it across the intersection.

The coffee shop looked and smelled the way Grace knew it would, even though she had no recollection of ever before stepping inside one. Upholstery a little shabby, mixed aromas of bacon and coffee thick in the air, hurried waitresses in pink uniforms and single men hunched over plates of eggs. Two strings of weak Christmas lights circled the counter near the cash register. They blinked on and off, unheralded. They looked as though they'd been in position for years, not weeks.

Grace found herself wondering where she'd spent her last Christmas and with whom.

Mac ordered buttermilk pancakes, so she did too. She bypassed coffee and drank milk. Maddie had told her that caffeine was bad for taut nerves. Grace had already known that, another one of those loose memories that rattled around in her head like the last peanut in a can. And just about as worthless.

"The service is slow," Mac said.

"The waitress has probably been on her feet all night," Grace said. "She's probably trying to pay the rent and support some bum of a boyfriend. Maybe she has two or three jobs. Cut her some slack."

He raised his eyebrows, but made no further comment.

When the food did come, it was hot and plentiful. Grace found the pancakes gummy and hard to swallow, but when Mac said something about how eating a big breakfast meant they wouldn't have to take time to stop for lunch, she polished off half the stack.

Time not eating meant time traveling closer to some kind of conclusion...

As he drank the last of his coffee, Mac said, "What are you staring at?"

"Your eye. I'm sorry I slugged you."

His fingers grazed his face as he said, "I've been slugged a lot harder than this and lived to tell the tale. Combine this shiner with my stubble and I'm going to look like a derelict by the time we get to Miami, though. I'll shave when we stop for the night."

When we stop for the night, Grace thought, anxiety seeping around the heavy edges of the pancakes.

Hours wasted.

No option, though. The man had to sleep sometime.

He pulled out his wallet, no doubt looking for a tip.

He said, "Let's use the facilities and then get out of here."

Sounded good to her.

A HEAVY GROUND fog shrouded the highway for the first few hours of driving after they left the diner. The freeway was a blur, the driving as dangerous as it was dull. Eventually, the skies cleared some and Mac stared at gauzy scenery he was too tired to appreciate. He tried recalling song lyrics to stay alert, then switched to imagining what life would be like if you couldn't remember your past.

No family. No friends. No history.

No mother. No loss.

He thought of the surly way he'd felt when Grace had asked him about Jessica. At least her image was there for him to relegate to the slush heap. His choice, his decision. His past.

Same with his mother. She hadn't been much, but at least he could recall her face. Sort of.

Grace could remember nothing of her past and so had tried to understand his. Given her set of circumstances, he realized, he would do the same thing and he was sorry he'd snapped at her.

After all, what else were they supposed to talk about? She had a history of about thirty-six hours and the only people she'd met were his people and the only one who had treated her more or less like anyone else was Maddie Cooper. A little of his annoyance with Maddie's gossip dissipated.

Grace had fallen asleep a couple of hours after the diner which had been a relief. At first, wound up tight with anxiety, she'd fired question after question at him. He hadn't taken this many walks down memory lane since—well, since never. She'd wanted to know where he went to school, what kind of girls he dated, what holidays were like, his aunt's entire history. And he'd indulged her up to the point when she started skating on thin ice, asking him to once again travel into areas of his past that still hurt. Then he'd said enough was enough and she'd drifted off to sleep.

Unfortunately, it wasn't as easy for him to let go of the memories she'd awakened. His mother. Jessica. Rob Confit. Three people he'd loved and lost. Too late now for fixing anything. A man did not prosper who wallowed in the disappointments of the past. Suffer what you must, accept what can't be changed, get on with things. That was his credo and it had stood him well through the years.

It occurred to him that the events of the last year had all led up to this point. The disillusionment with the force, the harassment, the task force and facing his demons on a nightly basis—he just felt a little shock worn. Then Grace had stumbled into his path and now look at where he was.

Not far enough south, that's where. He did a few mental calculations. His hope was to drive as far as St. Augustine, Florida, which was still a long way away. Once there, he'd fall into an eight-hour coma and take off again for Miami early the next morning. This time tomorrow, they'd be close to their goal. He tried to imagine a positive conclusion to their visit at the *L'Hippocampe* boutique.

It had to be the right boutique on the right day with the right employee present. It was one thing to offer a name to a salesperson, who could then look it up on their computer. It was another to hope for instant sight recognition.

In short, their quest seemed naive and hopeless.

Night was closing in so he switched on his headlights. As he did so, he glanced in the rearview mirror, something he did every few minutes, always expecting to see a black car following at a safe distance even though tracking a car on an interstate highway was a lot harder than in the city. This time, he felt his heartbeat accelerate and some of the weariness vanish from his limbs.

There was a headlight askew a few cars back.

His worn out brain searched the recent past. He'd seen that headlight before. In the fog, two states ago, that's where he'd noticed it. The driver's light pointed up and out. In city lights, it might not be noticeable, but here on the open highway, it was like a beacon.

He'd seen that car before.

Chapter Six

As Mac sped up, the car with the skewed headlight disappeared behind them. Hands gripping the wheel, gaze continually darting to the rearview mirror, he eventually slowed down. Sure enough, the wacky headlight came into view within minutes, coming on fast, then slowing and blending in with the other traffic.

His mind raced.

Grace made a sound in her sleep. He glanced at her in time to see her hands flutter in her lap. She said, "No," softly but urgently, like a wounded, frightened child, and his heart twisted in his chest.

Her next, "No," was louder and more violent and her hand batted at a dreamscape foe. He spared a hand from the wheel to shake her shoulder and murmur her name.

She awoke with startled eyes that stared right through him. He saw recognition flood her gaze and then a wan smile. "You okay?" he asked.

"I was dreaming," she said.

He glanced back again and mumbled, "A nice helpful dream maybe, with names and addresses?"

"Sorry, nothing concrete." Smothering a yawn, she asked, "Where are we?"

"Just outside Macon, Georgia."

He could feel her staring at him. Did she sense his uneasiness? He was trying his best to mask it, still unsure if the car six or seven vehicles back was connected to them or not.

Finally, she said, "Mac, you have to be bushed."

"Another three or four hours—"

"No. You haven't eaten since breakfast. We'll get up early and make up the time in the morning. It's dark in here, but damn, you look like hell. Stop at the next exit and get a motel. You know I'm right."

His mind whirled. What he knew was that a car with a weird headlight had been behind them for hundreds of miles. He also knew the car that had trailed him in Billington had crashed into a newspaper machine on the driver's side. Not a serious accident, but enough to whack a headlight out of alignment.

Was this their tail? He blinked a few times, cursing the fatigue that pulled on him like gravity. What had it been, forty-eight hours since he'd slept? He felt dull-witted and stupid.

"What is it?" she asked.

Get off the road, his inner voice demanded. *You can't fight when you're this tired. You can't plot a nice little trap when you can't think. You can't protect Grace.*

Hell, maybe that car buck there is a station wagon full of vacationers.

"Mac?"

"You're right," he said. He slowed down and watched as the car with the bad light passed him. Late-model, dark, impossible to see the occupants in the poor light. He waited until the car was far ahead before he took one of three possible exits, speeding up, turning, then turning again. He'd seen signs advertising a roadside inn with underground parking, and now he told Grace what to look for as he studied the mirror.

"Up ahead, on the right," she finally said as he almost turned the wrong way down a one-way street.

Soon they were deep inside the ground, parked in the darkest recess. Minutes later, he registered them as Mr. and Mrs. Weston, using a fake ID he carried for just such a purpose. He noticed with relief that the place had a lounge and a restaurant, which meant they could order up dinner.

Soon after that, they were inside their room.

What now? He could think of nothing to do but wait. He made a few calls on his cell phone, one to check that his aunt and the Coopers were okay and another to Lou to see if anything had broken on Jake's murder case. He idly asked about missing persons as well. Both calls had the same result. Everything was fine, nothing new to report.

After that, he stared at the plush bed, torn with conflicting emotions about how he'd like to put it to use. Part of him wanted to crawl between the sheets and black out. A bigger part longed to coax Grace in with him and do everything in the world but sleep.

The trick would be to do neither, at least not for a few hours, until he was sure they were safe.

"You look like a caged tiger," Grace said from a chair in the corner.

He tried smiling.

"Want to tell me what all that fancy driving was about or shall I take a guess? You saw something—"

"I don't know what I saw," he said honestly, rubbing the

back of his neck, weary to his bones. "I'm a careful kind of man, Grace. Not a risk taker."

"I don't believe you," she stated frankly.

"Well, it's true. Risks are for fools. I'm a dull, ordinary guy who just wants to safely escort a client home. That's why you hired me, right?"

"Technically, your aunt hired you," she said.

"Not exactly," he said. "I didn't accept her money."

"What do you mean? I thought you were going to let *her* finance this venture? I was going to pay her back."

God, she looked good sitting in the chair, even with her body kind of pitched forward, weight on the balls of her feet like she might make a run for it if he turned his back. She looked alert and healthier than he'd so far seen, her bright aura the total opposite of his burned-out fatigue. Of course, she was a decade younger and she'd slept most of the day away.

"I'm betting that anyone who can afford a five-hundred dollar bra can afford my fees. I'll keep the receipts and when this is all over, I'll bill you, okay? Meanwhile, I don't want to be my aunt's employee, I want to be yours. Do you understand?"

She thought for a second and nodded.

"Good. By the way, Aunt Bea's doctor sent your blood work off to the lab. They should have an answer tomorrow. I'm going to take a shower. Why don't you order us some dinner from room service? I'd like a straight bourbon and a medium-rare steak. No potato, extra vegetables. And Grace, don't open the door to anyone, okay, no matter what? Promise me?"

"Why?" she snapped, eyes sparkling with curiosity.

"You are the most hard headed—"

She waved him away with her hand, which he took to be as close to a promise as he could expect. Of course, if he told her about the car with the headlight, she'd no doubt dutifully cower in the corner, but damn, he hated taking that bit of fire out of her eyes. It looked good in there. Way too good to extinguish with a string of maybes.

Grabbing his duffel bag, he closed the bathroom door behind him. He heard Grace pick up the phone and order their dinner.

THE SHOWER revived him a bit, as did a shave and a change of clothes. It was the first time he'd really seen his face in days. The shiner Grace had given him the night before went a long way toward explaining why the check-in clerk had seemed fidgety.

He was tying his shoe when he heard a knock on the outside door. He pushed the bathroom door open, glanced at Grace with a stay-put look in his eyes and retrieved his gun, which he then tucked in the waistband of his jeans. It felt cold against the small of his back.

He looked through the peephole and found a gangly youth with a food cart. If this was their tail, he'd either started his life of crime at a tender age or affected a very ingenious disguise.

Mac opened the door slowly.

The kid was tall and awkward, still in his teens, Mac guessed, though technically, a kid that age shouldn't be delivering liquor. Mac felt kind of bad for even entertaining the thought this youngster could be dangerous, so after he settled their bill with cash, he tipped the kid twice as much as he should have, which earned him an enthusiastic shake of the hand.

"You didn't order yourself any dinner," Mac said as he lifted the lid off the single plate and found his steak. No vegetables. Giant potato. They never got it right. He covered it again and picked up the drink.

"I'm not hungry," Grace said from her chair where she flipped through the television channel guide without looking at the pages. "I'm too nervous to eat."

He put the gun on the dresser and sat down on the edge of the bed. "Come here," he said as he took the first sip of his drink and felt it spread a warm glow inside his body. With a lift of the glass, he offered to share it with Grace. She hadn't ordered herself anything to drink, either, but she shook her head and stayed in the chair.

"Please, Grace, come here," he repeated, patting the spread beside him.

Setting aside the magazine, she rose gracefully, still wearing Jessica's slacks and sweater, though the clothes were going to be way too warm for Miami.

The thought ran through his head that Jessica had never looked this good in either piece of clothing. She'd been a pretty woman, but she hadn't moved like Grace.

Grace stood over him for a second and he bent his head back to look up at her. The light in the room came from a single lamp and it cast her face in shadows. Setting aside the drink, he took one of her hands. Maybe he should come clean with her. He said, "Grace, sit down, please."

She sat beside him, bringing her face into full light, so close her features commanded all his attention. Big blue eyes, small nose, full lips. Short black hair. Rounded cheeks flushed like peonies.

Hell, he wasn't even sure what a peony looked like....

She barely touched his bruised cheekbone. Her touch was casual but for some reason he couldn't explain, electrifying. Galvanizing. Why that one touch should send a shudder right into his groin was one of nature's little tricks, he mused, played out every second of every day by the good people on the planet Earth as they looked at and touched one another in subtle ways that changed their corners of the world forever.

Damn, he was turning into a philosopher after one lousy sip of bourbon!

He caught her hand. His lips grazed her fingers.

"What are you doing, Mac?" she whispered, her full attention on his mouth, not his eyes, as though she couldn't tear her gaze away from his lips. He found her concentrated focus to be incredibly sexy. It drove what little rational thought he still possessed straight out of his mind.

"Nothing," he said, his voice husky, desire spreading through his body.

She seemed as mesmerized as he was by the way their fingers twined of their own accord. Their gaze met again. She whispered, "Then why does it feel as though you're doing something?"

No answer to that. It was part of the mystery. He didn't know what to do with her or with himself. He only knew what he wanted to do.

She further blindsided him by slowly leaning closer until her lips touched his. She pulled away at once as though his mouth had shocked her. He supposed it was her own boldness that surprised her. It sure as hell surprised him.

But that one chaste kiss was the spark that started the fire. He put a hand behind her head and pulled her to him again, and after the briefest of moments, she came with a sigh that quaked her slender body. When their mouths touched this time, there was no pulling back.

At first, it was like the first bite of food after years of starvation. Greedy, consuming, no moment for thought or even breathing. All moisture and warmth and tongues sliding against each other. At first, it was all sensuality and nothing more.

And then passion kicked in, that craving that surpassed hunger, unstoppable, insatiable. They fell back against the bedspread and he pinned her with his upper body, his hand sliding under her sweater, against her bare skin, his fingers flicking over the silk of her bra, her tender breasts warm and soft beneath the silk.

She aroused a host of emotions in him, so many they collided in his heart like bumper cars at the fair. Tenderness and lust, watchfulness and abandon, a sense of danger, a sense of need. He wanted to make love to her for a week. He wanted to fall in love with her. He wanted to see her fall in love with him. He wanted to know she would never take another breath without thinking of him.

That she would never kiss another man without thinking of him.

Her hand circled his neck; she pressed up against him. Her body was strong and sensual. He responded in all the predictable, delicious ways. With one hand covering her silk-clad breast, his finger grazed the tiny sea horse. The diamond, tiny as it was, grated against his nail.

Like a man grabbing a trapeze moments before a fall, he came to what remained of his senses.

He was her lifeline.

He was the float she needed to grab so she wouldn't drown, the vine hovering within reach over a pool of quicksand. She had placed all her hopes in his discretion, his judgment, his experience, and he was about to squander it all for a few hours of bliss.

And maybe, just maybe, that's why she was sucking on his earlobe and grinding her hips against his. This whole interlude might have more to do with Grace's understandable primal instinct to bind him to her than because she found him so damn lovable.

His hand slid off her breast and from beneath the sweater. Holding her close, he pulled them both back into a sitting position.

She rested her face against his. He could feel the warm exhalation of her breath against his cheek and eyelid. It seemed more intimate than their kisses. He couldn't imagine what she was thinking. His own thoughts were hopelessly tangled like a huge ball of fishing line snagged on a waterlogged branch deep below the surface. Tenderness for her. Concern for her situation. His loss, her loss.

All of it illuminated by the skewed glow of a twisted headlight.

At last he said, "I—"

She cut him off. Her voice was breathless and soft. "Don't."

"But—"

She pulled away a little and put a finger against his lips. "Don't," she repeated, tears suddenly filling her eyes.

"Grace—"

"I feel so useless," she said at last, and then confirming all his doubts, added, "Like I'm wasting your time—"

He hushed her with a hug, studiously ignoring the way she filled his arms. When she finally looked at him again, her eyes were moist but the tears had stopped.

"But more than that, Mac, for a moment I completely forgot I might be a married woman," she said. "I'm ashamed of myself."

"Grace…"

Casting about as if for a safe topic, her gaze settled on the food tray. "Your dinner is getting cold," she said, rising and pulling the tray close to him.

He admired her attempt to reestablish boundaries. He should do the same thing, he should talk to her matter-of-factly about the possible tail, about the possible danger lurking outside the door.

But he couldn't. She wouldn't meet his gaze.

Hell.

If he was right, the tail would find them on the highway the next morning, might even know where they were right at that moment. Mac had all night to plot a trap.

Why keep Grace up all night worrying?

"I'll eat if you'll eat," he said, and so they sat side by side on the edge of the huge bed, him cutting the steak, her dutifully eating an occasional bite, her eyes averted. He was too wiped out to drink alcohol and remain vigilant, so he took minuscule sips while she polished off most of the bourbon and all of the potato. With luck, the drink would relax her.

It seemed to work. After dinner, desperate for something to do that would fill in the time until bed and supersede the need for intimate conversation, he asked her to dig the cards out of the purse his aunt had given her. She agreed reluctantly and then shuffled them with a fluid motion that mesmerized him.

"Do you know how to play poker?" he asked her. "I have a pocketful of loose change."

She dealt their hands on the bedspread as he split the coins between them. "Seven card stud, deuces wild, ante up," she said.

He stared at her for a moment. This was a side of her he hadn't seen. An hour later, one dollar and fifty-eight cents poorer, he was glad when she begged off. "Time for me to take a shower," she said, gazing at the carpet.

He rolled the dinner tray out into the hall and locked the door again, knowing he was going to spend another night on guard duty.

He flipped on the TV so Grace wouldn't ask him to play cards again after her shower. It was a little embarrassing to get creamed at poker by a sweet-faced young woman who wouldn't meet your eye.

And he didn't want to talk to her again, either.

GRACE STOOD under the shower for a long time, letting the hot water pound her head and shoulders.

She'd spent the last hour acting like she didn't have a care in the world, trying so hard to make things normal her head pounded with the effort.

She'd been ready to make love to Travis MacBeth. If he hadn't had second thoughts, they'd be lovers now.

She pushed her fingertips against her forehead. It didn't take a genius to figure out the complications of a physical relationship between herself and Mac. Big one: she might be married. There might not be an answer waiting for them in Miami. They might have to return up north. She might have to relent and go to the police. She might be a felon. Perhaps her amnesia was a direct result of a guilty conscience. What if she'd murdered her husband? What if she was on the run from the law?

But why the memory loss, why the drugged state, why the needle marks in her arm? Why?

Best-case scenario—she regained her memory during the night.

Then what?

An end to this nightmare.

What would happen to Mac?

She'd become yet another woman who used him and left him.

The sexual tension throbbing between them didn't matter, nor did the fact that it was perfectly clear he shared her longing for intimacy. None of that mattered.

She wouldn't use him.

She wanted to run.

She stared at the doorknob and pictured turning it, walking out into the room, telling Mac she wanted a soda or a magazine from one of those little shops she'd seen signs advertising as they crossed the lobby. She tried to picture him agreeing to let her walk out of the room alone.

He wouldn't do it. He'd either go for her or insist on coming along.

So, if he went down there alone, what would stop her from leaving while he was gone?

Why don't you just fire him? an inner voice posed.

Because Mac wasn't the kind of man you could just fire. But the other reason was because she couldn't bear the thought of losing him forever.

Not until she had to, anyway.

All she wanted to do was get away for a while.

He would simply have to accept the fact that she wanted to be alone. She'd tell him straight. He'd be angry, but that was his problem.

Towel dried, she slipped on gray pants and a long, ivory top. She had to admit that Mac's ex-wife had nice taste. And yet the more complicated Grace's feelings for Mac grew, the more she hated wearing clothes that had once belonged to another woman.

Taking a deep breath, she opened the door and marched resolutely into the room.

All that resolution, all for nothing. He was asleep atop the bedspread, hands crossed over his chest, head kind of tilted as though he'd nodded off without meaning to. The only illumination in the room came from the TV. She approached quietly and looked at him for a moment in the flickering light.

Such a handsome, rugged, masculine man. So big and powerful and oddly innocent looking in his sleep. She stared at his lips and then at his hands, and her head felt light. She thought of him coming home to an empty house with a note on the table and his wife gone forever. She thought of the things Mac's aunt had told her, the way Mac was drummed out of the police force, the accident in the army.

She stared at him. He was a man used to going it alone, to coping with things in his own way. To calling the shots. In some ways, she thought, he was as solitary as she was.

She turned away and pulled a blanket from the closet shelf, draping it over his recumbent body, and then tried adjusting the pillow beneath his head so he wouldn't wake up with a stiff neck.

Why hadn't he asked for a room with two queen beds instead of this one king that had been offered? Or had he? She couldn't recall what he'd said to the woman who checked them in downstairs, only that as far as this motel was concerned, she was Jane Weston, wife of James Weston, the man now asleep on the bed.

That's why he hadn't made a point of asking for two beds, she realized. A married couple would want one bed and that's what they were supposed to be.

Mac was thorough.

Her reason for running was sound asleep, but that fact didn't change the antsy, got-to-move feeling still coursing through her veins.

She gently dislodged her hand and resettled his head on the pillow, relieved when he didn't stir.

Crossing to the chair in the corner she'd commandeered as her headquarters, she retrieved the little purse Aunt Beatrice had given her. Slipping it over her shoulder, she took the card-key and quietly let herself out of the room, careful to test the knob to make sure the door locked behind her.

She realized at once that she should have left him a note but was reluctant to chance going back into the room to do so now.

As she walked down the hall with increasingly sure-footed steps, she realized that for the first time since awakening in the alley, she felt…strong.

It felt good.

MAC WOKE UP instantly, pushing aside a blanket he didn't recall pulling over himself as he rose to his feet. He cursed the fatigue that had lulled him to sleep. One look around the room told him what he needed to know—Grace was gone.

How long? He switched on a lamp and checked his watch. It was ten o'clock. When had they eaten? Six-thirty? Seven? How long had she been gone? Two, three hours? Where would she spend that kind of time?

He checked the table she'd commandeered. The little purse was gone, though the slightly worn-looking deck of cards was not. He checked the top of the dresser—his car keys were as he'd left them. He pocketed them out of habit, even though he'd used the time Grace was in the shower, before he fell asleep, to call a car rental place that promised an early-bird delivery right to the underground parking lot. The plan was to leave here as the Westons in a sleek new rental car, the Coopers' wreck gathering dust in the bowels of the inn. Of course, this meant he'd have to replace the Coopers' car or come get it later. That dilemma could wait.

He shrugged on a jacket to cover the gun tucked in his waistband holster and pocketed his cell phone, all the while cursing his decision not to tell Grace he suspected they'd been followed. By trying to protect her feelings, he'd jeopardized her safety. A stupid mistake—it just went to show the dangers of getting emotionally involved with a client. He should have explained instead of leaving her in a fool's paradise where she felt safe enough to leave the room, to venture out where he couldn't protect her.

His first instinct was to go to the lobby, which he did. A few people milled around, but no Grace. No suspicious-looking single males, either, which was something of a relief, though the guy leaning against the elevator button had shifty eyes. Or was drunk. Maybe both. Maybe neither.

Mac rubbed his own eyes and took a deep breath as the button pusher stepped aboard the elevator and sagged against a new set of buttons.

Calm down, he told himself sternly and tried to think like Grace.

Clothes. She hated wearing Jessica's old clothes. He saw signs promoting a boutique downstairs and took the steps two at a time.

A placard in the door of the boutique indicated it had closed precisely at 9 p.m. Ditto the beauty and sundry shops. More signs announced more possibilities, so he kept walking. Door after door opened off the corridor, some with names mimicking Georgia towns. Atlanta, Columbus, Athens, Pine Mountain, Tifton. Conference rooms, he supposed, closed and locked for the night.

At the end of the hall, he made a turn. The corridor widened at this point, forming another lobby much like the one upstairs, only smaller. A coffee shop occupied the left side, one of those wide-open-to-the-public places. At the very end of the corridor he saw a door with street access to encourage local patrons. He hadn't realized until that moment that the inn was built on a slope, with the lobby above actually on the second floor. No wonder it had underground parking. What else had he missed in his semidazed state?

He searched the few late-evening diners, but there was no sign of Grace. Part of the right side of the small downstairs lobby sported an elaborate coffee stand shaped like a peanut lying on its side. A sandwich board proclaimed Goober's Espresso. It, too, was closed up tight for the night.

A dark door with a neon cocktail glass above it assured drinks. Another sandwich board set up in front promised live entertainment. On this Wednesday night, it sounded like an Elvis impersonator was having a go at it. The place was booming but poorly lit and Mac entered slowly.

As his eyes adjusted, he listened to an aging Elvis sing along with a karaoke machine in a warbly voice that sounded more than a little like the late-night crooning of a lovesick cat. When Mac could finally make out the details, he saw that the man's voice wasn't the only shaky thing about him. His dance steps—if those arthritic shufflings could be called dance steps—were painful to watch. A dingy white body suit, tattered scarf and slick black wig were crowning touches.

Had Elvis lived, this is what he'd look like. Haggard. Wrinkled. Approaching senior discount years. No wonder the lights were low.

Elvis held a handful of plastic leis. As he sang "Blue

Hawaii" off-key, he crooned to individual women in the audience, all of whom looked more mortified by his attention than flattered. But one woman sitting alone at a small table in front, an open wine bottle by her elbow, already wore two leis. Elvis was drifting her way again, dangling a third like a prize. No wonder he focused on her; the woman he appealed to was the only one in the room who seemed willing to meet his gaze.

Grace.

Chapter Seven

Grace.

Dressed differently, shopping bags piled at her feet, but Grace.

For a moment, Mac was so blown away by the transformation in her that he couldn't focus on anything or anyone else. Gone was the country club, buttoned-down look, the worried, frightened, preoccupied expression. In its place was sexy chic. A shimmering copper-colored dress wrapped her body with a suppleness that mimicked her flesh. Smoky drops twinkled on her earlobes and on her wrist. She'd bought herself black heels, which made her legs look long and lean, even when sitting.

However, as dazzling as the clothes were, it was what he could see of her face that truly stopped Mac in his tracks. Lips curved, eyes sparkling, cheeks glowing in the dim light. She looked vibrant and carefree, like any beautiful young woman out for the night, happy to be singled out for attention even by an aging wannabe Elvis wearing a ratty costume.

She was having fun.

Elvis was down on one knee, crooning to her. Mac didn't like the way this guy's act drew attention to Grace, but he couldn't think of anything to do that wouldn't make it worse, so he propped his behind on a bar stool. He ordered a beer when the barkeep came his way.

"Interesting Elvis," he remarked as he slid a ten onto the counter.

"Yeah, well, sometimes you have to take what you can get. Harry couldn't come in tonight."

"What do you mean Harry couldn't come in?" Mac said, his attention now focused on the bartender instead of Grace. "You mean the employment agency sent you a replacement?"

"What employment agency? Harry works alone. He called in sick at the last minute. This clown was sitting at my bar, heard me take the call, and offered to be Elvis. Told me he'd done it before. He was about Harry's size and all Harry's stuff was already here and I thought, why not? He's a little old, but so what? It had to be better than *another* open-mike night, right? Wrong!"

Mac's gaze returned to Grace, but this time another figure caught his attention, too. A lone man dressed in dark colors sat in a dim corner. He was tall and bony, angular, but his size wasn't what drew Mac's attention, it was the way his gaze stayed riveted on Grace, who was in the process of receiving her third lei. The man's right hand rested in his jacket pocket, and the predatory expression that dominated his sharp features as he gazed at Grace sent a chill of premonition down Mac's spine.

Elvis managed to get back on both feet. He leaned close to Grace. It looked as though he whispered something to her. She stood abruptly, stumbling over her shopping bags, pushing on Elvis, who tripped back and collided with the microphone stand. Grace's table went over next, the half-full bottle of red wine spraying an arc as it flew across the stage, the full glass shattering and spilling its bloodred contents on the hard-wood floor. Women screamed, men yelled.

Mac jumped to his feet. A large woman planted herself in front of him, blocking his vision. He pushed her aside in time to see Grace leave the lounge, walking stiffly in front of the man Mac had noticed just moments before, her body rigid. She wasn't carrying her shopping bags. Elvis called out at her to come back as the bartender hustled into the fray in an attempt to straighten things out.

Mac only noticed these last few things out of his peripheral vision as his attention was now focused on getting past the large woman who had once again assumed her former position. As he sidled past her, he kept an eye on Grace and her companion. He expected them to turn left, toward the corridor that led back upstairs to the main lobby and the guest rooms.

But they didn't. Turning right, the man opened the glass door and ushered Grace outside. He stayed so close to her that there was no way to separate them without risking Grace. Mac had seen similar scenarios often enough to put two and two together. Grace wasn't being given a choice where to go or with whom.

She was being forced outside. And he'd bet the farm her abductor pressed a gun against her ribs.

Mac pulled his five-shot revolver from its holster as he slid out the door after them, sticking close to the side of the building, avoiding the light that poured from the restaurant windows. The lightweight .38 carried a big bullet and an even bigger kick. He knew his firing options were limited. He searched the sidewalk ahead until he saw two people walking toward the rear of the complex.

Plans hatched and fizzled in Mac's brain as he kept to the

shadows, trailing them. He thought about his grandiose plans to trap the guy and make him tell them what he knew. But how did you trap someone who'd already snapped up the bait?

There was no time to call for help, no time to do anything but follow and wait for an opportunity to get Grace away from her abductor.

It appeared as though Grace was being directed to the employee parking lot out back. If the abductor had parked back there, he would no doubt force Grace into his car. Mac couldn't—wouldn't—let that happen.

They'd pulled far enough ahead that Mac chanced breaking into a run, crouching low. He circled the line of cars, then dropped to his stomach and peered beneath half a dozen parked vehicles. The pavement was wet, the light was terrible. He heard the clacking sound of Grace's heels before he actually saw two pairs of feet materialize a few cars down.

A car door opened. The man's voice was low and insistent, Grace's higher pitched but just as determined. She seemed to be arguing with the man about getting in the car.

Good for you. Make a little noise, cover my approach...

He slowly began edging his way closer, determined that Grace not enter that car. Statistics proved her best chance for survival was to resist being driven away. And her chances got even better when you factored in her wild card: him.

Peeking over the giant fin of a very old Cadillac, he saw something that gave him hope. The abductor pointed a knife at Grace. Not a gun, a knife. An ugly knife, to be sure, one with a long blade that must be scaring the daylights out of Grace. He glanced at her face, and felt both alarm and pride. She looked absolutely terrified, but she also looked angry.

Mac took aim at the man's forehead, but before he could

squeeze off a shot, another noise sounded in the parking lot behind him. The abductor apparently heard it, too. Ducking his head behind Grace's head, his left arm snaked around her waist and yanked her against his body while his right hand held the knife against her throat, the blade gleaming in the distant overhead lights.

Mac kept his eyes on his target. He could hear footsteps approaching, but he dared not turn. If the approaching figure was an accomplice of the abductor's, Mac figured he might relax his hold on Grace and move his head into clear range. As soon as that happened, Mac planned on shooting him.

And then all hell broke loose.

As gunfire came from behind Mac, Grace's assailant released her. She disappeared down between the cars, out of view. Mac couldn't tell if she'd been shot or not. Meanwhile, the knifeman yelled. More bullets flew. The knifeman took off at a run in the opposite direction. Pounding footsteps behind Mac suggested the gunman was in hot pursuit.

Mac didn't care who shot or knifed whom, as long as Grace wasn't the victim. But where had she gone? Dodging between cars, he finally caught sight of her. She'd collapsed onto the pavement in a whorl of coppery silk. She lay on her back, face upward, still and silent.

Without stopping to think, he ran to her side and crouched over her to protect her. "Grace," he whispered, searching in the miserable light for a sign of injury, blood, a bullet hole. "Grace," he repeated.

Her eyelids fluttered open and his heart constricted. "Daniel?"

The unexpected name jarred him, but he kept his voice even. "Lie still," he said as he patted her torso with his free hand, pushing the plastic leis aside, expecting to find a sticky gunshot wound between her breasts, a knife wound across her throat. He could still hear running footsteps and the occasional thump of a silenced gun. He needed to get Grace on her feet and out of danger—

"I'm okay," she said, eyes searching Mac's face. He helped her sit. "That man shoved me down. I hit my..."

Her voice trailed off as her eyes grew huge. She was looking at someone or something behind Mac. He felt a shudder run down his spine. He'd allowed himself to concentrate on Grace to the exclusion of guarding his back.

Someone was standing there. He couldn't see who, but he could feel a weapon trained between his shoulder blades and he could see the alarm grow in Grace's eyes.

Raising his .38, he turned quickly.

And there stood Elvis, arm extended, fringe dangling from his sleeve, gun in hand.

Without uttering a single word, the Elvis impersonator lowered his gun and turned abruptly, taking off at a dead run back toward the building.

Mac turned to Grace. Nothing made any sense but his instincts said to get her out of that parking lot before the abductor or Elvis decided to come back and tie up loose ends.

Grace read his mind, scrambling to her feet, awkward in the swirl of shimmering fabric that wrapped around her legs. One heel had broken sometime during the fracas. He took her arm and together they made their way back into the shadows, skirting the building, Grace limping, Mac listening for any sound that heralded a new attack.

"We're getting out of here," Mac said through clenched teeth.

"What about our things?" Grace gasped as he all but dragged her across the landscaped berms.

"We're not going back for anything," he said. The parking garage was deserted. Grace's undamaged shoe made a horrible racket and without his asking her to, she paused long enough to pull off both shoes and carried them clutched against her chest as they continued on to the car. They reclaimed the Coopers' sedan, hunkering down in the seats for a moment, waiting. When all remained quiet and still, Mac started the engine.

He was torn with indecision. He had no way of knowing if Elvis had wounded or killed Grace's abductor. He wanted to leave. Now. But their prints were all over the room upstairs. He knew that to the police, disappearing guests plus a shooting victim in the parking lot would equal murder suspects. Yet how did they casually saunter back through the inn to their room? And once there, how could they possibly clean it so thoroughly that a fingerprint wouldn't show up under investigation? And what about the registration card on file down at the desk? His prints would be all over it.

And if the abductor had gotten away? Would he now be lurking outside their room, waiting for them to return?

The dangers of lingering seemed more immediate than the benefits of trying to tie up loose ends that most likely could never be completely tied up anyway.

He realized later that it never crossed his mind to call the cops.

Grace was shaking hard. Her teeth clattered. Her knees trembled.

How could they be certain the kidnapping was related to Grace's situation? Maybe the kidnapper was a serial rapist who picked up hapless women in bars.

Maybe his choice of Grace was simply a coincidence.

Sure. Like Michael Wardman's, aka Jake's, murder. Just a coincidence.

As he drove away from the motel, a couple of thoughts topped all the others: *Who in the hell was the vigilante Elvis impersonator and what did he have to do with Grace?*

And who was Daniel?

FROM THE CORNER of his eye, Mac saw Grace hesitantly touch her neck as she sat there with closed eyes. He switched on the heater.

"Grace," he said softly.

Her hands fluttered to her lap as she turned to look at him. The sparkling pinpoints he'd noticed earlier on her earlobes caught the dashboard lights and shimmered right along with the whites of her eyes. He made himself look back at the road as he said, "Are you okay?"

She murmured, "Yes." He had the feeling she was afraid to try a sentence, afraid that a scream would escape instead of words. Trying to keep her centered, he said, "It's okay now. There's no one following us. It's okay."

She nodded as he dredged up a phony smile. The truth was that he longed to slam on the brakes and hold her, not only for her sake but for his own, to reassure himself that she was okay because he'd almost lost her tonight. He'd come so close that the taste of it still lingered in his mouth, like gunpowder hanging in the air. She could have been knifed or thrown into that car. Once the shooting started, she could have been hit by a flying bullet.

He'd almost failed her. His feelings for her had almost cost her her life.

Who the hell was Daniel?

It was the first time she'd uttered any name and he knew they had to talk about it. Could it be she'd recognized her abductor, that *he* was Daniel?

She finally whispered, "I'm okay."

"You've had a rough night," he said.

"So have you," she mumbled.

"It's not the same."

"I could have gotten us both killed," she added, her voice losing its quiver. "To listen to a lousy Elvis impersonator, for God's sake. To drink a glass of wine. To be…normal…for a minute."

He reached across and flicked one of the ragged plastic leis still dangling around her neck. "Yeah, but look. You came away with nifty souvenirs. Grace, who is Daniel?"

She repeated the name softly. "Daniel?"

"That's what you called me in the parking lot. When I leaned over you."

"When you leaned over me," she repeated. She pressed fingertips against her temples and grimaced. "I remember. Daniel. Leaning over me."

"Was he the man who tried to kidnap you—"

She shook her head violently. "No, no. Daniel. There was a needle."

He spared her another glance. "But, Grace. Who is Daniel?"

"I remember a needle," she said. "A man, leaning over me, sticking me with a needle." She rubbed her temples again, looking at him with an agonized expression. "Hurting me," she whispered.

"But you can't remember who Daniel is?"

"My husband…?" she murmured with a question in her voice that faded away.

Her husband! Her husband had shot her up with a needle? Her husband had scared her witless? Was she striving to stay true to a man who had all but sacrificed her for some unknown reason? To rescue a man who was the direct cause of her current situation?

All along, he'd been darting glances between the road ahead, the rearview mirror and Grace. Now he saw a pair of headlights behind, coming on fast. He held his breath as the lights grew huge, flooding the Coopers' car with light. At the moment it whizzed past. A low-slung convertible, top down, a woman behind the wheel. She disappeared up the road as quickly as she'd come from behind.

Mac relaxed a little and turned back to Grace. "Are you okay?" He realized it was an absurd question and couldn't imagine why he kept asking it.

She didn't bother to answer him, but her hand had once again strayed to touch her throat.

In the ensuing silence, he tried to recall everything they'd left in the motel room. His cell phone was in his pocket and he carried his wallet and gun as well. He said, "Grace, what all did you leave behind? If we have to go back there, we'd better do it now before we're any farther away."

"Clothes," she said. The brisk way she said it announced that she was trying hard to think clearly. "The little purse your aunt gave me is in one of the shopping bags I abandoned in the cabaret," she added, "but there's nothing in it except money. I guess the bartender will take out enough to cover the bottle of wine I ordered, then store everything else."

"I guess," Mac said. He thought of possible consequences. If Elvis had killed the kidnapper and then the kidnapper's body was found in the parking lot, the cops would question everyone in that motel. Eventually, they'd find the bartender or the stout woman who had blocked Mac's way. One of them would recall seeing Grace leave with the dead guy—his imposing size would identify him if nothing else did. One of them would recall Grace. They'd search the bags she'd left.

He said, "What exactly did you have in those shopping bags?"

"Um…clothes. That's all. And the purse, like I told you."

"Any mention of my aunt in the purse? A card or a name tag maybe?"

"No. Just cash and the card-key to our room. Your wife's old clothes were in one bag and a few toiletry items were in another. And clothes, like I said, just panties and a pair of jeans. A sweatshirt. Socks."

Okay, they'd lift Grace's prints from the shopping bags and match them to the room. They'd get a good physical description of her from the salesgirl or the barkeep. Ditto of him from the desk clerk and the boy who'd delivered room service.

His prints would be a piece of cake to trace. Army records, police force. No problem. Grace would be more difficult. Unless she, too, had served in the service or held a government job or committed a felony, and how in the world did he know that she hadn't done all three?

He didn't.

Who was Elvis?

Grace said, "Mac, I've been thinking. There was something familiar about that man. I think it was same guy I saw in the alley that first night. Before you found me."

Mac felt his heartbeat triple. "The tall man with the dark eyes. The man in the rain?"

"When he stared down at me in the parking lot, I had a definite feeling of déjà vu."

"Déjà vu originating from the last few days, you mean?"

"Yes."

Had they just come face-to-face with Jake's murderer and the answer to the puzzle of Grace's identity?

And was that answer now bleeding to death in a parking lot behind them?

"When he told me to get in that car, I asked him if he knew me," Grace added.

"Good thinking. What did he say?"

"He didn't respond. Besides arguing with me about getting in his car, the only words he spoke were when he poked that awful knife in my side and warned that if I didn't do as he told me, he'd kill you."

"He knew about me?" Mac said, thinking aloud.

"Absolutely."

So much for the coincidence of the abduction.

"Mac, who in the world was that Elvis? Why did he come to my rescue?"

"We can't know for sure that he actually came to your rescue," Mac said.

"He shot at the bad guy."

"Maybe what happened was between them and not because of you."

"He didn't hurt us when he could have."

True. Mac said, "I have trouble pegging him as an aging superhero in an Elvis disguise."

She tried to laugh. She seemed to realize how strained it sounded and stopped.

A new thought buzzed Mac's brain. He hit the steering wheel and all but slammed on the brakes. "Grace, your underwear. Did you leave it in the bathroom? It's the only clue we have—"

"I'm wearing it," she reassured him. "I washed it out and

dried it with the blow-dryer. The material is so thin it dried in nothing flat."

Mac pressed down on the accelerator again.

"I had fun picking out new clothes," she said softly. Her voice sounded oddly petulant. "And makeup. Even a little jewelry."

"What did Elvis say to you?" he asked her. "Before you pushed him."

She was spinning the bracelet on her wrist. "Crazy stuff," she mumbled.

"What do you mean?"

"I mean his words made no sense."

"Then why did you push him?"

Glancing up, she said, "Because he tried to cop a feel."

"He what!"

"He touched my breast. And it wasn't an accident. He knew what he was doing. Up close he looked like a lecherous gnome in a black wig. He touched me. He said something I could barely understand so I pushed him away."

"Try to remember what he said."

"Something about B.O."

"As in body odor?"

"I don't think so. Something like, 'B.O. says go home.' What does that mean?"

"I think it means Elvis knows who you are."

"Great."

She was quiet for a time before adding, "The kidnapper obviously knew who I was or how did he know to mention you by name? The nasty little Elvis impersonator seemed to feel I wouldn't mind a friendly grope. What does that say about me, Mac? What does that say about the kind of woman I must be?" She tore at the bedraggled leis and dumped them at her feet. "I don't want to talk about it anymore," she announced.

And with that, she turned as much of her back to him as possible before leaning her forehead against her window.

Mac kept driving, too tired now to even be tired. His thoughts traveled in concentric circles, but he wondered if Grace was right.

What kind of situation had she gotten herself involved in before she lost her memory? Would she ever be able to accept the woman she'd been once she started recalling what had happened to her?

He had no idea how things like this worked. Did people undergo personality changes with amnesia? Did they stay the same only without their memory?

He stole a glance at her. It was too dark to see much and her back was turned to him anyway.

He checked out the rearview mirror, half expecting to see a whacked headlight lurking in the distance, but the road was all but empty. No one back there seemed to care about them one way or another.

He tried to think of something he'd done right since leaving Billington and couldn't come up with a thing.

The memory of Grace's lips flooded his mind. The feel of her skin…

No. Especially not that…

AS THE HOURS of the night passed in an endless progression of miles, Grace stared out the window, trying not to relive the moment she'd felt the cold touch of the steel blade against her throat. She hated knives. She hated the thought of their cruel steel slicing through her skin.

She was tired of feeling like a victim. Tired of feeling as though she'd been run over by a truck. Her emotions were always getting the best of her. Fear and worry and anxiety and whatever it was she felt for Mac, all of them a tempestuous brew gurgling away in her gut, shooting occasional flares into her brain.

Well, no more.

It was time to use her head instead of her heart.

And her head was finally beginning to work again. She could sense faint rumblings in the recesses of her mind. Shadows. Lurking figures. The feeling of anxiety that had plagued her from the beginning now gnawed at her like an angry rodent trying to eat its way out of a maze. The car didn't move fast enough, and as she sat there in the dark, she imagined sprouting wings and taking flight.

Once in a while, out of pure fatigue, her eyes drifted closed and she jerked them open with a start. Every time she relaxed, those fuzzy images in her mind kind of took over, like bullies on a playground, pushing other thoughts aside, looming like thugs. She couldn't imagine what they would do to her if she allowed herself to fall asleep. She just wouldn't. She didn't want to find out.

And she was constantly aware of Mac. How she longed to slide across the seat and snuggle down beside him. How she longed to feel his warm arm flop across her shoulders, to feel his hunger for her. He was real, the only real person in the world, more real than she was. She wanted him to want and need her, even though she knew such desires were selfish. So she kept to herself and tried to picture another man, a man who had once slipped a ring on her finger and vowed his love.

But he was a phantom.

A new memory surfaced with daybreak. "I remember the sun rising over the ocean," she said, her forehead pressed against the cool glass of the window.

It was the first time either of them had spoken in hours. Mac glanced at her before looking back at the road. "That means you remember watching the sun rise on the east coast," he said. "Hopefully it means we're going in the right direction."

"And I remember swimming in the ocean," she added. "I like the ocean. I like the buoyancy when I float in salt water. I like the feel of the sand between my toes when I walk on a beach. I like the sun on my face."

It was the first time she could recall knowing things about herself, backed up with physical sensations she could recall and not just vague feelings. It made her feel wonderful and she hugged herself with the pure joy of it.

"Have you remembered anything else about yourself while you've been sitting over there?" Mac asked. He was in the process of exiting the freeway and she glanced at their gas gauge. It was time for a fill-up.

"No," she admitted.

He nodded once and then surprised her by pulling into a motel parking lot. This time, it was a small place next to the freeway with no underground parking, though Mac pulled into a slot at the back between two huge trucks. It seemed kind of out in the open to Grace, but she knew Mac well enough by this time to assume he had his reasons for the choice. Besides, what concerned her more than the safety of stopping was the prospect of hours spent cooped up in a tiny room. She didn't want to go to sleep. She dreaded it.

Mac said, "I know you're anxious to keep going, Grace, but there's a limit and I've just about reached mine. We're in

Florida now, only a few hours away from Miami. I look like hell and you don't look much better. We need to get some sleep and then find ourselves some clothes that aren't wrinkled or torn. You need to do something about getting your hair back to its natural color and I need to shave. There's no use walking into a fancy store looking like derelicts."

"You're right," she said. The dark circles beneath his blue-green eyes were so pronounced it paled the bruise from the shiner. She felt terrible for putting him through the physical dangers of the past few days. She hoped she was wealthy enough to compensate him for the risks he had taken on her behalf, though the more troubling thought was that there was no way to make up for the emotional hazards to which she'd subjected him.

"I figure the man who tried to abduct you is dead, dying, or otherwise out of commission," Mac continued. "Otherwise, I don't think Elvis would have run away like he did, nor do I think we would have made it out of that parking lot alive. And since Elvis seems to know exactly who you are and where you live, I don't think we have to worry about him sneaking up on us."

"I agree," she said, willing to agree to almost anything if Mac could just shut his eyes for a while and not look so hurt. She could fidget. She'd do as he asked and sit tight.

Damn! She missed her cards already.

Once in their room, he closed the drapes and hooked the Do Not Disturb sign on the doorknob.

And once again, they both stared at the bed as if it were the symbol of everything they desired and couldn't have. As, indeed, it was. The silence was awkward as neither of them made a move to turn back a cover.

Chapter Eight

"This is ridiculous," Mac finally said as he stripped off his belt and put that and his gun in its holster on a bedside table. "Okay, so we have…feelings…for each other. So we'd both like to make wild, passionate love. It isn't going to happen. We both know it. That's the bed and we need to just buck up and get into it without worrying about…things."

His little speech brought a smile to Grace's lips. She watched as he pulled off his T-shirt. The muscles in his upper body rippled when he moved, the fine dusting of hair on his chest looked soft and comforting.

"It would help if you stopped staring at me as I undress," he said softly, eyes smoldering.

"Sorry," she said, and then aiming for the same matter-of-fact tone he'd used, added, "You're an awfully good-looking guy. I've always been a sucker for hairy chests."

They both realized the import of her words at the same time. Another memory, this time about her taste in men. She tried to extrapolate the revelation into a full-blown husband, but it wouldn't happen. With an apologetic smile, she went to the bathroom and attended to toiletries. Wearing nothing but his jeans, Mac took his turn next.

He looked great bare-chested, wedge-shaped and strong and powerful. He would look perfect in the ocean, she thought. Graceful. She bet he was a great swimmer.

Grace slipped off her torn, oil-smudged dress and got between the covers. Her plan was to lay very still until Mac fell asleep, then sneak out of bed and sit in the chair by the window. Memories could float to the surface when she was awake and could control them—she had no intention of allowing them free rein in her subconscious.

Mac came out of the bathroom. He stripped off his jeans and climbed into the bed wearing boxer shorts.

"I figured you for a briefs man," she said.

"Nope. Boxers. Why the sudden interest in my underwear?"

She turned on her side to face him and found him lying on his side facing her. The light in the room was extremely dim, thanks to the curtains, but she could see the gleam of his eyes and the flash of his teeth. "Turnabout is fair play," she said. "You've been ogling my undies for days now."

"Strictly professional interest," he said, reaching over to run a finger along the bra strap that had slipped down her arm.

She hoped he didn't feel her shiver. She said, "Is that so?"

"Absolutely," he whispered.

"Mac, do you like to swim in the ocean?"

"I've never done it," he said.

"Never?"

"Billington isn't well-known for its oceanfront property."

"But you were in the army. I saw your picture at your aunt's house. You've traveled."

He shrugged. His shoulders were bare above the sheets, and his skin looked dark and tantalizing against the white linen. "A little. Mostly the desert. There wasn't a lot of time for frolicking on the beach."

"You served in the Gulf War, didn't you?"

"How do you know that?"

"Your aunt told me."

"It's not something I'm fond of remembering," he said, his tone suggesting this line of questioning was over.

But she wasn't done. "That crash you mentioned, the one that killed your friend. You were on that helicopter with him."

He was silent for so long she was sure he wasn't going to comment. Not that she needed him to. She'd heard enough conversation at Mac's aunt's house to know that he'd been aboard. He finally sighed deeply and said, "I couldn't save Rob," he said. "I tried…but I failed."

"That's not the way I heard it," she whispered.

She could feel his laserlike glare on her face as heat suffused her cheeks. She added, "I heard that because of your quick thinking and training, Rob stayed alive long enough to be rescued."

"For all the good it did him," Mac said.

"At least he died in a hospital and not in the middle of a desert," she said. "That must have been a comfort to the people who loved him."

"Grace," he interrupted, his voice firm but not unkind. "I know your curiosity about my life stems from your frustrated curiosity about your own life, but please, can we give this topic a rest?"

"I don't understand why you blame yourself," she said.

He just stared at her.

"Like you blame yourself for your wife's infidelity. I even think you blame yourself for not saving the wino last year or that poor man in the alley."

The stare turned into a glower.

"Mac?"

"Question-and-answer time is over," he said firmly.

This time, there was no doubt in Grace's mind that he meant it. He closed his eyes. She figured the gesture was as much to punctuate his intent to stop their conversation as it was to fall asleep. After a couple of minutes, she said, "Let's buy bathing suits and go swimming tomorrow."

His eyes opened, pinning her with their intensity. "This isn't a vacation."

"I know, but maybe the water will be therapeutic. Maybe it will hasten more recollections."

He smothered a yawn in his fist. "That sounds reasonable."

"Does everything always have to sound reasonable to you?" she teased.

He closed his eyes again, and this time, an aura of abandonment followed. His face, in repose, looked lean and vulnerable. He said, "Hmm."

The way he relaxed reminded her of the way a child abandons their concerns at night. Had her own baby looked like this when he or she went to sleep? Was that why the memory seemed so poignant to her?

Did her baby miss her? If she never remembered who she was, would her baby even remember her? She couldn't help asking one final question. She whispered, "Mac?"

Without opening his eyes, he murmured, "Hmm?"

"You must have *some* fond memories of your mother," she said.

He was silent.

"I know you were young when she left, but there must be something that stands out, something of her that…remains."

His eyes half opened as his lips gently curved into a wistful smile. "Every morning," he said softly, "she would ask me about my dreams of the night before. I'd tell her as much as I could remember, then she'd tell me what the dream meant. I remember her voice, kind of far away and whimsical, and the soft look of her eyes."

"You must have been very young," Grace said.

"Yes. But I learned quick. If I couldn't remember a dream for her to interpret, I'd make something up."

"To prolong your time with her," Grace said.

"To keep from disappointing her," he said, yawning into his fist.

Grace felt for the stretch marks she could barely discern by touch. As her fingers grazed her skin, she knew, she absolutely *knew* she had a child somewhere.

Anxiety all but choked her. She closed her eyes and bit on her fist, determined to stay strong, trying to conjure an image, unable to form anything more tangible than a feeling. But this feeling was real.

She had a child, and the child was alive.

She knew it.

ACCORDING TO the digital alarm clock provided by the motel, it was five o'clock when Grace jerked awake. Mac's pillow was bare.

Had he abandoned her?

She switched on the light and looked around the empty room, heart pounding in her ears. A note beside the lamp caught her attention.

I've gone out to get a few supplies. Stay in the room. Please. I'll be back soon.

She took a deep breath and got out of bed. Nine hours of sleep should have refreshed her, but she felt sluggish instead. At least her sleep hadn't been fraught with monstrous shadow people. *Or knives...*

She decided to take a quick shower and had just put back on her once pretty coppery dress when she heard a noise at the door. She opened it with a welcoming smile.

Mac stood there, card-key in hand, arms juggling plastic sacks and newspapers. "You didn't even ask who it was before opening it," he said with a frown as he walked past her. "Lock the door, use the chain," he added.

She did as he asked. "Who else would it be but you?" she said. "Yum. What smells so good?"

"It could have been Elvis or the guy from the parking lot," Mac said. "It could have been someone else, someone who hasn't introduced himself yet." He dropped a bag on the small table flanked by two chairs that took up the corner of the room. With a sigh, he added, "Breakfast is served."

"You mean dinner," she said, opening a foam cup of coffee and taking a sip.

"I mean breakfast. We slept all of yesterday and through most of the night."

She pulled the cup from her lips. "But it's dark outside—"

"The sun hasn't come up yet. I found one of those twenty-four hour stores a few blocks from here and picked up a few things. I gassed up the car and bought us a couple of breakfast burritos. Do you like breakfast burritos?"

She shrugged. She was hungry enough to try almost anything, but she couldn't get over the hours they had wasted sleeping. The tension in her stomach came back with a vengeance.

Mac separated what appeared to be four different newspapers into sections as Grace unwrapped their food. She handed him his share and he handed her half of the newspapers. "Look for any mention of a shooting or a knifing taking place night before last night outside of Macon," he said. He took a bite of the burrito and grinned. "Not bad."

She couldn't believe the change in him. Gone were the hollows beneath his eyes. Even the shiner had all but faded away. Gone also was the weariness. He seemed revitalized, ready to tackle the world. It took all her willpower not to pull him out of his seat and force him into the car.

They were so close....

Instead, she focused on the wee tendrils of optimism she felt sprouting in her own heart. Mac's enthusiasm and his clear, bright eyes gave her hope that this ordeal would be concluded before another night fell. Trying out a positive outlook, she said, "Today's the day."

Mac looked up from scanning the front page of a newspaper. "Today is what day?"

"Today is the day we get an answer," she said, discovering that giving voice to a good thought was like pumping gas into an empty tank.

He folded the paper down and almost scowled at her. "The underwear store is a long shot," he said softly.

"I know," she said. "A million-to-one chance. I guess I'm feeling lucky."

He turned his attention back to the newspapers and she felt a little of her unwarranted optimism fade. She buried her head in the newspaper and scanned every headline.

After several minutes of silence, disrupted only by the rattle of paper, Mac said, "There's nothing in here. Did you find anything?"

She glanced down at the Atlanta edition in her lap. "A hit-and-run in downtown Covington and a man who shot his best friend over a bagel. Nothing about a dead man in a parking lot outside of Macon."

"Nothing here, either. Of course, it might be yesterday's news by now."

They rustled through the rest of the papers but found nothing pertinent. "Why don't you call the place where we stayed and ask the desk clerk?" Grace asked at last.

"I imagine they have caller ID," Mac said. "If there was a murder, the police will be on the lookout for calls like that. Too risky." He shuffled around at his feet until he pulled from one of the shopping bags a pair of red plastic flip-flops. "For you," he said.

She took the shoes and put them on her feet. "Nice," she told him, wiggling her toes.

"Better than nothing," he said.

"Did you get me a box of hair color?" she asked him.

He glanced at her hair. "I really think you ought to go to a salon for that."

"But the time that would take—"

"Is time well spent, Grace. If we're going to saunter into an uppity place like *L'Hippocampe,* we'd both better look more the part."

"But Mac—"

He leaned forward and patted her knee. "Grace, your dress is torn and smeared with grease and those flip-flops aren't going to win any fashion points. A couple of hours getting ourselves prepared will pay off in the end. It's not even 6 a.m. Trust me."

Like she had a choice! He held the car keys, he was in charge. She bit her lip and nodded, glancing at the nightstand clock.

"Check out the bag from the store," he told her. "I bought you a present."

She dug into the abandoned sack and felt her fingers close around a small, rectangular box.

"You shouldn't have," she said, smiling as she withdrew a new deck of playing cards.

"Just don't ask me to play poker again," he grumbled.

AFTER THEY each chose a change of clothes, Mac used the time Grace spent having her hair colored to use a remote Internet connection located in the middle of the shopping mall. From his vantage point, he could see the front of the salon and the main entrance of the mall. He found nothing in any online newspaper about a murder in the right spot at the right time.

Did that mean Elvis had only wounded the man and that the man had subsequently escaped? Or did it mean Elvis took the body with him?

He could still see the Elvis impersonator jogging back toward the motel. Empty-handed. Well, except for the gun.

The abductor must still be out there, waiting for another chance to nab Grace.

He couldn't even begin to fathom what Elvis's role in all this was.

He was so deep in thought that it took him a second to realize the striking blonde leaving the salon was actually Grace. Her hair was still short, but now it was shaped and framed her delicate face. The color and cut made her blue eyes sparkle, her lightly tanned skin glow.

She'd chosen a form-fitting deep blue blouse and a slinky white skirt, which rode on her slender hips. White sandals wrapped her toes and ankles. He'd been with her when she bought these clothes and he'd marveled at how she'd just pulled them off the rack. How she ended up with such a sexy ensemble without hours of plotting and planning was a mystery to him.

He was mesmerized by the way she walked, too, without affectation but with the grace he'd always noticed in her, as though she owned whatever pavement on which she placed her feet. And his weren't the only male eyes glued to her swaying hips. While Grace had made a very pretty brunette, she made a truly dazzling blonde.

"You look…stunning," he said, walking up to meet her. She'd applied makeup sometime during the past couple of hours, and she'd applied it with real skill.

She smiled as she took his arm. The two of them kept walking toward the exit. Even her smile looked different.

"It's going to take some time getting used to you this way," he added.

She touched her hair. "I kind of hoped I'd look into a mirror and my name would pop to mind," she admitted.

"No such luck?"

"'Fraid not."

"Well, I assume this is what you usually look like, which is the whole point. Maybe someone else will look at you and your name will pop into *their* mind."

"But you don't really believe that will happen, do you?"

"No. I'm sorry, but I don't."

"I'm nervous, Mac."

He nodded. He could feel the quiver in her arm as it rested against his side.

As she strode out of the mall beside him, he felt a stab of regret for not making love to Grace when he'd had the chance.

The Grace of a day or so ago had needed him. The Grace of today looked well on her way to discovering herself and he had the distinct feeling she wouldn't need him or maybe anyone else once she had.

He metaphorically shook his head to clear such thoughts. His job was to keep Grace safe. His objective was to help her rediscover her identity.

After that, he needed to go home and help track down the man who had stabbed poor old Jake to death.

Not Jake. Michael Wardman.

Unless the killer was hurt and wounded somewhere behind them.

Or alive and kicking somewhere up ahead...

"ANYTHING LOOK familiar?" Mac asked.

Grace had been both expecting and dreading this question. As she peered out the car window and took in the sights of Miami, she had to admit nothing struck a familiar chord.

Not the faded blue skies or miles of white, sandy beaches. Not the pastel buildings or hoards of people walking down the sidewalks. Not the skateboarders, the vagrants, the tropical shirts, the shoppers, the sidewalk diners. Not the smells of spicy food, the palm trees rustling in the slight breeze, the afternoon light slanting across the pavement.

Nothing.

But it *felt* right.

Feelings weren't enough, however. She was sick of feelings. She wanted clear-cut pictures, irrefutable proof. "No," she said, striving to keep the disappointment out of her voice.

It was three o'clock in the afternoon and they'd been driving without a break since leaving the mall. Mac's eyes were hidden behind sunglasses, but she was well aware of how often he checked the traffic behind. She was also aware of how often his gaze drifted to her, how often it lingered a heartbeat, and she wondered if it was because she looked so different or if it was something more.

How could he have feelings for her that went further than mere physical attraction when she felt so invisible?

She made herself look away.

She didn't want to, though. She wanted to stare at him. As they rolled closer to a possible conclusion, she was afraid she was about to lose him.

She'd chosen a long skirt to hide the scabs on her knee, a long-sleeved blouse to cover the fading bruises on her arms. Mac looked sophisticated and sexy as all get-out in linen slacks and a bronze shirt. She'd chosen his clothes as he didn't seem to know how to shop for anything other than blue jeans and gray suits.

Mac drove directly to *L'Hippocampe,* finding it on a side street after admitting he'd memorized directions on the Internet while he waited for her. The shop was narrow, with gilded gold lettering on the door and an arrow directing patrons to a small parking lot in the rear.

They got out of the car and walked around to the front, Grace gripping to her chest the small brown bag that held the beautiful bra on which she pinned all her hopes for an easy resolution to this nightmare.

The air was warm and redolent with the aromas of the nearby sea. They could hear laughter and music in the distance.

He had his hand on the door. She felt a tornado of apprehension rip through her body and put her hand over his. "Mac, wait. What if you're right? What if no one in here knows me? Then it's all over."

"No, it's not all over," Mac said.

"What would we do next?"

"If they don't know you in here, we'll find a place where we can watch our backs and wait for your old pal Elvis to show up," he said.

"Or wait in a dark alley for a limping, bleeding former kidnapper to wander across our path?"

"Exactly," he said, and surprised her by leaning down and brushing her lips with his. "Don't put all your eggs in this one basket," he murmured against her cheek. "It's a long shot. It's always been a long shot. Too many variables. Too many conjectures. We aren't without a plan B."

"Plan B," she repeated.

He straightened up and grinned. He had such a nice grin. Even with the sunglasses, she could see the way it crinkled the skin at the corners of his eyes.

"There's always a plan B, baby," he said softly. And with that, he opened the door.

Stepping into *L'Hippocampe* was like stepping into a very ritzy lady's boudoir, all done in gold and white, with draping fabrics reflected over and over again in floor-to-ceiling mirrors. Grace found the place strangely comforting and wondered if she'd ever before walked through the front door.

The carpet was deep and plush, the dainty French provincial furniture stained white with gold embellishments. There was no visual clue as to what the store actually sold.

As the front door silently closed behind them, a wall of dark gold curtains in the back parted. A woman wearing a white suit and a discreet smile appeared. With her upswept colorless hair and multiple strands of oversized pearls circling her long neck, she looked dated, but as elegant and as ageless as the room. Both the woman and the boutique were jarring notes of antiquated civility, especially as they existed only a block from the wild, vibrant world of Miami Beach.

"Good day, Mrs. Priestly," the woman said. "How nice to see you."

Mrs. Priestly!

A name, handed out casually, just like that.

Mrs. Priestly...

A sharp intake of breath from Mac, a stuttered, "You...you know me?" from Grace, whose knees sagged as Mac's grip on her arm tightened.

The woman came to a stop a few feet in front of her. "Of course I know you. You're Katrina Priestly." A gentle smile curved her lips as her voice softened. "How are you?"

Her tone was oddly solicitous, but the comment itself was offered in such a restrained way that Grace didn't know what to make of it. Struggling to keep her head on straight, she stammered, "I'm fine...I..."

Words failed her. A blizzard began howling through her mind. She glanced up at Mac. He'd taken off his sunglasses and looked as shocked as she felt by this woman's offhanded gift of her identity. He recovered quicker, however, and said, "Mrs. Priestly wasn't sure you'd recall her. It's been a while since she's been here."

The saleswoman shook her head. "No, not so long. She was here a few weeks ago. Maybe three months. That's all."

"Are you sure?" Mac persisted.

"Please," the woman said, gesturing to the two chairs fronting a desk. Mac guided Grace into one of the chairs and took the other as the saleswoman seated herself behind the desk. She opened a drawer and withdrew what appeared to be a large ledger.

The woman opened the book and leafed through the pages until she uttered a soft exclamation of success and turned the book so they could see the entry.

October 2: Mrs. Katrina Priestly, four 66-01, one 66-06, one dozen 66-26.

"Is this some kind of code?" Mac asked.

"It means Mrs. Priestly bought four of our neutral brassieres, one black and one dozen panties. It says here they were shipped on November 1."

Grace opened the paper bag and brought out the bra. After a cursory inspection, the saleswoman said, "It's one of ours, though I can't be certain if it's from this order or the one before. May I ask what's going on? Does this have anything to do with the…accident?"

Mac started to speak, but Grace cut in. "The accident? What accident?"

The saleswoman's expression mutated from sympathetic to alarmed.

"Mrs. Priestly is confused—" Mac said, his voice dropping as he apparently searched for a good explanation.

The saleswoman provided it herself. "Oh, my. I didn't realize you were aboard the plane, too." She patted Grace's hand and added, "Please let me say again how shocked we all were. Your husband seemed such a dashing young man. Is there anything we can do for you? Anything *I* can do?"

Grace couldn't have uttered a word if her life depended on it. A wave of nausea washed through her body. Her head felt like exploding. She heard Mac's voice and made out a few words.

"—so you can see that Mrs. Priestly is having a rough time

right now. Would you please write down the last address you have for her?"

"Of course," the saleswoman said, producing a small card and copying information from a different book. Grace stared at the woman's hand as she wrote, trying to concentrate. Her heart felt like it was up around her tonsils. She could barely breathe. She stood abruptly and almost fell over. Mac grabbed her arm and steadied her.

The saleswoman's gaze flickered between the two of them again. At last, she said, "I lost my own husband a year ago. I understand how…difficult…this must be for you. I'm terribly sorry."

Flashes exploded in Grace's head like muffled fireworks. She stared at Mac and the saleswoman without clearly hearing either one of them. Their mouths moved, their eyes cast her sympathetic glances. She had to do something, she had to faint or run away—do something, *anything* to escape the storm in her head.

Darting frantic glances around the room, she saw her reflection here, there and everywhere, so many times, so many blond women, so many dazed blue eyes.

One moment, she was standing there, and the next, she was on the sidewalk, the brilliant sun blinding her, leaning against the rough bark of a palm tree. Memories banged against each other. Nothing made sense.

She felt two warm hands grip her shoulders. She turned to collapse against Mac.

"Grace," he whispered against her hair.

She shook her head. *Grace* wasn't right. Nothing was right.

Next thing she knew, she was sitting in the car, Mac leaning over her, fastening her seat belt.

She felt so odd. Lowering her head into her hands, she closed her eyes.

"It's okay," Mac said, but she knew he was wrong.

Nothing was okay.

MAC SAT BEHIND the wheel for a few moments, unsure of his next move. Grace wouldn't meet his gaze; in fact, her head remained buried in her hands and she was ominously still.

Her husband had been dead a little more than two months. She must still be reeling with grief, he thought, a stab of jealousy hitting him square between the eyes. He'd expected to feel jealous of a living man, but of a dead one? How futile was that?

He finally got out of the car and turned on his phone as he walked a distance away. It took a couple of calls to reach Aunt Beatrice's doctor, George Handerly, the man Aunt Beatrice had introduced to Grace as her accountant, the doctor who had taken a blood sample from Grace and had it analyzed.

The doctor spent the first few moments relating the results of Grace's drug tests. He rattled off substances easily available on streets across the nation, from Miami to Billington. The drugs were so ordinary that knowing their names was of no help. There was no way of knowing if they'd been self-administered or forced upon her, but their presence did explain Grace's initial confusion and overriding fatigue.

But not her memory loss.

The doctor said he'd examined Grace when he took the sample and that it had appeared to him that she had suffered a blunt trauma to the head sometime before. But not a terrible one, and he was perplexed why she had amnesia.

Unless it was hysterical amnesia or caused by drugs they hadn't tested for…

Mac related Grace's reaction to the saleswoman's disclosures. He wanted to know if he should take Grace to a hospital. He also told the doctor that the saleswoman had provided a few additional facts about Grace after she left the store. If she didn't recall them on her own, should he tell them to her?

"Don't barrage her with facts. And given how paranoid she seems to be of doctors, I'd skip the hospital for now. You said you know where she lives?"

Mac glanced at the paper the woman inside the store had used to write down Grace's last known address. "I think so," he said.

"Take her there," the doctor said. "Maybe her husband or her family will be available to help her through this. Ideally, she has a doctor you can consult. Take her home."

"Her husband is dead," Mac said.

"Just take her home," the doctor repeated.

Mac clicked off his phone with a heavy heart.

Grace's husband had died in a single-engine plane crash almost two months before. The saleswoman wasn't sure of every fact, just that Daniel Priestly had died way before Christmas.

In other words, Grace's memory of her husband leaning over her, threatening her with a needle, didn't seem to have anything to do with her current plight. Maybe his sudden death explained what sent her off the deep end though.

Was there a deep end?

How could he know for sure? The drug angle was fuzzy. Grace ending up a thousand miles from home was suspicious. He still couldn't swear Michael Wardman's death was connected to Grace. Even the would-be Macon abduction might have been motivated by the simple desire to take Grace back to Florida—not to harm her but to return her.

With a knife at her throat?

But hadn't Elvis told her someone or something called B.O. wanted her back home?

As he slid back into the car, he looked over at her. She was staring straight ahead, hands folded in her lap. When he just sat there, she finally turned to face him. Whatever makeup she'd applied in the salon that morning had done an admirable job of holding up to her tears.

"I'm remembering things," she said, pain flashing in her eyes.

"What kind of things…Katrina?"

"Kate," she said softly. "Call me Kate. Danny is dead. In a plane crash, before Thanksgiving."

He watched the tears stream down her cheeks and felt a new flash of jealousy. He wasn't proud of it, it was just there.

Her eyes suddenly grew wide. "My babies," she cried, grabbing for her seat belt. Fumbling with the buckle, she added, "Mac, start the car. Now, please, I don't have one child, I have two. Twins. Oh, my God. Where are they? Who's looking after them? Please, Mac, hurry."

The memory of her children seemed to have come out of the blue, sudden and violent. Her distress was contagious. He knew Boward Key was south of Key Largo, and as he wound his way through traffic toward Highway 1, he couldn't help but wonder what kind of situation he and Grace were about to encounter.

"Hurry," she pleaded, sitting forward and straining against her shoulder harness.

Chapter Nine

Images rolled through Kate's head like the reels in a slot machine, the kind with three spools and three windows. So far, just the images of her children had coalesced. Danny's face was a blur. She couldn't seem to line up the three matching parts; they kept jangling to a stop a little off-kilter.

On the other hand, every mile they traveled revealed more familiar scenery. Miami, the crowded streets, the sun and palms giving way to Florida Bay, gulls, tidal flats, mangrove trees—it all began to feel like home.

"Why don't you try talking about things as they pop into your mind?" Mac suggested. "Maybe if you kind of start at the beginning, I can get a handle on what's happened to you before we get down there."

"All you have to do is find my babies," she said with a steely coldness to her voice that surprised even her.

"Tell me about them," Mac said.

She spared him an impatient glance. He was driving as quickly as he could; he was only trying to prepare himself. Clasping her hands together, she said, "Their names are Charlie and Harry and they look alike. Except to me, they don't. They're eighteen months old. They're cute and clever and energetic and noisy and oh, I don't know, what is it you want me to tell you? They're my babies. They're my reason for living."

"Calm down," he said softly. "Tell me about their dad."

She took a deep breath.

"For instance, where did you meet him?" Mac persisted.

And in that instant, the tumblers aligned and Danny's face appeared in her head. The memory of their first meeting came back with a clarity that momentarily startled her. They hadn't been close when he died, but the moment when she first met him was fresh in her mind in a way it hadn't been for a long time.

And she knew she wouldn't tell most of it to Mac.

"Try," he coaxed.

She found other faces lurking in her mind now. "I have a brother named Tom," she said.

Mac had obviously expected details about her husband. He said, "Well, okay, that's a start."

"Tom and my dad own a string of car washes in Oregon. I always thought that was funny because they say all it ever does is rain up there, so why do they need car washes?"

He cracked a smile. "What about your mother?"

"They divorced when I was very little. I lived with Mom and her new husband in San Francisco, Tom was older. He wanted to go with Dad. I left home at eighteen."

"That's young," he said.

"Well, my stepdad had a temper. After one particularly hairy fight, I just moved out."

What she'd done was run away after her stepfather got a little too friendly and her mother refused to believe it. And, truth be known, she'd been barely seventeen, not eighteen.

"Where did you move to?" Mac asked.

She shrugged. "Here and there."

"Are you purposely being vague?" Mac asked, sparing her a quick glance.

"It's still fuzzy," she lied.

She cast him an under-the-eyelash look and thought about explaining what it had been like after leaving home, damn near penniless with few skills on which to draw. She'd flitted here and there, she'd made some questionable liaisons, she'd gritted her teeth and taken care of herself.

Mac would understand. He wouldn't jump to erroneous conclusions about her like Danny had. He'd be sympathetic. He'd listen.

Wouldn't he?

What if he doesn't? a niggling voice squeaked. *What if he decides you aren't worth helping? How will you get your babies back? How can you risk that?*

She pressed her fingers against her temples as other memories began to float to the surface. They left her mouth dry.

"What about Danny?" Mac said.

For a second, she relived the moment she'd looked into Danny's eyes and fallen in love. At least, that's what she'd thought she'd fallen into.

Mac said, "Where did you meet him?"

"At work," she said truthfully enough. "I was a…waitress. He came in and one thing led to another. We got married three weeks later."

Mac whistled.

"I thought I'd found the love of my life," she explained.

"And what about him?"

"Danny was looking for a way to rebel against his father.

A few weeks later, I was pregnant. And sixteen months after the twins were born, Danny's plane crashed."

"The saleswoman said he was on his way home from a trip to Vegas."

Kate rubbed her forehead again. The mention of Las Vegas threw her; she hadn't heard the saleswoman say anything about Vegas....

"Danny liked to play cards," she mumbled.

"He was a gambler?"

She nodded.

"Did he go often?"

A surge of bitterness all but lifted her off the seat. She said, "Danny did whatever he wanted, whenever he wanted. He loved to fly. That little plane was his passion. Well, that and gambling. He was the only child of wealthy people with his own money, thanks mostly to his grandfather's trust. After college, Danny didn't seem to have a single goal in life except to fritter away his money, none of which he'd actually earned himself."

"Oh, Grace," Mac murmured, probably in reaction to the acerbic tone of her voice. He didn't seem to notice he'd used the wrong name.

But even Kate was having a hard time thinking of herself as Kate and not Grace, especially sitting next to Mac. Talking about Danny, remembering the good times before the stress of the bad times, made the old feeling of despair reappear behind her chest bone.

But more than that she realized she liked being Grace better. *Grace* was a blank page with a million opportunities. *Kate* had baggage.

Tears welled in her eyes. *Kate* also had Charlie and Harry, and they were all that mattered. Her feelings, Mac's feelings, the truth—none of that meant a thing, not when compared to the needs of Charlie and Harry.

And what they needed was what she needed: to be together.

"Danny couldn't seem to understand how much I just wanted him to…care," she said softly.

"So why did you stick around?" Mac asked, wearing his inscrutable cop face.

Already aware of how flaky she must sound to Mac, she felt reluctant to admit that she'd been about to leave Danny when he died. She'd been plotting it in secret, waiting for the right time. How did she confess this to a man whose wife had scribbled him a note as she ran out the door with her new boyfriend?

She mumbled something about the children.

"What about Danny's family?"

"His dad is a doctor in Boward Key. *The* doctor, if you know what I mean. He grew up poor in Chicago, then moved south after becoming a physician. He married Paula Boward, the only daughter of a land developer responsible for all sorts of things up and down the Florida Keys. Boward Key is named after Paula's grandfather."

"What's she like?"

"She's a Southern girl from the old school, the stand-by-your-man type. A little wishy-washy, but I think she truly loves her husband. Everyone loves Dr. Priestly. And he knows it, too." She wasn't sure why, but as she'd talked about Danny's father, she'd felt a tightening in her vocal cords as though someone was choking her.

Mac's gaze flicked to the rearview mirror. He finally said, "Grace—I mean, Kate—hold on a moment. What happened to *you?* How did you end up in Billington?"

"I don't have the slightest idea," she said, which was the truth.

"Think back. You and your husband were having marital trouble. Then he died. What did you do?"

"Nothing," she said. *Nothing but covertly plot an escape. Nothing but wait for probate to clear so you could get the hell out of Florida.* Biting the inside of her cheek, she said, "I thought about going up to Oregon. I haven't seen my dad or Tom in five or six years."

"You didn't want to stay near your in-laws?"

"No," she said. Her head began to throb again and her throat felt tighter than ever. Deciding what not to say was as hard as deciding what to say.

"You're not close to Danny's parents," Mac said.

"No, I'm not."

"Why exactly?"

"Why?" She pressed her fingers against her forehead. "Because Dr. Priestly hates me."

There it was, out in the open, and still she felt no better. Having said it, she now realized she had to explain it. Very carefully, she said, "I wasn't exactly the kind of woman Dr. Priestly had in mind for his one and only son."

"He disapproved of you?"

"Yes."

"Why?"

"Oh, Mac, does it matter? I don't think anyone would have been good enough for his little boy. Certainly not a girl like me, with no education and no money of my own—I just wasn't good enough for a Priestly, that's all."

"And he told you this?"

She shrugged. "When Danny and I would argue, he'd retaliate by telling me how his dad felt about me. Dr. Priestly wanted Danny to divorce me, even after I became pregnant. And then Paula sometimes told me things he'd said, to try to explain his behavior, I guess…let's just say I was very aware of his feelings about me."

Mac looked properly incensed, which warmed her heart.

"And things just got worse after Danny died," she added, "because then there was money to worry about. Oh, not like in the old days, when I supported myself, or as though there was never enough. The problem after Danny died was that there was too much. Trust funds for the boys, assets, stocks, land deeds…money I suspect the Priestlys believe I have no right to. It's a mess."

"Money is a great motivation for all kinds of mayhem," Mac said.

Kate grew wistful. "For two years, all I wanted was to get out of there. It looks like I got my wish, doesn't it? Now all I want is to get back."

Mac kept his gaze straight ahead. He said, "So, tell me the very last thing you remember."

She worked on organizing her thoughts, picturing the day over a week before when she'd taken the boys to see their grandmother. "I remember being at my in-laws' house," she began slowly, wanting very much to get it right. "It's close by. The boys and I took the shell path down by the water. They like to throw rocks. My father-in-law was supposed to be away at a medical conference in Orlando."

"So, you remember walking to your in-laws' house, that's it?"

"Yes. No, wait, there's more," she said uneasily, memories pummeling her brain now like flashes from a strobe light. She rubbed her eyes. The past was not only coming back, it was beginning to taunt her. As her thoughts morphed into words, some of the pressure in her head seemed to dissipate; she talked fast, her heart racing.

"Paula was there," she said. "She was…distraught. She said Dr. Priestly thought I was responsible for Danny's death! He told her that if Danny had loved me more, he wouldn't have had to fly away so often. I was hurt, of course. I tried to explain about gambling addictions, but she was crying by then. We were standing on the stairs and then Dr. Priestly was there…"

She trailed off because the memories had collided with one another and left a huge, black hole.

"So the doctor wasn't at a conference after all?"

"No. I don't know." She closed her eyes completely, and once again saw Danny leaning over her with a needle.

Danny with his gray eyes—

No! Not Danny.

She gasped. "It was Dr. Priestly who attacked me, Mac. Not Danny. Daniel Priestly. I must have said something about moving away, I don't know for sure, but I can remember the expression in his eyes." She shuddered with the memory of the glacial indifference that had stared right through her.

Mac made a noise in his throat. "Your father-in-law! Are you sure, Kate?"

Was she sure? "I think so," she said, tears welling in her eyes as panic rose in her throat. "Yes. Mac, the children must be with him and Paula. Hurry."

MAC TRIED not to glance too often at Grace—not Grace, not Grace…Kate—but the former cop in him was having trouble with her story.

Or would it be more accurate to state that the former cop in him was having trouble with *her?*

Who was this woman?

Why did she skip over the details of her past?

He had to admit that her evasiveness disturbed him. In the last few days, he'd come to admire what he'd seen as her innate honesty. He thought they'd developed a kind of mutual trust unlike any he'd ever shared with a woman. All that seemed to be crumbling now. He hated the doubts about her story that were beginning to take a stranglehold on his mind.

Had he built his reality of her on shifting sand?

He put aside what he hoped was rash disappointment and concentrated on what Kate had said, and what she'd said about her father-in-law was troubling mainly because, in Mac's opinion, it was so improbable.

Why, for instance, would a well-respected man—a physician—attack his dead son's wife? What would be the purpose? Because he didn't want her taking his grandchildren out of state?

If the old guy really thought Kate was unsuitable to raise his grandchildren, he'd hire a slew of lawyers and go to court to prove it, wouldn't he?

For money?

If the gambling son had money, it figured the parents had even more, didn't it? Besides, hurting Kate wouldn't help them get her share. Even if she died, whatever was hers would revert to her children.

Kate was still sitting forward in her seat, her hands twisted around the shoulder harness.

"We'll go to the police, first," Mac said. "You need to file a complaint. If you're sure your father-in-law moved you between states, that's a matter for the FBI."

"No," she said with conviction. "Absolutely not."

"Listen, Kate—"

"I said no. Boward Key is named after my mother-in-law's grandfather, for heaven's sake. I told you Dr. Priestly is well-known—but that's just part of it. He's well-loved, too. No one else sees him the way I do."

Mac felt a renewed sense of alarm as Kate talked. She sounded paranoid. He said, "Okay, first we'll go to Dr. Priestly's house and knock on the door. We'll find out what's going on."

Her response was immediate. "We can't just knock on the door. I told you, Dr. Priestly attacked me. I can't just go waltzing into his house—"

"*You* won't go waltzing into his house," Mac interrupted. "I'll go."

"No."

"Then we'll call your mother-in-law and talk to her. Get the lay of the land. See if she can tell us what's going on."

"That's better," Kate said slowly, and he was relieved. She sounded reasonable again.

A moment later, she shattered this perception. "If it's true Dr. Priestly attacked me, then he's guilty of breaking all sorts of laws, right? He'll try to cover his tracks. He'll never admit he did anything wrong. So, he won't just hand me back my babies, not when he almost killed me to get them in the first place.

"So this is what we'll do. We'll wait until bedtime. Paula will put the boys to sleep upstairs. Gloria, their maid, sleeps in the next room, but she's a heavy sleeper. You're clever, you know about things like this. You figure out how to get into their house and we'll take my boys. It won't be against the law, they're my children. Then you can help the three of us disappear!"

Mac was thoroughly alarmed by the craziness of Kate's scheme. Had she been this erratic just a few hours ago before all these memories started coming back? And how many of the memories could be depended on? She was obviously distraught. Despite his growing apprehension, his heart went out to her.

"You're talking about breaking and entering," he said, struggling to keep his voice calm, hoping if he acted sensible, she would too. "Can you imagine how terrified your kids would be if we tried a stunt like this? Think, Kate."

"I'll be there with you," she said. "They're not scared of me."

Mac shook his head. "Kate," he said gently, "let's take this one logical step at a time. Let's not borrow trouble. I know you think your father-in-law is the cause of all your current troubles, but you don't know that for sure."

"I do, though, Mac! I remember—"

"But your memory isn't reliable," he said. "At first, you thought it was your husband who drugged you. Now, you think it's your father-in-law."

"I know it's him!"

"Grace—"

"Kate!" she snapped.

"I'm sorry," he said. "I'm sorry I keep getting your name confused."

She stared at him in response.

"Honey, independent of who did what, there is at least one man with a big gun following us, and he isn't your father-in-law or anyone else you recognize, right?"

"You mean our Elvis impersonator."

"Exactly. The man who spared us. The man who shot at your would-be abductor back in Macon. And don't forget *him,* either. We don't know if he's dead or alive."

He saw her hand fly to her throat and he knew the memory of that knife blade still haunted her.

He added, "You told me Elvis said to go home. He said someone or something called B.O. wanted you back in Florida. If your father-in-law shipped you out, why would he send a man with a knife to bring you back? It doesn't make sense."

Eventually she said, "You're right. It doesn't."

"We just don't know for sure what's going on," he reasoned, "but breaking the law right off the bat is overkill. Trust me, okay?"

Her answer this time took even longer to come, but finally he heard her whisper, "Okay."

Just in time, too, as a big sign on the side of the road had just welcomed them to Boward Key.

MAC PULLED INTO the parking lot of a convenience store and turned off the engine. Kate reminded him of a boiling tea kettle, almost levitating from her seat with anxiety, hands shaking with pent-up emotion and nerves. Any second now and she'd start whistling.

"Now what?" she said.

"Now we need a plan."

"Then you believe me?"

He hedged by counting things off on his fingers. "If things are as you remember them, Kate, then this is what we know. One, your mother-in-law is grief-stricken. Two, your father-in-law lost his marbles and attacked you. You still don't remember the time between seeing them both and being under attack, is that right?"

"Yes," she admitted.

"So we don't know how you got to Billington, we don't even know for sure *where* your children are. Let's go to your house," he continued. "Let's make sure your kids aren't there. For instance, do they have a nanny?"

"Of course not. They have a mother. What would they need a nanny for?"

"I don't know, I just thought rich people had nannies."

"Not me."

What he was hoping was that someone—a nanny, a gardener, a neighbor, anyone—would be around Kate's house and that that person would recognize her and corroborate some of her story.

"Nellie," Kate said softly. "I've forgotten completely about Nellie."

"And Nellie is—"

"The housekeeper. What day of the week is it?"

"Tuesday—"

"Then she'll be there even if the children aren't. Probably."

Another thought struck Mac. "Kate, what's the last calendar date you recall?"

She wrinkled her brow. Her blue eyes looked fathomless to Mac. She was so lovely that he yearned to take her in his arms. It wasn't that he didn't believe her, he told himself, it was just all so complicated. She finally said, "January ninth. I took the kids to see their grandma on January ninth. I remember because it was the two-month anniversary of Danny's crash."

"Today is the eighteenth. You've been gone over a week."

"And you found me when, a couple of days ago?"

"No, more like five days ago."

Her frown deepened as though time had gotten away from

her. He added, "It took us four days to get down here, but of course, we slept through most of one twenty-four hour period."

"And we spent hours today getting my hair dyed and going to *L'Hippocampe*."

"Exactly. So, say it took someone a couple of days to drive you to Billington, where were you for the two days preceding that?"

She shook her head. "What does it matter?" she said at last, obviously frustrated.

"I'm just trying to figure out what's going on."

"Just get my babies back for me, then we'll figure out what happened to me. I have money, I know that now, so you will get paid."

Now he was frustrated. "This isn't about money," he snapped.

"Of course it is. You're a private eye, I'm a wealthy widow due to inherit even more. Now drive me to my house and help me or I'll find someone who will!"

She shocked him with that statement and he stared at her as though she was a stranger because suddenly, that's exactly what she was.

Her eyes filled with tears as she studied his face. Reaching across the seat, she touched his cheek with trembling fingers. "I'm sorry, Mac. I just don't understand why we're wasting time in this parking lot. Please, take me to my house. It's down the road a ways, I'll show you how to get there. Maybe my in-laws hired Nellie to stay and care for my boys. Maybe I'm all screwed up and Charlie and Harry are playing in their own yard waiting for Mommy to come home. I just don't know anymore. Please, please help me."

He put his hand over hers and kissed her palm, breathing

in the scent of her for a moment, her skin soft and fragrant against his lips.

And he thought.

Was she as confused as she sounded? Did she really believe the words she spoke? Had she abandoned the idea that her father-in-law had attacked her and carted her off to Billington, Indiana?

He lowered her hand and looked into her eyes. He saw the woman he'd come close to making love to, the woman who needed him, the woman he felt he'd known for half a lifetime instead of a few days.

The woman who was now the most singularly important person in his life. Talk about cruising for heartbreak. He could feel it in his bones, as if he had a trick knee that warned of impending storms.

Hurricane Grace.

Kate. Hurricane Kate.

He started the car and followed her directions.

HER HOUSE WAS a single-story sprawling white structure that sat back away from the shores of Florida Bay. A large patio surrounded the building on the water side, while huge trees and rolling waves of low-lying plants anchored it to the grass on the other. A fence encircled the land side of the property. The only sign that two small boys lived there was a wooden play structure on the lawn, all but hidden by flowering shrubs.

The setup shouted money.

"My in-laws live less than a quarter of a mile south of here," Kate said as he drove the car through the open gate, traveled the circular driveway and parked under a graceful portico. One of the doors of the garage was open, revealing an empty spot;

Mac could see the rear bumper of a large, dark SUV parked behind the closed door beside it. An old red car was parked in the breezeway connecting the garage to the house.

As Kate unclipped her seat belt, she added, "Good, that's Nellie's car. She must be here. This house is on the same property as the big house. They both belong to my in-laws. I'm still living here only by virtue of their generosity. I can't wait to move, but then, that's the story of my life."

He wasn't sure what she meant by that. He opened his mouth to ask, but a challenging look from her changed his mind.

As Mac hung back a little, Kate walked briskly across the rock patio and tried the knob of the front door. He had to admit her boldness jolted him. He realized at once that was just the shock of seeing her know where she belonged, what was hers, who she was.

"It's locked," she said, banging on the wood with her fist.

"Is there another door?" Mac asked.

"The laundry room door is off the breezeway," she said, turning. But at that instant, the front door flew open and a plump woman, with graying red hair and wearing a white apron and black running shoes, stood framed in the doorway.

She cried, "Ms. Katrina," and engulfed Kate in a hug that all but swamped her.

Mac heard Kate utter, "Nellie," with obvious relief in her voice.

Mac felt another unexpected twinge of loss. This was yet another step in her journey away from him. How selfish was he that such a thought should even creep into his head?

Kate finally disentangled herself from Nellie's arms. "Where are Charlie and Harry?" she demanded, her voice desperate. "Nellie, where are my babies?"

Nellie looked to be on the far side of forty. Laugh lines were currently at odds with the frown wrinkling her brow. "They're with the doctor and his wife, up in Fort Myers," Nellie said, grasping Kate's hands. "They're fine, Ms. Katrina, honest they are. The doctor said you drove off last week but he didn't know where you'd got to. I've been worried sick."

In two strides, Mac was at Kate's side.

"Dr. Priestly said she drove away from his house?"

Red curls went every which way as Nellie first shook her head and then nodded. "Maybe from his house, maybe from here, what does it matter? All I know is that her car is missing."

With some urging, Kate allowed herself to be led into a wide entryway decorated with potted palms and baskets of orchids. It looked like the lobby of a posh resort.

"Come sit down," Nellie said softly. "I'll make something to drink."

"Why are they in Fort Myers?" Kate said, her voice beginning to sound numb. It was as though all her energy had been focused on getting here and finding her children, as though hearing they were not near had broken something inside her.

Nellie said, "The doctor had...business up that way. He and the others will be home first thing in the morning, Ms. Katrina. Please, come sit down. You look exhausted. I know you don't like iced tea, but I just bought a whole bag of lemons. Let me make you some lemonade." Nellie cast Mac a suspicious look.

Nellie seemed to have come to a decision about him, and Mac wondered on what basis she had made it. Her occasional glances radiated disapproval, yet he could think of nothing he'd done since meeting her that she could disapprove of.

He needed to get Nellie alone and talk to her.

"Why don't you take Nellie's advice, Kate," he said gently. "Grace" had almost slipped out and he was grateful he'd caught it in time. Gesturing in the direction of the living area, where upholstered wicker furniture commanded a peaceful view of the patio and the water beyond, he added, "Catch your breath. I'll help Nellie with the lemonade."

Kate ignored him, flashing anxious eyes at her housekeeper instead. "You said they'll be back tomorrow?"

"First thing in the morning."

"When did you last see them? The boys, I mean."

"Just two days ago when I packed their clothes for the trip. Ms. Katrina, what's going on? Are you sure you're okay? The doctor warned me that if you came back you might not be…feeling well."

"What else did the doctor tell you?" Kate asked, her voice trembling.

"Nothing. Honest. He just said that he didn't know where you'd gone, just that you were upset when you left. He assumed you met up with one of your… friends…from the old days."

Her voice trailed off as her gaze strayed to Mac and then back to the tiled entry floor.

Aha. He was the nefarious "friend."

Nellie's declaration seemed to be the last straw for Kate. She sagged at the knees. Mac caught her. Nellie rushed into the living room and tossed pillows aside to make room for Kate on one of the sofas. Kate sank onto the soft white cushions with a sigh worthy of a woman three times her age and then leaned her head back. Mac was dismayed to see how wounded and how hurt she looked.

And so vulnerable.

And oddly out of place.

The room was done in shades of white and ivory, with touches of pale yellow and sky blue. Kate, wearing the sapphire-blue blouse and a skirt just a tad on the racy side didn't quite fit in. An oil portrait on the wall behind the sofa caught her in an off-the-shoulder white dress. Golden hair curved around her face and fell in gleaming waves halfway to her waist. Sitting in her lap were identical little boys with flushed cheeks and bright blue eyes. The painting of Kate and her twins looked like a portrait of three angels.

Nellie escaped to the kitchen and after making sure that Kate was okay, he followed.

The housekeeper was busily halving lemons as she glanced behind Mac, presumably to make sure Kate hadn't followed him into the kitchen. When she was sure they were alone, she leveled a steely-eyed gaze at him and said, "Thanks for getting Ms. Katrina home safe. You can go now."

Mac leaned against the counter. He was suddenly very tired. "Far be it for me to rile the dander of a woman wielding a big, sharp knife," he said with what he hoped was a beguiling smile, "but it's not that easy."

"The doctor warned me that Ms. Katrina might show up with some gigolo—"

This was what wearing expensive clothes did for a man? Make him look like a gigolo?

"I'm hardly that," he said sternly, trying to look like a hard-boiled detective toting a big intimidating weapon, which he wasn't. He'd locked it in the glove compartment before entering *L'Hippocampe,* many hours ago. "I'm a private detective. I'm trying to discover what happened to Katrina Priestly nine days ago. I want to ask you a few questions—"

"Now you listen," Nellie said, using the knife like an extension of her hand. "I work for the doctor. If you think I'm going to stand here and gossip about this family to some stranger, you're nuts."

Mac said, "You work for Dr. Priestly, not Kate?"

"Absolutely. And you will never on this earth find a kinder, gentler man than the doctor. I don't know what kind of scheme you've got running—"

"I told you, I'm working for Kate—"

"Then it's true what the doctor said. Poor little thing, suffering so much after her husband died. She's gone out of her mind, hasn't she? She even looks different! What happened to her hair? She's thin and pale—"

"Nellie," Mac said, trying to calm the woman down. "Kate is going to be fine. If there's anything you can tell me about Dr. Priestly to shed some light—"

Nellie interrupted him this time, eyes blazing. "If you think I'm going to stand here and listen to you slander the doctor's good name, you're out of your mind."

"Now what have I said to make you think I want to slander anyone?" he said calmly. "Come on, just a question or two. For instance, do you work here every day?"

Still scowling, Nellie said, "Not every day, no."

"How about the day Kate took the boys over to her in-laws? Did you work that day?"

"No. Ms. Priestly told me not to come in that day. She wasn't one to go out to the country club, you see, and with Mr. Danny just deceased, she'd taken to doing for herself and staying real close to her kids. There wasn't a lot for me to do."

That meant Nellie hadn't been in the house when Kate left

on foot. "You said the doctor told you Kate was upset when she left his house?"

She looked at him like he was trying to trap her. She finally said, "They'd had a fight."

"Who had a fight?" he snapped. "Kate and Dr. Priestly?"

"As if it's any of your business," Nellie said.

"What about the boys—"

"The boys are with their grandparents," Nellie said, "and I have to admit that after what I've seen here this afternoon, they belong with those fine people. It's a good thing little Charlie has a grandpa to take care of him when he's so sickly."

"The boy is sickly?"

Nellie's shifting eyes betrayed conflicting feelings. She looked as if she were struggling between disclosing more information to put him in his place, or clamming up to do the same thing. Much to Mac's relief, she settled on the first ploy and said, "That's why they took him to Fort Myers, to see a specialist."

"What kind of—"

"Never you mind."

"Kate has a right to know—"

"*They'll* tell her what she needs to know," Nellie insisted. "At first, I was kind of alarmed when they mentioned going to court, but now I can see why they have to do it."

"The Priestlys are going to court?"

"They've already been," she said.

"Then—"

Nellie's eyes narrowed. "You're a sneaky one, getting me to talk about those fine people."

He decided not to point out that it hadn't really been all that hard. He said, "Just tell me—"

"I've already said too much," she said, turning back to her lemons.

He stood there for a moment, but it was clear that Nellie had stopped talking, as witnessed by the lemon halves flying hither and yon. He returned to the living room to find Kate exactly as he'd left her. She must have heard him coming, because she turned her head his direction when he was halfway across the room.

For a second, the portrait on the wall and the woman on the couch gazed at him with the same blue eyes. It seemed to Mac that *Kate* was in the painting, and *Grace* was on the sofa. He realized at once that this was a presumptuous conclusion to reach, and he concentrated on the real woman as he sat down next to her. Kate, not Grace.

"I'm going to get a motel and then take a look around town," he said.

"There are plenty of empty rooms right here," Kate said. "You don't have to get a motel."

"I think I do," he said, nodding toward the kitchen. "Kate, why is Charlie considered sickly?"

"He has allergies," she said. "They're not bad. I'm careful. His pediatrician says he'll grow out of them."

It was on the tip of his tongue to mention that her in-laws had started court proceedings, presumably to gain custody of her twins, but he decided against it. Honestly, the woman didn't look as though she could take another blow. With a wistful sigh, he recalled the way she'd appeared earlier that very day when she'd walked out of the beauty parlor looking like a million bucks, confident and excited and hopeful.

Back before she remembered who she was...

"You have to believe me," Kate said so softly he sat down beside her to make sure he caught every word.

He said, "Believe what?"

"Believe that my father-in-law is responsible for what happened to me. That it's imperative we get the boys away from him."

He wanted to believe her. He *ached* to believe her. He wished he could rattle off some glib lines of reassurance but the truth was that he didn't know what...or whom...to believe.

It jarred him that the doctor had gone to court. It's exactly what he had expected a law-abiding man to do: rely on lawyers and the judicial system, a system that always favored a mother unless the grandparents were upstanding, influential members of society and the mother...wasn't.

He said, "Maybe if you get some sleep. Maybe by morning, your head will clear."

"My head is clear right now," she protested, but her eyes looked confused.

"Nellie said Dr. Priestly told her that you had an argument with him before you left. Do you recall what it was about?

She shook her head. "I don't remember an argument."

"And you still don't remember the last few minutes of your time there?"

"No."

He gently took her hands in his. "Kate, I'll ask around tonight. Maybe I can get wind of what really happened here."

"You'll ask around? About me?"

He stared into her eyes, and dissembling, said, "About your father-in-law."

She nestled her head against his chest and he fought the

desire to kiss her forehead, to gather her tightly in his arms and hold her for the next several hours.

"I promise you I'll figure out what's going on," he told her and he meant it. "Don't give up."

She gazed up at him. "I will never give up," she said softly. As seductive as her clinging had been, the conviction he could see burning behind her eyes was downright galvanizing. At that moment, he would have slayed a dragon for her. Instead, he pulled her close and kissed her.

She was a free woman, at least when it came to a husband, and this was the first time he'd kissed her knowing that he wasn't trespassing, so to speak. It was the first time she'd kissed him with the weight and the richness of her past alive and kicking in her cognizant mind, and he wondered for one split second if it would change things between them.

And in the next instant, as they drew apart and stared intently into each other's eyes, he knew that nothing was different, not when it came to this primal connection that transcended time and place. He might not trust her memory of the events that had preceded her troubles, but he did trust the truth of what he saw in her eyes. Their mouths drifted together again; this time, the kiss was a tender promise.

"Ahem—"

Nellie.

They split apart like guilty lovers.

Mac swore under his breath as he met the acrimonious gaze of the housekeeper. He'd just confirmed every bad thing she thought about him.

That didn't matter. What mattered was that she not think badly of Kate.

He stood abruptly and, hoping Kate would understand, said, "I never should have kissed you like that. I'm sorry."

She looked bewildered. He wished he could warn her that though she seemed to like and trust Nellie, the woman worked for her father-in-law and seemed to think the world of the man. Surely Kate knew that already. Since his back was to Nellie, he tried a quick wink and added, "I'll call you later from my motel. Goodnight…Kate."

He could feel Nellie's gaze drilling holes in his back as he let himself out the door.

Chapter Ten

For the first time since the trip began, Mac registered under his real name. The motel had the feeling of an anomaly in Boward Key. Obviously not fancy enough to be frequented by tourists, it was still a little too respectable to be classified a flophouse. It was moderately priced, reasonably clean and somewhat private. There was no air-conditioning, but a beat-up old fan twirled nicely over the bed. He felt right at home.

He changed out of his Florida Keys "gigolo" clothes and back into his jeans. His cell phone was all but dead, so he plugged it into the wall to recharge, sat down on the bed and plopped the motel phone in his lap. Moments later, he listened to it ring in Billington, Indiana.

Leo Gerald had nothing new to report on Dr. Michael Wardman's, aka Jake's, murder investigation, but, in answer to Mac's next question, took the motel number and promised to call back within the hour.

It was more like two hours later when the phone finally rang, jarring Mac awake. He'd made a few phone calls after talking to Leo and then fallen asleep, sitting up with the phone in his lap. Years of practice had him answering it in a voice no one would suspect was just seconds away from unconsciousness.

"You owe me," Leo said. "I had to talk to my wife's brother's retired father-in-law to get you this name."

"Glad I could help cement family bonds," Mac said, reaching for a pencil and a slip of paper.

"You ready? Take this down. Neville Dryer. He's been on the force down there for two or three hundred years. My retired contact knows this guy from the old days. I get the feeling it's a cozy little town, the kind of setup where everyone knows everyone else's business."

"I think you're right," Mac said. "And I hope to bring you home a lead on that investigation of yours."

"Good. The newspapers here are having a field day with this whole thing. Calling for an investigation, the whole nine yards. Chief Barry is madder than hell. I think he senses his ship is sinking."

"Maybe if he'd worried more about what was good for the community and the cops who work for him and less about the mayor, he wouldn't have to worry about getting his feet wet."

"I didn't hear you say that," Gerald said with a nervous laugh.

"Hell, Leo, it's not like I haven't said the very same thing right to the man's face. Thanks for doing this for me."

"You can buy me a beer when you get home."

Mac hung up the phone with a smile on his face. What he missed the most both from police work and the army before that was the comradeship. Going it alone got kind of…lonely.

Or maybe he just missed Grace.

This time, he didn't even pretend to think of her real name because he knew that to him, Katrina Priestly would always be Grace, his Grace.

He shoved himself off the bed. It was time to see what Officer Neville Dryer had to say about Dr. Daniel Priestly.

KATE WALKED AWAY from her linen-and-lace bedroom with a feeling of escape. She hated that room and everything it stood for. All the broken promises, all the glitz without substance, all the nights of lying alone on three-hundred-dollar sheets while her husband amused himself elsewhere.

It was also good to escape the tomblike quiet of that house. She missed her boys with an ache that wouldn't go away because it was tinged with real fear. What story had Dr. Priestly concocted to explain what had happened? Whom had he told it to, besides Nellic?

Kate had idly asked Nellie if her father-in-law had left town nine days before and Nellie had mentioned the conference he went to in Orlando, the one Kate had thought he was already at when she brought the kids over to visit Paula. Had *he* driven her to Indiana? Could Mac find out if he'd really attended that conference?

It was cool and she buttoned the white sweater she'd pulled on over her blouse as she walked down the rolling grounds toward the water.

Mac had just called and told her his motel room phone number. He'd seemed distracted. That, coupled with the way he'd apologized for kissing her earlier—even if it was mainly for Nellie's benefit—heightened her feeling of abandonment. Nevertheless, when it occurred to her that someone should physically check out the Priestly house, she'd immediately thought of Mac. He hadn't answered his phone and the motel didn't have an answering machine. Why hadn't she thought to take his cell phone number?

She would check her in-laws' house for herself to make sure they were really gone and not holed up inside, hiding her babies from her. She wouldn't put a stunt like that past Dr.

Priestly and she knew Paula would always bow to her husband's demands.

Near the water's edge, she easily picked up the trail that led between the two houses. Covered with crushed shells, it glowed in the moonlight. There'd been a time when she loved this path; it had seemed so exotic. Back when she first married Danny, the house and grounds had struck her as terribly romantic.

This Florida estate was a far cry from the little tract house she'd grown up in in California. A world away from the cramped apartment she'd shared with two other girls after she left home. Coming here had been like landing on another planet. At first she'd felt like a fairy-tale princess with her very own knight in shining armor.

Thinking of the first days with Danny always made her feel sad, and thoughts of him now led directly to thoughts of Travis MacBeth. Was she falling in love with him, or was she just so damn dependent on him she couldn't tell the difference? She didn't want to glom on to another man out of weakness. She'd decided months ago that's what she'd done with Danny. Danny's father thought she married Danny for his money, but that wasn't true. She'd married Danny for the fantasy of his devoted love.

The two things were entirely different.

She didn't want to do the same thing again. A man like Mac deserved a woman as strong as he was.

Not a woman like his ex-wife, a woman who ran out on him.

She bit her lip as she realized the duplicity of criticizing Mac's ex-wife when her own first line of defense was to run. She'd done it when she left home at seventeen, again when she married Danny; she'd planned for it when her marriage began falling apart. She'd wanted to do it a half dozen times since waking up in that alley, too, and, face it, part of her wanted to run away right now.

If she had her boys, she would. She'd put them in her car and drive—

What car? It was missing. The only car in the garage was Danny's big old SUV and she hated the gas guzzler. Besides, even if she could drive away, where would she go?

Not to Mac. Despite her growing feelings for him, she was afraid to tell him everything about herself. Afraid he'd be disappointed in her, afraid he'd take that disappointment out by turning away from her, and she couldn't risk that. She needed him to help her reclaim her children.

Kate was aware of how formidable an enemy she had in her father-in-law, but she also knew how crazy her story would sound to anyone else, especially anyone living in Boward Key. The man would never own up to what he'd done and she'd probably never be able to prove it.

That was okay. She was not after retribution. She was after her babies.

Mac was apparently out asking questions about her father-in-law. Wouldn't that inevitably lead to people speculating about her and what many thought of as her colorful past? Wouldn't a full disclosure of the facts sound better coming from her than from one of Danny's old buddies or a member of Dr. Priestly's country club set?

Of course it would. She made up her mind to talk to him as soon as she could.

The mental gymnastics fled as she rounded a copse of low-growing palms. The winds rustled in the fronds as the Priestlys' big house came into view. The estate, lit from one end to the other, dominated a small promontory. The lights meant nothing; no doubt Gloria and her husband Eduardo were in residence, whether or not the Priestlys were home.

She would have to get closer.

What, and peer through a window? Trigger the alarms? Get the cops out here to arrest you?

You could knock on the door like old times.

The idea made her stomach lurch.

It might be the only way.

Memories flashed behind her eyes again and this time they included Paula Priestly's frantic voice screaming, "No, no!"

She couldn't go back into that place when Dr. Priestly might be there. What would keep him from attacking her again? Where might she end up next time? How would she find her way back without Mac?

How would she find her way back *to* Mac?

But Charlie and Harry might be in there. You have to find out for sure.

Shaking with nerves, she nevertheless crossed the grounds and knocked on the back door. This door opened directly into the kitchen and was cracked almost immediately by Gloria, who had spent more of her life in Florida than Cuba. She wiped her hands on her apron as though Kate had interrupted dish washing.

"Are the Priestlys here?" Kate asked, hating the tremor she could hear in her voice and vowing to make sure Gloria stayed by her side if they were.

"The Mr. and Mrs. left for Fort Myers day before yesterday," Gloria said, speculation about Kate's appearance at the back door after nine days' absence showing in her dark eyes.

"How about Harry and Charlie?" Kate asked. "Are they already in bed—"

Gloria shook her head. "Oh, no. The reason the Priestlys drove to Fort Myers in the first place was to consult with a specialist for Charlie. The Mrs. is so worried—"

"Charlie isn't well?" Kate gasped. "What do you mean?"

"His allergies," Gloria said. She seemed to read the alarm in Kate's eyes as she hurriedly added, "The doctor just wanted to make sure everything that could be done for him was being done, that's all. You know how he is with those babies."

"They have a pediatrician, right here in Boward Key!"

"But he's not a specialist," Gloria said patiently. "Why don't you come on in, Ms. Katrina? You can look around if you don't believe me. I'll get Eduardo to run you home in the car. It's chilly outside and you look—"

Kate didn't want to hear how she looked. She mumbled a polite no thanks, and hurried away as the door closed behind her.

Charlie was sick. It didn't happen very often, but when he did get wheezy, he always liked her to hold him and read to him; now her arms ached with emptiness. She closed her eyes and almost felt her two small boys snuggle against her.

She had to get them back. She had to talk to Mac.

The wind rustled the reeds and palms on her right, the water lapped gently against the rocky shoreline on her left. She picked up her pace as she once again found the shell path and began the quarter-mile walk home.

So focused was she on contacting Mac that at first she didn't hear the sound of shells crunching behind her.

Nor did she witness the moonlight gleaming off the steel

blade of a knife. The man who wielded the knife followed her progress with a cold precision that had no place in such a lovely spot.

NEVILLE DRYER was a florid man with buzz-cut gray hair and silver wire-framed glasses resting near the tip of his nose. He had to be nearing sixty. The extra fifty pounds he packed around his gut and the cigarette drooping from his lower lip suggested he wasn't into health fads.

Mac could hear dispatch coming from somewhere toward the back of the cinder block building and the click of a keyboard from an adjacent cubicle. Familiar sounds, friendly in their dispassionate way. Mac felt right at home sitting in front of Dryer's desk, one leg propped on top of the other. He missed being a cop, and for the first time in his life, seriously considered settling somewhere other than Billington to pursue what he felt in his heart was his true vocation.

Dryer perused Mac's license, then stared at Mac over the top of his glasses. "What can I help you with, Mr. MacBeth?" he asked as he handed the license back to Mac.

"I need local knowledge," Mac said, hoping Dryer was as bored as he looked.

"About what?" Dryer asked, stubbing out the cigarette, for which Mac was truly grateful.

"I need to get a feel for the Priestly family."

He was met with a steady, semihostile gaze.

"I'm working for Katrina Priestly," he added, dismayed to see Dryer's lip curl upon hearing Kate's name. "I'm trying to figure out what happened here a week or so ago. I need background."

He was studied again and he'd just about given up hope of

any information when Dryer nodded briskly. "That's some client you have there."

Mac let the comment slide. He had no idea where it came from or what it meant. "I'd appreciate any help you can give me," he said.

Dryer's swivel chair creaked as he leaned forward, took off his glasses and set them in his out tray. Resting his heavy forearms on the cluttered blotter, he said, "Well, first off, I'll tell you that Doc and Paula Priestly are both pillars of this community."

"I'm not saying they aren't," Mac said firmly.

Dryer nodded and seemed to relax. "You know about their son, Danny, I suppose?"

Mac nodded.

"Well, him dying like that just about killed his poor mother. She's still reeling. No one could believe it when Danny's plane went down last November. Danny was one of those kids who seemed to have it all. Looks, money, good at sports…the whole nine yards."

"Know of any trouble he had with gambling?"

Dryer pushed himself back in the chair as he thought. "I know he enjoyed a good game. Heck, he was returning from a trip to Vegas when that little plane of his went down," he said at last. "Never heard he had a problem, though. Hate to see some ugly rumor start now that he isn't around to squelch it."

"How about his parents?"

"You'll never meet a nicer man than Doc Priestly. He's worked his butt off making sure our little community hospital stays open—half the town owes the man some debt of gratitude. Paula's big into helping out wherever she can. They had their son a little late in life, but that just made it all the sweeter."

"And Katrina?"

A pause was followed with, "One of the kids who works here calls her a hottie. I have to warn you, she's crazy though. This last stunt of hers is going to cost her big."

"I assume you mean her leaving town."

"You know about that, huh? That's what I mean, all right."

"I was wondering why no one here filed a missing persons report."

Dryer leaned forward again. "There's no cause to report someone missing who purposely leaves, is there?"

"And how do you know she purposely left?"

"Did she tell you differently?"

"I'd rather not say."

Dryer peered at Mac and then grumbled, "Is she making some kind of allegation?"

Mac returned the stare and said easily, "Not at this point. I was just wondering aloud how you knew she left of her own accord."

Dryer sat back again. "The little lady has a history of running off," he said. "No one ever says much about her absences, certainly not the doc or Paula, they just pitch in and make sure the kids are taken care of till she gets it in her head to come home. I hear she has a little bit of a drug problem, but that's just hearsay. Anyway, this time, one of her kids got sick and the doc had to get him medical help. That's why he petitioned the court for temporary guardianship of those two little guys, so he could take proper care of them. Otherwise, I imagine he would have covered for their mother again. 'Course, Judge Linstad thinks as much of the doc as the rest of us do."

Mac was growing increasingly uncomfortable with the information he was gathering. While Dryer was obviously biased in favor of the elder Priestlys, he also seemed level-headed and the picture he painted of Kate as an insufficient, drug-abusing mother was damning. Mac cleared his throat as he continued. "Did the doctor mention that an altercation of sorts preceded her…departure?"

Dryer's brow wrinkled. "Oh, I know what you mean. Yeah, the doc said she demanded money. Said she threatened to take the kids away forever if he didn't pay up. She wouldn't say what she needed the money for and when he refused, she got mad and ran off in a huff."

"But she's set to inherit a good sum," Mac said.

"Maybe she needed it sooner rather than later, you know, to pay someone off or settle a debt. Maybe she got tired of waiting around for probate to clear. For some people, there's never enough, fast enough. For a woman like her, well…"

"But—"

"Listen here," Dryer said, sitting forward yet again. The chair groaned in protest. "Your client might look like an angel, but take it from me. She's a shrewd one. Danny found her in a Vegas strip club, hustling drinks, dealing cards, dancing with her clothes half off—well, it doesn't take an old man's imagination to figure out why the boy married her. Bringing her back here, foisting her off on his folks…some people say she took Danny's death hard, but it seemed to some of us that she recovered real quick."

Mac stared at Dryer without blinking. All Kate's equivocating about where she went after leaving home and how she met Danny suddenly made sense to him. He could think of only two reasons for her to hide these details. One, she was ashamed of them. Two, they shed light on her character and what had happened to her on the ninth of January.

Either way, uneasiness was beginning to give way to anger. He felt manipulated and duped by the one person he'd begun to treasure. Dryer was staring at him. Mac said, "She seems to adore her boys—"

"She got pregnant about a week after she and Danny tied the knot. My wife says she wanted to make sure she tied herself to all that Boward money."

"And what do you say?" Mac asked.

Dryer shrugged his beefy shoulders as he lit another cigarette, taking a long pull and expelling a cloud of smoke. After a moment, he posed his own question. "Why exactly did Katrina Priestly go and get herself a hired gun out of Indiana?"

Mac had no way to answer this question that didn't reveal more than he was currently willing to disclose. He tried a shrug and a mumble about being a friend of the family.

"You mean *her* family?"

"I mean she's a friend of my aunt's," Mac said.

Dryer nodded. "And why does she feel she needs a detective?"

Another tricky question to answer. Should he mention the gunman they'd encountered on their trip south, the definite threat to Kate's life, her conviction that her father-in-law was responsible?

Even though she'd told him she wouldn't swear out a complaint, in all good conscience, how could he not? Though she'd evaded the truth with him, how could he not assure her safety by being truthful with the lawman sworn to protect her?

He said, "There's been some trouble—"

Before he could explain, Dryer sat forward again, his eyes narrowed. "Woman like that attracts trouble," he said, tapping his cigarette against an ashtray. "She's practically defined by it. Any trouble she's having, you can damn well be sure she brought it along with her."

And then Mac knew. Officer Dryer was never going to believe Kate's story about her father-in-law, not without proof. Dryer had a history with these people; maybe he was one of the half of the people of Boward Key he'd mentioned who "owed" Doc Priestly. Mac said, "She's anxious to resolve family disputes and get her children back where they belong."

"I believe where those two babies belong is now in the hands of the court to decide," Dryer mused, flinging the chair back again.

"So you think the grandparents will continue to try to gain custody, even though their mother is back in town?"

"More or less have to, don't they?" Dryer said. "Their daddy is dead, their mother is unreliable or worse and what with Charlie being sickly it's a good thing those kids have their grandparents to raise them." He leaned close and lowered his voice. His breath smelled like old socks. "If you ask me, it's the best thing that could happen to those little kids. Give them some stability in their lives. No one needs a mother who runs out on them, now do they?"

Mac's own mother's face appeared behind his eyes and he blinked rapidly before saying, "No. I don't suppose they do."

SOMETHING—an echo, an extra sound between steps —*something* alerted Kate to the fact that she wasn't alone on that path and she stopped abruptly, holding her breath.

Shells crunching behind her stopped a millisecond later.

Expecting that Gloria had sent Eduardo after her to make sure she got home safely, she whirled around so fast she almost fell over.

A tall shape ran down the path toward her. She started to tell Eduardo to go home when she realized this man was much taller and thinner than Eduardo. And then the moonlight hit the object in his hand and Kate stifled a scream.

She spun on the balls of her feet and ran.

She knew this path by heart and she knew it petered out up ahead as it met the broad sweep of grass leading up to the house. She could think of nowhere on that gentle, moonswept slope to hide until she got almost to the deck. Her sandals weren't made for running; she knew she would never make it.

On her left was a shoreline of small rocks and then the black water of Florida Bay.

No cover there, she thought, unless one considered the water itself. She'd never been swimming here, but she had been boating, and she knew it was shallow toward the shore but quickly deepened.

Kate stopped thinking. Stumbling over rocks, slipping on slime, she forged ahead without stopping. Her breathing was so loud it pounded in her ears. At any moment, she expected an arm to grab her around the neck, a blade to slice through the back of her sweater and pierce her heart.

When the cold water splashed as high as her knees, she lowered herself flat on her stomach. Splashes behind her signaled the killer had entered the water. She pulled herself along, fighting to keep her head down, cursing the moonlight that played across the surface ripples. The cool temperature of the water went all but unnoticed in her haste to put a safe distance between herself and the monster with the knife.

When the water was deep enough, she swam as fast as she could underwater, instinctively traveling as far from her last position as her inhaled breath would take her, kicking off her sandals as she swam, thinking, thinking as her loose clothes grew heavier and hindered her movement.

She could try to make it back to the Priestly house, to their dock. If she could get out of the water unseen, Eduardo or Gloria could help her.

The attack came after you left the Priestly house, an inner voice shouted against the drumming of her heart. *Are you crazy? You can't go back that way!*

There was an old pier north of her house. She could swim to that. It was a long swim, but the lethargy that had claimed her since coming back home was gone, washed away by water the color of ink and the determination that whoever was stalking her wasn't going to win.

She *would* get to dry land, she *would* reclaim her babies, she *would* move as far away as humanly possible.

With or without Mac.

She'd worry about how to get back to her house once she made it to the pier. First things first.

She surfaced, trying hard not to gasp for air, though her lungs ached. As she dog-paddled in place, she tugged off her sodden clothes, desperately raking the shoreline for a sign of her pursuer as she fought stubborn buttons. She finally recognized a tall shape in front of the palms, out in the water.

Did he have a gun, too?

She didn't know.

As her assailant switched on a flashlight and played the beam across the water, Kate let the last of her garments slip away. Then she took a deep but noiseless breath, closed her eyes and slithered silently into the depths, away from the light. She swam north.

IT WAS LATE AND THE TWO TACOS Mac had bought at a drive-through and eaten in the Coopers' car sat heavy in his stomach.

As he drove back to his motel, questions kept buzzing his brain. Had Kate really run out on her kids? Was she really a gold digger? A stripper?

Why had she kept secrets from him?

He tried to drum up a scenario that fit. She'd admitted that after her husband died, she wanted to leave Boward Key. Was it possible she had decided to do so, only without her children? Had she approached her father-in-law and asked for an advance on her inheritance so that she could make a break? When he refused, had she gone off on her own, maybe thinking she'd get settled and then retrieve her boys? Had she then met up with foul play that landed her in Billington or had some old crony of hers chosen that moment to track her down?

That fit in with the Elvis impersonator groping her in the bar right after he warned her to go home. Hadn't she wondered aloud, way before her memory started coming back, if she was tied up with unsavory people? Had she known this guy two years ago?

Since her memory returned, had she reconsidered her decision to abandon her children? Was she embarrassed to admit she'd done so? Was she scared that she'd made such a giant mistake that she might never get them back? Or did the fact that she seemed to have forgotten the pivotal few moments before everything went awry mean she'd also forgotten her own decisions and actions?

Or was she lying to him?

When it came to Kate, he hated trying to create worst-case scenarios, but she had asked him to kidnap her children from their grandparents. He had to gather information and no matter how he felt about Kate, he had to find out *who* she really was, not who she thought she was or who she wanted to be. Or who she wanted him to think she was.

He rubbed the back of his neck as he pulled into the motel parking lot.

Having thought the worst, now he could think in other directions. How about the two guys in Macon, Georgia?

Okay. One of them had tried to abduct her. Apparently, if he took Kate's word for it, this guy had been the first person she saw when she woke up back in Indiana. Why hadn't he just killed her then, if that was his plan? The second time, in that parking lot, maybe it had been too close to other people, too dangerous even for a knife. But the first time, in that abandoned alley? Why hadn't he knifed her as he had apparently knifed Jake?

And how had she gotten into the alley in the first place? How had she ended up in Jake's clothes and why had Jake then been murdered?

He was getting ahead of himself. He turned off the ignition as he thought about the Elvis impersonator.

The man had told Kate that B.O. wanted her home and then he'd fired at the abductor, presumably to make sure Kate had a chance.

Why?

How did an Elvis impersonator, who happened to also know Kate, end up performing in a roadside inn they themselves hadn't know they were stopping at until the last moment? He must have been following them. So, assuming that Elvis and the abductor were separate agents, which one of them drove the car with the wacky headlight? Had there been a whole parade of Indiana cars traveling from Billington to Boward Key?

Who were these men? For whom did they work?

And what did they have to do with Kate or the elder Priestlys?

He pushed his room key into the lock, opened the door and stood there without turning on the light. Then he closed the door without entering.

There were no answers for him inside that room.

The answers were a mile away, in Kate's head. He needed to talk to her—not tomorrow morning, but right at that moment, before her in-laws brought the children home from Fort Myers.

He desperately needed answers.

Chapter Eleven

Mac rang Kate's doorbell. When that didn't work, he tried banging with his fist. He was about ready to go to the car, retrieve his gun from the glove box and shoot the damn lock when Nellie opened it at last.

"I want to speak with Kate," he said.

"Ms. Katrina has been asleep for hours," Nellie said.

"Then we'll wake her."

The housekeeper seemed to grow roots into the floor. "*We* most assuredly will not. If you must see her, come back in the morning, though if you ask me—"

"Thing is, I'm not asking you," Mac said, and with a firm push, snapped the door out of her hand. As she protested his audacity, he took a chance that the bedrooms were situated on the north side of the house and started down what looked to be the appropriate hallway, Nellie nipping at his heels.

"Of all the unmitigated gall," she sputtered. "I've half a mind to call the police."

"Ask for Officer Dryer," Mac said. He stopped in front of two closed doors and said, "Which one?"

Nellie was so angry with him that she refused to indicate which door was Kate's. He tried one knob, and pushed open the door to find two cribs and a plethora of neatly arranged stuffed animals and plastic trucks. He tried the other and found the master suite.

"I can't believe your nerve," Nellie said, still right behind him.

He stopped in front of a huge bed draped in cream and shades of tan, with fluffy pillows and roses everywhere. If this wasn't a marital bed, he'd eat all six frilly throw pillows, and a stab of red-hot jealousy poked right through his gut. Ignoring the jealousy, he regarded the tousled but empty sheets, the hand of solitaire laid out and half played on the lace coverlet, the framed photograph of Kate's sons lying face up on a pillow. "Where is she?" he said.

Nellie had already opened the folding doors to a walk-in closet crammed with clothes and now she was turning on the lights in what appeared to be a huge attached bathroom. She turned startled eyes to him. "I don't know. She went to her room some time ago. I just assumed…"

They both looked at the glass door leading to the patio.

"Call the Priestly house and make sure she isn't over there," Mac directed, and for once, Nellie didn't protest. He checked the door. It was unlocked, and a jolt of alarm rattled him. Had someone entered this room and forced Kate to leave?

He shouldn't have left her alone!

Nellie was off the phone in a flash. "Gloria said she was there almost two hours ago, wanting to see the children. She told them the Priestlys had taken them up to Fort Myers. I already told her that. Why did she go bother Gloria?"

"Because she's worried sick about her kids," Mac said, impatience making his voice brusque. "It's not a long walk between the houses, is it?" He felt a little better knowing she had apparently walked to the big house under her own steam.

"Just a few minutes. Maybe she decided to take a stroll."

"Or a swim?"

"Not out there," Nellie said.

"You stay here, I'll go look for her."

With that, he let himself out the door and crossed the patio. As he stepped onto the grass, the door behind him opened and Nellie hurried outside. "Take this," she said, handing him a flashlight. "Dr. Priestly lives south of here. There's a path along the shoreline."

"Thanks," he said, and took off at a run.

THE MUSCLES in Kate's arms and shoulders throbbed with fatigue. When she finally saw the gray silhouette of the old fishing pier jutting out into the bay, she felt like crying with relief.

Eventually, she reached the pier. She knew from the times she and Danny had visited here that it was too unstable to climb on, even if she could have figured out a way to shimmy up the rotting log supports.

No one fished here anymore, and the beach wasn't particularly attractive for late-night strolls, facts for which Kate was grateful as she waded through the mud and turtle grass. Of course, it wasn't tourists or fishermen she was nervous about.

Common sense said her attacker would never dream she'd swim this far north, that the shoreline was too broken up by buildings for him to have followed her without knowing her ultimate location. She still felt uncommonly naked standing there, and it wasn't just because she'd stripped down to her underwear.

How was she supposed to get home?

Was it safe to even go home?

What did she do now?

MAC HAD SELDOM in his life felt as helpless as he did at that moment.

He reviewed the two options he thought he had. He could call the police and tell them that the woman they were already convinced was a total flake was now missing…again. He had no proof she hadn't left of her own volition. Nellie couldn't find the clothes she'd been wearing, so presumably, she'd still been wearing them. Ditto, her shoes. He'd searched every inch of the shoreline, from Kate's property to the Priestly house, and he hadn't found one iota of evidence that anything untoward had happened to her. Gloria confirmed that Kate had knocked on the door hours before and that she'd been distraught when she left.

Or he could wait.

He didn't like either choice and settled on a third. After getting Nellie and Gloria to promise to call if Kate showed up, he went back to his motel. It was only a mile or so, and the monster SUV lurking in the closed part of the garage was still there. It made sense she'd walk.

The streets back to the motel were depressingly empty, as was the porch in front of his room. He had the door open and was half-inside when his cell phone started ringing. Heart slamming against his ribs, he answered.

"You should see the results of the latest poll," Bill Confit said, his voice booming with confidence.

Mac sat down on the bed, facing the door he'd left ajar. It took a second to get past the fact that the caller wasn't Kate. He said, "I take it you're way out ahead."

"Way out. If things keep going like this, the election will be a landslide."

"That's great, Bill."

"And if it is, young man, the first thing I'm going to do is go to the city council and ask for Chief Barry's resignation."

"You'll be doing the city a favor," Mac said, distracted by his continuing worry about Kate. What should he do next? Give up and call Dreyer? "Listen, Bill, I need to get off the phone—"

"No, you listen," Confit said, suddenly serious. "If all goes according to plan, I want you to take over as chief of police."

Mac was sure he'd misheard Confit. His mind had been drifting….

"Mac? You still there?"

"I guess I'm speechless," Mac said. "Bill, I'm flattered you think I could handle the job—"

"Of course you can. You're the last honest man in Billington. Don't let me down. This city needs you."

Despite his worries about Kate, possibilities ran through Mac's mind. Ways to clean up the police department, ways to build bridges to unite the divergent sections of the community. And along with these lofty goals came the allure of vindication. He'd no longer be the whistle-blower, the outsider, the man who had sabotaged his chance to fit in by speaking out.

"You think about it before you say another word," Confit said. "Call me when you get back to town. Night, Mac."

Mac clicked the phone off and sat there for a moment, stunned. Him a police chief? How could he ever say no to such an opportunity? Why would he?

As he sat there and speculated on the whimsy of fate, he gradually became aware that a car had pulled into the spot in front of his room. Headlights illuminated the drawn curtain. He heard voices. A door slammed. The headlights receded as his door swung fully open.

He knew immediately that the svelte shape standing in front of him was Kate.

He was up and at her side before she could utter a word.

"What happened to you?" he asked as he flicked on the weak overhead light and took a good look at her. Her hair was wet, she was wrapped bosom to knee in a red-and-white checked cloth. A fine layer of mud covered her bare legs and feet and streaked her arms and hands.

"It's a long story," she said, clutching the cloth to her chest as she swung his door shut.

Conflicting emotions bombarded him. Joy at seeing her alive and well. Fury that she'd put him through hell for the last hour and a half. Concern that something had obviously happened to her. Disappointment that he'd had to learn about her past from a stranger instead of directly from her. And there were more emotions bubbling below these, as well. Too many to name, let alone acknowledge.

For a moment, relief won. He pulled her into his arms and kissed her forehead. When she looked up at him, he kissed her lips, relieved when she relaxed enough to kiss him back until her very compliance seemed to reawaken the anger that had never been far from the surface.

"Where the hell have you been?" he demanded as he held her at arm's length. "Do you have any idea how much worse you've made things? Why didn't you tell me you were a stripper in Vegas when you met your husband? Why didn't you mention that you habitually left your kids with their grandparents? Is it true you have a recreational drug habit?"

Some of the steam seemed to dissipate as accusations dressed up like questions tumbled from his mouth.

But there was more. "And how about that fancy underwear

you look so lovely in, huh, Kate? If your husband didn't love you, why did he buy you stuff like that? Why did he have your portrait painted? Why did he hang it above his sofa?"

Staring up at him with tired looking eyes, she said, "I see someone told you...about me."

"Officer Dryer."

"And what were you doing talking to a police officer?"

"Trying to find out about your father-in-law, whom, I might add, is up for sainthood."

She twisted away from him and paced his carpet, leaving muddy footprints in her wake. "So this Dryer told you all about my sordid past. How I married Danny for his money, how I wormed my way into poor Dr. Priestly's life."

"More or less," Mac admitted.

"And how my revered in-laws have had to fill in for me because I'm such a dismal mother. How even now, they have Charlie seeing some allergy specialist up in Fort Myers."

Mac nodded.

She stopped dead in her tracks and said softly, "Isn't it odd how the police know all these details? Almost like the good doctor keeps them informed, isn't it? Why do you think he does that?"

"Maybe they're friends," Mac said.

"Sure," she said.

Mac was beginning to wish he'd approached Kate with compassion. He was almost sure it had been one of those subterranean emotions he'd ignored. Anger had been the wrong approach. Anger had been what she expected from him. Not what she wanted, but what she'd come to expect from men. He could tell that now. Too bad he hadn't been able to tell that five minutes ago.

He held out a hand, but she turned her back on him.

"Kate," he said. "I'm sorry."

She whirled around to face him again. "You're sorry? That's it? Sorry?"

"What happened to you tonight?"

"Nothing," she stated in a way that very clearly said whatever had happened to her was none of his business.

"Listen, Grace—"

"Kate," she corrected him. "My name is Katrina Priestly. Why can't you remember that?"

"Maybe because in some ways, I wish you were still Grace," he mumbled.

"Well, I'm not Grace," she said, eyes blazing. "Furthermore, I've never been *Grace*. You made Grace up, you made her be what you wanted her to be. I'm just Kate. Okay, I hustled drinks in Vegas. I dealt cards. I was too short to be a showgirl, so I tried stripping. Once. I hated it, so I quit. But on that one lousy night, who should happen to waltz through the door but Danny Priestly. Danny wanted a sexy, wild adventure. What he got was a wife. He didn't want children, either, but he got those, too. I bought the fancy underwear for myself, and by the way, it's a whole lot cheaper than your aunt's friend led her to believe. And my portrait came about when an artist Danny played poker with paid off an old debt with a painting."

"Kate—"

"Furthermore, for the record, I left my boys with his folks twice, and both times, they knew exactly where I was going. They knew that I was trying to get their son to come home to his kids and I was never even away overnight. I have never used drugs. Period. End of story. I bet I have better morals than half the people you know."

"I never said—"

"But you *thought* it," she fumed.

"You didn't help matters," he said. "You could have told me the truth right from the beginning."

"I did tell you the truth. I just didn't tell you every detail. It's none of your business if what I used to do for a living embarrasses me now. What is your business is helping me get my children back. I'm paying you for that, not for judging me."

He stared at her in stunned silence. She lowered her gaze as though considering the impact of her words. He finally mumbled, "I am not judging your past," he said. "I couldn't give a damn about your past. You're more than a client to me and you know it."

"And maybe that's the crux of the problem," she said softly.

"Maybe it is."

She met his gaze again, defiantly. He wasn't sure what to do. He wasn't a quitter, and he still felt there was a whole lot more story here than he knew. But he didn't know if he had the heart to stick around and ferret out the truth.

More than ever, he felt that once this issue was resolved in her favor, *if* it was, Kate would take her children and disappear from his life. He had disappointed her just as much as she had disappointed him.

He finally repeated, "What happened to you tonight?"

"Someone tried to stab me," she said, her voice weary.

"What!"

"While I was walking home from the Priestly house, someone tried to kill me. I escaped by dodging into the water and swimming up the coast to a rotten fishing pier. An old man and his wife happened to be parked nearby. They gave me the picnic tablecloth out of their trunk so I could cover up and drove me to your motel because, quite frankly, I was afraid to go home alone."

Mac rubbed the back of his neck and tried to put one coherent thought next to another as he stared at Kate.

His Kate.

She added, "Doesn't that prove Dr. Priestly is involved?"

"I don't know," he said.

"I wasn't attacked until *after* I visited the doctor's house. And I don't think he went to that Orlando conference, either, Mac. Maybe you could check. I think he drove me up to Billington—"

"I made a few phone calls today," he interrupted. "Dr. Priestly did go to the conference. He gave the keynote speech on the evening of January ninth and he led a workshop on the tenth. He was back here by the eleventh, seeing patients. In fact, he was here every night until two days ago, when he and his wife took your kids to Fort Myers."

She seemed to wilt.

"I checked on Paula Priestly, too. She never left town."

"How did you—"

"Nellie. I questioned her when I was at your house this evening, looking for you. She saw Paula Priestly every day of the week last week, Kate. She was over there a lot, helping Gloria with your kids."

"Well, I never really suspected Paula," Kate said.

"The point is, neither of these people had the opportunity to take you to Indiana."

Mac sat down on the edge of the mattress and gestured at the one chair the small room provided. Kate sank onto the seat. "Remember when the Elvis impersonator told you someone named B.O. wanted you to go home?" he asked her.

She mumbled, "Yes. So?"

"Remember how you felt he seemed comfortable with the fact that he could grope you?"

Rubbing her hands along the wooden arms of the chair in a restless gesture he could only assume mirrored the state of her nerves, she stared at him. She finally said, "I don't understand where you're going with this."

"You don't remember this Elvis guy from a couple of years ago?"

"No."

"He's not someone from your past, Kate? Someone from Vegas? B.O. isn't an old boyfriend or boss—"

She stood so abruptly that the picnic spread fell to the floor and, once again, as she had so many times before, she stood in front of him wearing nothing but very fancy underwear.

"So you think someone from my past is trying to get rid of me for some Hollywood-type reason? Maybe I was a mobster's girlfriend and witnessed a murder? Maybe I'm a runaway call girl—"

"Kate," he said, standing. He leaned down, picked up the cloth and held it out. She refused to take it, as though accepting even this would put her in his debt and she no longer wanted to owe him anything. "I'm just asking if it's possible you may have brought this trouble with you. Officer Dryer said—"

"No," she said emphatically. "I can't believe you would believe the word of a stranger over me."

"You've been confused," he said. He didn't add that she'd already lied to him.

"Is that how you do it?" she said, tilting her head.

"Do what?"

"Push women away? Do you lure them into feeling secure

with you and then start doubting them when your head gets in the way of your heart?"

"That's not fair," he grumbled, wishing she'd cover herself up. How was he supposed to think straight?

Part of him wondered what she'd do if he pulled her against his chest. Would she come, reluctantly at first, then willingly? He didn't think so. He said, "My love life is not the point. Did you get a look at the guy with the knife? Was it our friend from Macon?"

"I think so. He had the right build, kind of tall and spindly. He kept one arm real close to his body."

Mac rubbed his neck again. The tension across his shoulders seemed to throb exponentially to his powerlessness to help the one woman in the world he…cared about.

"I want to go home," she said. "Will you please drive me home?"

"I don't think it's wise for you to go back to your house. We need to call the police. I checked that path and didn't see any sign of trouble, but they'll have more men and better lights—"

"Oh, yeah. Let's get them out here right now so I can show them my undies and give them all something else to hold against me. No way. The Priestlys will be home tomorrow. Maybe they'll hand over the kids without a fuss."

He stared at her for a moment, unsure if she'd just said what he thought she'd said. "Are you implying that you're not sure your father-in-law is behind all this?"

She blinked rapidly, obviously holding back tears. "I don't know. I remember Paula being upset, I remember the surprise of my father-in-law still being home, I *seem* to remember his eyes as he leaned over me…" Shivering, her voice petered out and she finally took the tablecloth and wrapped it around her body. "He told the police I left there by myself?"

"Yes," Mac said. "Is it possible, Kate? Even remotely possible?"

She shook her head, unshed tears making her eyes glisten. She said, "I don't know. But I have never, ever heard of someone called B.O."

"Stay here tonight," Mac said, surprised at how much he hoped she'd agree. He needed to tell her about the Priestlys taking her to court and he just couldn't think of a way to do it that wouldn't devastate her. Plus, what she'd said about him pushing women away was beginning to prickle. He wanted time with her—time to talk, to reconnect. He wanted to trust her again. And he didn't want anyone else trying to hurt her. "You'll be safer here. We can talk."

"I have to go home. I'll set the alarm system and stay inside, but I have to go home." She glanced at her muddy arms and hands, and added, "I need to clean up and get ready for tomorrow. If I stay in this motel with you, it will confirm everything everyone thinks about me."

"Then I'll stay with you—"

"No, you were right to refuse that offer. Best if we sleep a mile apart from each other. It'll look better."

"You're in danger," he said bluntly.

"I know. But I have to prioritize things. Number one—get my boys back. Number two—trap the jerk who's trying to kill me and make him spill his guts."

Mac shook his head. He hadn't made it on to her list. His hands itched with the need to hold her. Hold *on to* her. One thing for certain. He wasn't going to let her face the Priestlys without warning her about their intentions. He said, "Kate, there's no pleasant way to tell you this, so I'm just going to say it. Your in-laws are taking you to court."

She stared at him without blinking.

"Kate?"

"They didn't waste any time, did they?"

"If somehow they're innocent of all this, then maybe they really are concerned. I'll help you talk to them, I'll help them understand what you've been through—"

"Let's get real," she told him, the edginess back in her voice. She began pacing again as she spoke. "If Dr. Priestly didn't orchestrate all this, he'll never believe I'm suitable for raising his grandchildren until I can prove in court that what happened to me was not my fault. And if we can't trap that jerk with the knife, maybe I'll never be able to prove it, I don't know. At the moment, it all seems kind of hopeless to me. But I *am* going to get my babies back."

She stared defiantly at him and he understood the unspoken message. In the end, to keep her children, Kate might have to steal them. Was he ready to help her do such a thing?

The honest-to-God answer was that he wasn't sure.

"When we get back to my house, I'll write you a check," she added. "For services rendered. For services yet to be rendered."

"Not yet," he told her, feeling as though he hadn't rendered a single service other than falling for her, which was definitely a questionable one. "Don't pay me until this is over."

She stared at him a long time before saying, "I see."

He took her home, discouraged by the way she hugged the passenger door. He thought about her accusation that he was pushing her away. It seemed patently unfair to him that she couldn't understand his position. He was a man used to lining up his ducks. Experience told him facts didn't lead a man astray, whereas feelings were as trustworthy as a mirage.

He searched her house, Nellie on his heels, and stayed until the housekeeper had locked every door and window and punched in the security code. Back at the motel, he performed a few housecleaning chores, blotting the dry mud stains on a carpet no one cared about, then wiping down the chair Kate had used. He stared at the muddy bath towel in his hands. There was a hole the size of a beach ball in his stomach.

Why hadn't he asked Kate about her father-in-law's accusation that their last argument stemmed from Kate demanding money? It hadn't even crossed his mind to say anything to her about that. He'd been so focused on blaming her for everything that he hadn't even looked for ways to prove her right.

God, what a jerk he was.

Throwing himself down on top of the bedspread, he laid awake half the night thinking about Kate and her two cute little boys. Blond and blue-eyed, smiling in the photo on Kate's pillow, Kate's arms wrapped around their torsos in that oil painting above her sofa. Though he had never met the kids, their plight was as real to him as his own misgivings.

What if, way back when, Mac's own father had handed him over to his mother? Would he have spent his life wandering the city streets with her, helping her look for her next fix?

The difference hit him hard. His mother hadn't *wanted* him. Kate was desperate for her kids.

And he was desperate for Kate.

UPSET BY the conversation with Mac, Kate paced her bedroom and watched the clock. She kept going over and over what Mac had said.

Was it possible something had happened to her after she left the Priestly house? Was it possible she'd turned her dislike and distrust of Daniel Priestly into a subconscious vendetta against him? Were the memories of a needle and gray eyes as undependable as Mac said they might be? Or was she right? Was Mac trying to push her away?

She could always find another detective to help her, hopefully one more impressed with money and less anxious to understand every little detail. But hiring help wasn't the problem.

What she couldn't so easily replace was the way she felt about Mac. The way she trusted him and yearned for him to trust her. The way she would have given just about anything for him to unflinchingly back her up.

Even when your own memory is foggy and incomplete? Is it fair to ask the man to trust you more than you trust yourself?

She had to put Mac out of her mind and concentrate on her boys. Toward that goal, she tried to remember everything she could about the habits of Daniel and Paula Priestly—in her opinion, two of the most predictable people on the face of the earth.

Or so she had thought until she took her boys to their house for a visit and woke up half a dozen states away.

She reviewed their traveling habits. Dr. Priestly attended many in-state conferences and meetings. He didn't like to drive after dark, so he always stayed over an extra night and traveled first thing in the morning. Fort Myers was only about two hours away.

She could expect them home before noon.

MAC WOKE with a start, sensing at once that he wasn't alone. He fumbled on the nightstand for his gun until he remembered that it was still locked in the glove box of the Coopers' car. There was a cache of ammo in his duffel bag, which sat two feet away, but ammo without a gun amounted to pretty much nothing. A noise from a dark corner by the drapes jerked him upright.

"Morning," a voice said, as a shadow detached itself and moved toward the chair.

Grateful he'd gone to sleep fully clothed, Mac threw his legs over the side of the bed and switched on the lamp. The digital clock blinked 10:13. The room was warm, despite the fan twirling lazily overhead. A small man holding a gun sat down in the chair across from him.

Mac said, "Do I know you?"

The man sat back and crossed his legs, resting his right ankle on his left knee. He wore white socks covered with black squares, along with black trousers, a black shirt and a white vest. Snappy clothing for a run-of-the-mill thief, which Mac really didn't take this guy for. His thin lips and hollow cheeks looked vaguely familiar. The bald head looked wrong.

"I guess you know me best as Elvis," the man said.

Mac stared at him for a while before saying, "I should have expected you. Mind my asking how you got in here?"

"Piece of cake," Elvis said. "Don't be too hard on the management, though. They actually have fairly decent locks, but they're no match for Betsy." With this, he patted his vest pocket. Mac assumed it held a lock pick.

"And you're here because…"

"You have a problem with that lady friend of yours. Almost got herself killed last night."

"She's got a mind of her own," Mac admitted.

"Lucky for both of you I was following her back in Macon.

Have to admit, I was a little surprised to see her waltz out of that room alone. Could have knocked me over with a feather when she started trying on clothes, and then she sashays into a bar? I couldn't wait to see what she'd do next."

Curiosity got the best of Mac. "How did you wind up dressed like Elvis?"

He flashed a smile. "I admit it, I have a weakness for performing. When the bartender started spouting off about a no-show Elvis, I thought what better way to keep an eye on the little lady than to stand smack-dab in front of her. She'd just ordered a bottle of wine, so I knew she planned on sticking around for a while. Things were going great until I picked up on the fact that the guy who'd been tailing you since Billington had sneaked in behind her and was sitting off in a corner. I thought for sure all your fancy driving coming into town had thrown him off. What probably happened was he made me, too, by then. He probably followed me following you! What a gas, huh?"

"A real hoot," Mac said.

"Then you showed up, and I took matters into my own hands."

"By groping Kate?"

"I wanted her to get mad at me and run to you. Instead, she pushes the table over. Next thing I know, the tail nabbed her. This is one creepy dude. Not the kind you want touching your woman."

Mac regarded the smaller man. The unflinching self-regard he found staring back at him appeared as straightforward as it was outlandish.

Elvis seemed to sense his skepticism. "What can I say?" he mumbled, shrugging spindly shoulders. "I have a flamboyant streak."

"You also told her B.O. wanted her to go home."

"Exactly."

"So, who tried to knife her last night? The guy from Macon?"

"That's right. That knife must be his calling card. I was getting ready to intercede when she took off into the water. She took care of herself that time, but the girl's luck has got to be running thin."

"And just why does B.O. want her back here?"

"Well, now, you see, B.O. thinks she needs to start acting like a proper widow."

"In what way?"

"We hear she stands to inherit a lot of money from her late husband. She can't do that if she's dead in an alley somewhere, now can she?"

Mac put two and two together. "Her husband left gambling debts. B.O. wants her to settle them."

"Exactly. Danny-boy wasn't a lucky fellow with the dice."

"And this B.O. had nothing to do with Kate ending up in Billington, Indiana?"

"Now you're being stupid."

"So humor me."

As Elvis moved, Mac realized the black squares on the white socks were dice, the pips represented by sequins. "I got here a couple of weeks ago to scope things out," Elvis said. "Right about the time I'm getting ready to make a sales pitch to the pretty lady about honoring her old man's debts—or else—I see her classy little Mercedes leaving town, only she's not behind the wheel. She's all slumped over in the passenger seat.

"I start following. The trip took forever. Start and go, long delays, but never once did that girl get out of the car. I don't think she even woke up. Next thing I know, I'm in Indiana. Never been in Indiana before. Can't imagine why anyone would want to live there, especially in the winter. Anyway, the boss says to keep her in my sights, so I keep her in my sights."

"Then you saw the man who did this to her!"

"Yeah, I saw him. The same guy who forced her out of that bar in Macon, the same guy I winged, the same guy who attacked her last night."

"So if we go to the police—"

The small man stood so quickly the chair jumped back against the wall. "Nobody is going to the cops, especially not me," he said, waving his pearl-handled gun. "I saved her up in Macon. Okay, so I only winged him before he got away—if I hadn't come along, she'd be dead. I'm here this morning to tell you to keep a better eye on that girl 'cause that creep is back and I don't think he'll settle for another cross-country drive this time. Hate to see anything happen to such a pretty lady."

"Before B.O. gets his money."

"Exactly."

"Okay, just tell me a few things. Did you see Kate with anyone else? Her father-in-law, maybe?"

Elvis ruminated for a moment, obviously trying to decide if it mattered if he answered a couple of questions. Finally, he shook his head.

"While you were watching her up in Billington, did you see the creep buy an old bum's clothes right off his back?"

"He gave the old guy new clothes in exchange. And a few bottles of liquid refreshment."

"Did you see this same guy come back later and kill the bum?"

"I kept my eyes on the girl, not the creep. You had the girl, ergo—"

"Then did you follow me through Billington?"

"Just over to your aunt's place and then when you left with the girl. Cute little car switch you pulled, by the way."

"It obviously didn't work," Mac said dryly.

"No, but it wasn't your fault. Your aunt drives like an old lady. It took the other couple so long to merge into traffic while sitting under a street lamp that they might as well have taken out an advertisement." He pointed at his own bald head and added, "They both have white hair."

"When—"

"Nope. That's it," Elvis said, making his way slowly to the door, his gun trained on Mac's head. "Sit right there a sec, okay? And do us all a favor. Keep the little lady safe, keep her where we can find her. We'd hate to see anything happen to her before she has a chance to do the honorable thing by B.O. I, personally, hate making threats, but B.O. mentioned getting to her through her kids, so urge her to cooperate, will you?" With a nod and a wink like some kind of pip-squeak Santa Claus, he opened the door and slipped away.

Mac sat for a moment, digesting everything he'd just heard, and then picked up the phone and left a message for Officer Dryer. He'd no sooner replaced the receiver than it rang.

He snapped it up. "Yes?"

"It's me, Nellie," Kate's housekeeper said, her voice trembling.

"What's wrong?"

"Ms. Katrina has gone over to the Priestly house. I begged her to wait for you, but she was up all night, pacing, and this morning she just left. What should I do?"

"I'm leaving right now," Mac said, slamming down the receiver. He hung a Do Not Disturb sign on his door before locking it behind him.

Chapter Twelve

Kate twisted the doorknob of the Priestly estate, almost faint-
ing with relief when it turned silently in her hand and the door
glided open. Hope surged in her chest. She'd reclaim her children and be gone before anyone knew she'd even been here.

She'd seen them drive past the house a few minutes before.
They were people of habit, and Kate knew the first thing Dr.
Priestly did upon returning from a trip was to shut himself away
in his den to look over the mail that had accumulated during his
absence. Her mother-in-law, on the other hand, would retreat
to her room to freshen up. Kate figured she had a good half hour.

The boys almost certainly would be left in their suite, probably with Gloria in attendance. Gloria might question Kate's
presence, but she wouldn't forbid Kate to touch her own children. As much as Kate was determined to get the boys away
from this house, she was equally determined to see them, to
touch them, to hold them in her arms.

For an instant, she thought of Mac and her resolve almost
fled. She'd told him she'd stay put. Though it had crossed her
mind to call him when she saw the car drive past, she'd been
afraid he would try to talk her out of coming and that would
take time she didn't have.

The house opened into a huge entry, with a sweeping stairway off to the right. Flooded with midmorning light, the whites and greens of paint and plants complemented the hardwood floors and wooden trim. There wasn't a soul in sight, and Kate moved quickly.

She was halfway up the stairs when Daniel Priestly exited the den at the bottom of the stairs. Kate turned and saw his face the instant he spied her. She saw surprise flicker across his even features. At that moment, she heard a gasp come from above her and turned to find Paula Priestly on the landing above.

Dr. Priestly whispered, "You came back!"

"Yes," Kate said. On the drive over, she'd decided to play it dumb in the hope the Priestlys would be reasonable if they thought she held no grudge. "Of course I came back," she replied. "I'm a little unclear on what happened, but I never intended on leaving the twins here for long. You must have realized that."

Dr. Priestly gave her a shrewd once-over.

Kate's mother-in-law sighed. "We've been so worried about you," she said in her soft drawl.

Kate said, "Well, um, thank you for filling in for me. I'll just get the boys and get out of your hair."

Paula Priestly started down the stairs, but paused when her husband said, "Paula, dear, stay up there, will you? Stay near the children."

"But Gloria is with them."

"Please," he said.

Paula took a step back. Resting a hand on the balustrade, she addressed Kate. Her voice apologetic, she said, "Charlie has been quite sick, dear. I've been worried."

Kate advanced another step. "Then he needs me."

"What he needs is stability," Dr. Priestly said sharply. His voice held the old arrogant tone that set Kate's teeth on edge.

Paula Priestly said, "Come on up here, dear, and see the children."

Kate felt tears of relief spring to her eyes and started up the stairs only to hear Dr. Priestly snap. "Absolutely not! Paula, use your head. Kate, I'm warning you, stay right where you are."

Paula waved Kate back. "I guess Dr. Priestly is right," she said. "I'm sorry."

Kate appealed to her mother-in-law as the friends they'd been close to becoming. "I have to see Harry and Charlie," she said. "Surely *you* understand."

Paula's expression was difficult to decipher, and Kate puzzled on it for a moment while Dr. Priestly said, "Judge Linstad has granted us temporary custody." There was a menacing tone to his voice that tripled Kate's heart rate.

The door swung open and everyone turned as Mac appeared. He was unshaven and crumpled but so damn handsome, so big and real, that Kate felt her breath catch. She'd never in her life been so glad to see anyone. She imagined at least some of the fire in his eyes was directed at her for coming here without telling him, but that was okay, too. He said, "The door was open, so I—Kate, are you all right?"

"I was just going to get my kids," she said.

Mac looked from her face to Daniel Priestly.

The doctor said, "You must be Mr. MacBeth. Gloria told us you'd come looking for Kate last night. I gather she was missing…again?"

"My mistake," Mac said. "Tempest in a teapot."

"I see. Are you a friend of Kate's from the old days?"

"No," Mac said. "I'm her friend from when someone dumped her in an alley in Billington, Indiana, and left her there to almost freeze to death. Would you happen to know anything about *that,* sir?"

Kate felt a smile tug on the corners of her mouth. In that second, she realized she loved Travis MacBeth, warts and all. She said, "Mac—"

But Dr. Priestly upped the ante. "I don't have the slightest idea what you're talking about," he said, his voice appalled. He added, "Paula and I have no desire to make things any harder on Kate or our grandchildren."

"I see," Mac said.

"However, Kate, you have to understand that you can't just barge in here whenever you want."

"He says the judge issued them a temporary custody order," Kate said, hating the catch she heard in her voice.

Mac said, "May we see it?"

The doctor smiled. "Of course. I'll get it. It's in my den."

As he moved off toward the den, Charlie and Harry burst onto the landing above and shouted, "Mommy!" in unison.

Kate's heart just about leapt out of her chest at the sight of them. In a flash, she scrambled past Paula and fell to her knees at the top of the stairs, her heart almost bursting as her two perfect babies tumbled into her arms. She kissed them frantically, hugging their sweet-smelling bodies, gazing at their faces and laughing with the pure joy of seeing them.

Charlie looked rosy and healthy, and some of the worry about his health dissipated. Harry was trying to explain something about a boat or a goat, but neither child was a great talker yet and when they were excited, their speech became even harder to decipher. She sat down as they crawled onto her lap and touched her face with plump fingers.

This was happiness.

"You see, they're just fine," Paula said as Gloria hustled through the door of the twins' suite, slowing down only when she saw the babies cuddled against Kate. Her arms were full of their toys.

"I'm sorry, Mrs. Priestly. I just turned my back for a second, and they were gone. They must have heard their mother's voice—"

"Never mind, Gloria. After you get the children down for their nap, I'd appreciate it if you'd have Eduardo drive you to the store," Paula said. "I made a list. It's in my room."

"Of course," Gloria said.

Looking right at Kate, Paula Priestly added, "It's time for their nap, Kate. Let Gloria settle them while we finish talking. Go on, boys, go with Gloria."

"Come along, *nenes*," Gloria said.

"They're fine right here," Kate said, but even as she spoke, the boys scurried after Gloria, chattering and giggling, completely unaware of the tension permeating their mother.

Dr. Priestly strode back into the entry. "Judge Linstad signed this a few days ago," he said softly, holding a folded piece of paper. He handed it to Mac who examined it.

"Honestly, what were we supposed to do?" the doctor continued. "Charlie was wheezing, he needed medical help. We did what any concerned grandparents would do. Simon agreed what's important are the children, so he signed this temporary order. Kate will have her chance to speak in court."

Simon? Her father-in-law referred to the judge by his first name? Disheartened, Kate's gaze went from him to her mother-in-law.

"What in the world did *he* tell you to explain what he did to me, Paula?" Kate said calmly. "Why are you protecting him? Don't you recall screaming when he attacked me?"

Paula shook her head. "Oh, my. Daniel is right. You have gone out of your mind."

"No," Mac said. "No, she hasn't gone out of her mind. These things did happen. I saw the results."

Kate cast him a thankful glance.

Dr. Priestly looked pained to have to explain things to Mac. "There's another account of events, you know, one that isn't quite so preposterous. You may not know that Kate has a rather...colorful...past," he began, his voice dripping with distaste. "My son confided this to his mother and me. He warned us that some rather unsavory characters might show up someday. Apparently that's exactly what happened. After Kate left our house that day, she must have met up with someone from her past. We have a great deal of...sympathy...for this young woman's plight, but sympathy can only extend so far."

"How about the argument you had with her on the day she left?" Mac said, handing the court order back to the doctor.

Kate started to protest, but a swift look from Mac kept her silent.

"What does Kate say?" Dr. Priestly asked.

"She can't remember a thing that happened here after learning that you hadn't yet left for Orlando."

"I was just so sad that day," Paula said. "About Danny, of course. About my dear boy." Tears filled the older woman's eyes and spilled down her cheeks. Kate got to her feet and despite everything, felt a wave of sympathy as one woman to another, one mother to another.

Dr. Priestly cleared his throat. "I had a last-minute phone call from the hospital that morning, so I didn't leave for the conference as planned. I heard my wife crying and came out to see what the problem was."

"And what did you do?" Mac demanded.

The doctor looked at Kate with something approaching loathing, or so it seemed to Kate. Then he looked at his wife as though reluctant to get into this matter in front of her. He shook his head. "I was worried Paula would make herself sick, so I came in here to ask Kate to leave. When Kate saw me, she demanded money. She said she intended to start some nasty rumors about Danny if I didn't pay her off. She was tired of waiting for probate to clear. She wanted freedom. It was all very…upsetting, but I don't like to be threatened, so I stood my ground. She left in a huff. Left the kids, just like that. Paula eventually calmed down and I went on to the conference to fulfill my obligations. Since then, we've done the best we can."

Kate glanced at Mac, anticipating the scathing remarks he'd make on her behalf.

He said, "It's all very complicated, isn't it? Kate's memory is…fuzzy. I guess she could have gotten parts of this wrong."

"Mac!"

"Let's leave now, Kate."

"I'm not going anywhere."

"The court order is solid," Mac said firmly.

"I don't care if it's chiseled in rock."

"If Dr. Priestly presses trespassing charges against you, Kate, things will go from bad to worse."

"But he—"

"He's trying to help you, aren't you, Dr. Priestly?"

Dr. Priestly nodded at Kate, his eyes full of benevolence. "I truly am, Katrina. Leave now."

"Trust me," Mac said, holding out a hand.

Kate stared at him. As disgusted with Daniel Priestly as she was, he had presented no big surprises. He'd been arrogant with her, reasonable with Mac. Same old, same old. And, given the present climate in this house, trying to remove Charlie and Harry would result in a fight that would scare the daylights out of them. They were safe here for the moment.

But Mac! He'd fallen for Dr. Priestly's charm. He'd sold her out.

She walked down the stairs with a wooden smile on her face. She couldn't feel her feet. Heartsick, she walked past Mac's extended hand and out through the door.

Mac followed the big SUV back to Kate's house. He parked behind Nellie's old red car and had to run to catch up with Kate before she entered the house. Once she'd done that, he knew, he'd be lucky if he ever saw her again.

"Listen," he demanded, grabbing her arm. She turned to face him. The tears running down her cheeks didn't mitigate the fury blazing in her eyes.

"Let go of me," she said.

"Not until you listen. You know how you're always telling me we should trap the bad guy?" As he hoped, the question intrigued her enough to keep her from pulling away. "That's what we just did," he added. "We trapped the bad guy."

"What are you talking about?"

"We trapped the man who started all of this, your father-in-law. That's why I asked him about the fight."

She narrowed her eyes. "I don't understand—"

"You remember going to your in-laws' house. You remember Paula coming apart, then your father-in-law showing up. After that, it's all a blur except for some faint memory of her screaming and him leaning over you. Is that right?"

"With a needle."

"Yes, with a needle. You don't recall asking him for money."

"I would never do that," she said hotly. "And I would never walk out on my kids. Never."

"But he insists you did."

"So what? He's lying."

"Exactly. He maintains that you got mad at him and left the house and that sometime after that, you ran into someone you used to know who caused your trouble. You say you went into that house and woke up in Indiana."

"I still don't—"

"Honey, I might have worried that your memory of events was fuzzy or that you kept things from me, but I never doubted that you told the truth as you knew it. I think you would recall if you intended on blackmailing your in-laws for immediate cash. That would take some forethought. If you don't remember having that kind of intent, then you didn't ask for money, which casts every other thing he says into doubt. It means you very well might not have left that house on your own, and frankly, from something Elvis said earlier, I don't think you did."

Her eyes grew big. "You talked to Elvis? Today?"

"Yes."

"Then you believe me?"

"Yes," he said. "I'm ashamed I ever doubted you."

"But you did, Mac. I'm glad you believe me now, but it still hurts that you tried so hard not to."

"I tried hard not to?" he echoed, a hollow feeling growing in the pit of his stomach. "What is that supposed to mean?"

"It means you wanted to believe the worst of me so you could walk away from me before I walked away from you."

"That's absurd."

"Is it?" she said.

"We don't have time for this," he grumbled, chancing a look into her blue eyes, determined to tell her she was full of it. Something he saw in the brilliant irises stopped him, though, something he couldn't fight.

The next thing he knew, he was pulling her into his arms. She came willingly, meeting his kisses with kisses of her own, kisses that said everything and solved nothing. When they were in each other's arms, everything was as it should be.

Couldn't they just stay that way forever?

A movement behind one of windows that flanked the front door caught his attention and he reluctantly drew away from Kate.

"I think we're scandalizing Nellie," he said, smoothing the short blond hair away from her tear-stained face.

"She scandalizes easily. She thinks of me as a grieving widow. What I am is a terrified mother."

"I want you to know I'll help you any way I can to get Charlie and Harry back. When I saw you holding them today…when I saw how you loved them and how they needed you…I don't know, I guess I'm not making any sense—"

She studied him a moment before whispering, "Yes, you

are. You finally are." She ran one of her smooth hands down his stubbled cheek. "Thank you, Mac. We'll have to wait until this is over to figure out if you and I can ever really trust each other."

"I do trust you—"

"No you don't, Mac. You don't trust me in the important ways. There will be time to talk about this later. What matters right this minute is getting my boys back, but I don't want to ask you to do something illegal that will ruin your life. I don't want to make things harder for you than they already are."

"The only thing that will make things harder for me is losing you," he told her and he meant it with all of his heart. The thing was, he wasn't sure he hadn't already lost her.

As for Bill Confit and his job offer? If he participated in abducting these children, he and Kate and the kids would have to disappear forever. He felt a twinge, but pushed it aside. He'd always attempted to do what was right and his gut was telling him that reuniting Kate and those little boys was what was right.

Even if the law disagreed.

"At least you now know what my father-in-law is capable of," she said. "Now we have to concentrate on figuring out some legal way to get my kids back home."

"Things have just been happening to us," he mused. "We've been followed, you've been threatened. Elvis comes and goes at his leisure…it's time to take control."

She said, "You really saw Elvis again? Did he tell you what he meant when he said B.O. wanted me to go home? Did he explain why he saved me from the guy with the knife?"

"Yes, yes and yes," Mac said. "I'll tell you about it later. We might as well face Nellie now."

"Poor Nellie," Kate said as she searched the SUV key ring for the house key. "You know, Mac, it's just my word against Dr. Priestly's. I don't stand a chance with his buddy, the judge. No one in this town is going to take me seriously."

"That's why we need a new plan. The knife wielder is our ace in the hole. All we have to do is get him to talk. Plot a trap. Listen to me, I'm beginning to sound like you." Mac noticed the door was unlatched. He pointed it out to Kate.

"Nellie must have left it open for me," she said, reaching out to push it open.

Mac caught her hand. Lowering his voice, he said, "Would she do that?"

"I don't know. She never has before—"

"Follow me. Stay close."

From reconnoitering the house the day before, he knew the laundry room door opened off the breezeway connecting the garage with the side of the house. He found the door shut tight and tried turning the knob. It was locked.

"Do you have a key?" he whispered, peering down at Kate.

"It's the same as for the front. Mac, what's going on?"

"Probably nothing. Slip off the house key and give it to me," he whispered, as he pulled his gun from the concealed holster against his back. He'd reclaimed it earlier, after Elvis left his room, better late than never. "I'm just being paranoid," he added. "Stay close."

The key slipped into the lock. Mac soundlessly nudged the door open. He stepped inside, aware of Kate behind him, worrying that he should have left her outside but more worried that she would be vulnerable out there alone.

No doubt Nellie had opened the front door, seen them kissing, and left it ajar as she retreated in titillated horror. No doubt his current caution was not only unnecessary but ridiculous.

The laundry room was narrow and windowless. Mac gestured at Kate to stay back as he peeked through the doorway into the kitchen.

The first thing he saw was Nellie, sprawled on the floor, sightless eyes open, laying in a pool of blood.

The second thing he saw was a tall, thin man standing at the far end of the kitchen, poised and waiting, his left arm suspended in a black sling, a scabbard cinched to his right thigh. Mac knew that from that vantage point the killer had a clear view of the front door. If Kate had walked through that door, he would undoubtedly have leaped upon her and slit her throat.

It bothered Mac that he couldn't see the man's right hand or whether or not anything was in the scabbard. Reason said the killer held a knife but Mac couldn't take it for granted. He raised his gun, aiming.

At that moment, Kate must have seen Nellie, for she gasped, and in that still, quiet house, her gasp was as loud as a scream. The man by the refrigerator twirled instantly, firing a gun as he spun.

The bullet splintered the wood next to Mac's head. Mac pushed Kate to the floor and fired his .38.

Kate screamed.

The gunman fired again as he disappeared around the refrigerator. Mac fired off another shot. "Stay right here," he told Kate. "I mean it, Kate. Don't move."

"Nellie needs me," she mumbled, trying to stand, her face so white Mac was afraid she was going into shock.

"Nellie is dead. Stay here."

Skirting Nellie's body, Mac crossed the kitchen. A shot whizzed past his head. He craned his neck and glimpsed the sling. He fired.

In the foyer, he half expected to find the front door wide-open and the killer gone. But it was still just barely ajar as it had been when they first approached the house. He closed and locked it, made a quick search of the open living area to his left, then continued down the hall. Another bullet hit the wall to his right; a shower of plaster fell on Mac's shoulder. Mac darted around the corner and got off a couple of rounds as the killer disappeared into the twins' room. He heard a crash that sounded like shattered glass and ran down the hall, stopping in front of the twins' doorway.

A glance inside revealed an impromptu exit had been created by shattering the window located near a bright yellow toy chest on the east side of the house. Looking through the window, he saw glass sparkling on the broken branches of the bushes outside. The killer was nowhere in sight.

To make sure the broken window wasn't a ruse, Mac tore open the closet door and the connecting door to the bathroom. Then he hurried back to the kitchen, growing worried that the killer could have doubled back outside and entered the house again through the kitchen.

Nellie was still there, but Kate was gone.

He ran to the Coopers' car, gun still in hand, digging in his pocket for the keys. The big SUV was missing. He didn't know if that portended good or bad. Did the killer force Kate into her late husband's vehicle or had she left under her own steam?

If she had left of her own accord, there was only one place he could think of that she would go and that was the Priestly house.

MAC FOUND Daniel Priestly standing at the foot of the stairs as though he hadn't moved since they'd left a half hour before. The doctor jumped when he heard Mac slam the door behind him.

"Where is she?" Mac demanded. "There's a killer loose. Where's Kate? What have you done with her?"

"She ran in here a few moments ago," Dr. Priestly said. "She's upstairs with the twins."

"Was she alone?"

"Of course."

As Mac caught his breath, he said, "You're not going to get away with this. You may not know it yet, but the man who abducted Kate ten days ago just killed her housekeeper."

Dr. Priestly's tanned face seemed to blanch right in front of Mac's eyes. "Nellie? Dead?"

"Nellie. The woman who damn near worshipped you. That psycho you hired to kill Kate stabbed her. The police will find him, Doctor, I guarantee you. And the first thing he'll do is plea-bargain to save his own skin."

"I didn't hire a killer," the doctor protested. "I'd never do such a thing. A doctor saves lives, he doesn't take them."

Damn if the man didn't sound sincere. Mac said, "You're lying."

"No, no," the doctor said, spreading his hands as though trying to illustrate his innocence.

"You wanted Kate out of the way. You wanted her babies," Mac said. "You hit her over the head and drugged her and had her driven away from here. I don't know why you didn't just kill her outright, unless the plan was to get her so far away her death wouldn't throw suspicion on you. The police will investigate. Trust me, they will find out how you did it and why. And they'll find a way to connect you and your hench-man to a harmless old bum who wound up with a knife in his back." Leveling his gaze, lowering his voice, he added, "And if they don't, I will."

"You have it all wrong," Dr. Priestly insisted, taking a step or two toward Mac, coming to a standstill when Mac raised the gun he still gripped in his right hand to warn him off. "That's not the way it happened. I did drug Kate, I admit it, but she was already injured. I did it to save her life."

"You did it to save her life?" Mac repeated dryly.

"Yes, yes," the doctor said, furtively looking up the stairs, his voice a hiss. Mac began to wonder if the guy was nuts. "It was the only way. I never intended for anyone to die, least of all poor Nellie."

"Wait a moment," Mac said. "You say Kate was already injured. If you didn't hurt her, then who did?"

The doctor looked up the stairs again, and this time a look of fear skittered across his eyes.

Mac turned, expecting to find that Nellie's killer had come in the kitchen door and made his way up the back stairs.

Kate stood there, both hands on the balustrade, Paula Priestly behind her. Mac felt his heart thump double time. "Kate! Are you okay?"

"I—"

"Kate thinks she's remembered what happened right be-fore she forgot everything," Paula Priestly interrupted. "I could tell by the expression on her face when I walked into the twins' suite just now. She was standing by the boys' cribs, but she looked at me and I knew."

"It all came back to me when I saw…when I saw Nellie," Kate said through trembling lips.

"Only you can't really trust your memory, can you, dear? Even your boyfriend knows it's undependable."

"He's not my—"

"Of course he is. I saw the way he looked at you. Our boy dead only two months and you're already in bed with another man. But that's the kind of woman you are, isn't it? That's the kind of woman who trapped our poor boy and then had the audacity to think she could waltz away with control over my son's trust fund *and* his children."

"No. It's not like that."

Mac had had enough. "We're leaving," he said, starting up the stairs to help Kate retrieve her kids, aware that in so doing, he was drawing a line in the sand and stepping over it. This was where his career in law enforcement ended. He didn't give one single damn.

Those kids were Kate's, and hence, they were his. All four of them were going to leave this house together or not at all.

"I can't move," the love of his life whispered.

That's when Mac saw the tiny silver gun Paula Priestly held pressed against the back of Kate's head.

"I BOUGHT THIS GUN for my protection," Paula said. "Officer Dryer suggested it after we had a break-in a few months ago. You remember, Daniel, you were away at one of your conferences and I was here alone."

"Now, Paula—" Dr. Priestly began, but his wife ignored him.

"Our daughter-in-law keeps breaking into our home, threatening to take the children."

With the muzzle jammed against the back of her skull and

the stranglehold Paula had on her upper arm, Kate knew she was trapped. Behind her lay her sleeping babies. In front of her, down that graceful flight of stairs, stood Mac, holding a gun, his gaze unwavering. *Mac...*

He was as trapped as she was.

And it was her fault. She shouldn't have come back here. And then she thought of the twins sleeping just a few feet away and knew she'd had no choice—she'd had to come. Her fault was in leaving without them the first time.

"There's not a court in the world that would blame me for shooting her and you, too, Mr. MacBeth," Paula said. "Especially since I called the police soon after your first visit and expressed my concern that you might come again. Look at the way you're waving that gun at my poor husband."

"Why don't we both just put our guns away," Mac said calmly.

But he didn't know what Kate knew. It had all come back to her as she crouched in her laundry room, staring into Nellie's dead eyes. The interlude with Paula that Kate had recalled as merely unpleasant, had actually been horrific, laced with scathing vitriol and threats of violence. Not from Dr. Priestly, but from Paula. Kate had reacted to Paula's unexpected rage by announcing she was taking her babies far away. She'd turned to go collect them.

And then came the shove, from right here atop the stairs, the tumble down to the bottom, the pain and confusion when she opened her eyes and wasn't sure where she was or at whom she was gazing, until a man with gray eyes approached her with a needle and she was powerless to resist...

"I would be a fool to unarm myself with a man like you in my house," Paula said.

"Gloria and Eduardo will be back soon," Kate said.

"Don't you wish!" Paula scoffed. "No, dear, they just left and the market is up in Key Largo." She jabbed the gun hard into Kate's head and added, "Tell your boyfriend to put his gun on the third step and move away, Kate. Go on, tell him. You know I'll do what I must to protect my family."

And with that, she shoved Kate. Too scared to scream, Kate felt herself falling. Memories of the last fall came back with blinding clarity. At the last moment, Paula grabbed her by the collar and hauled her back. Kate grabbed her throat as her gaze met Mac's. She pleaded silently with him to hold on to his gun, to protect himself and save her children from these fiends.

He stepped forward and set his gun on the third step.

"That's better," Paula said. As she forced Kate ahead of her, she added, "Kate has an ornery streak. I believe it's inevitable for a woman with her distasteful background. Wouldn't you agree, Daniel?"

"My dear," Dr. Priestly said softly. "There's no need for a gun. There's been enough violence. We can talk or…something."

"Dr. Priestly is a mild-tempered man," Paula said proudly. "Ask anyone." She rested the muzzle against the top of Kate's spine and added, "You don't want Charlie and Harry to wake up to the sound of gunfire, do you Kate? Daniel, pick up Mr. MacBeth's gun."

Kate made a steady but slow descent of the stairs as Daniel Priestly picked up Mac's gun and held it like he might hold a ticking bomb.

"My dear husband doesn't like firearms," Paula said.

"They don't seem to bother you," Mac said.

"A good wife knows how to make up for her husband's

shortcomings. I know it sounds old-fashioned nowadays, but trust me, the power in a family is always the woman. Always."

"She has been manipulating all of us for years," Kate said as she took the stairs one at a time, her gaze glued to Mac's, watching for some sign that he had a plan. "She told Danny I cheated on him. She told Dr. Priestly that I made Danny's life miserable. She told me that Dr. Priestly hated me. She's been like some Machiavellian puppeteer, hiding behind counterfeit smiles, pulling strings to make all of us jump. She's the one who disapproved of Danny to the point he married just to spite her. She's the one who wanted to kill me."

"Don't give me all the credit," Paula said. "Daniel came up with the idea of a hired gun."

"This is becoming an untenable situation," Dr. Priestly said, Mac's gun now gripped tight with both hands. It appeared the doctor wasn't sure who he wanted to shoot more, Mac or his wife.

Kate met her father-in-law's gaze. "Sir, please. Your wife is…sick. Surely you can see she needs help. Give Mac back his gun—"

Paula's small but lethal weapon came down on top of Kate's head with a perfectly aimed thump that set stars to spinning. Kate stumbled on the stairs and fell, hitting her knee, pitching forward, caught at the last moment by two sturdy hands that had to belong to Mac. They both tumbled backward until the wall stopped them just short of crashing to the floor. The painting on the wall rattled against the paneling as Mac steadied her.

And for the instant his hands were in contact with her skin, Kate felt a surge of strength. Her heart soared.

Paula barked, "Both of you stay right there!"

Reality hit with a bang. Kate tried to open her eyes; the world was still spinning and she felt woozy. But she knew that leaning on Mac would hamper his movement and he was their best chance. She forced her eyes open, fought the nausea and stood on her own two feet.

Dr. Priestly had moved away, as though to distance himself from the whole situation. Paula had descended within a few steps of the bottom. She pointed her gun at Mac's forehead. Mac was still and watchful, his big body tense and prepared for action. Kate was scared to death for him.

"It's true," Dr. Priestly said, addressing Mac as though Mac had the power to forestall the current disaster-in-the-making. His words gushed like water from a clogged gutter spout. "Paula was furious when Kate mentioned moving away. She went berserk and pushed Kate down the stairs. Thankfully, the servants were gone, so no one else saw what she'd done. Kate came to eventually, but she didn't know who she was or what had happened to her."

"*You* shot her full of something that guaranteed she'd stay that way," Paula snapped. "And you're the one who called Bellows."

"Casey Bellows had done some work for a doctor friend of mine, a man with one too many girlfriends," Dr. Priestly said as though discussing a consultation with a specialist to treat a medical emergency.

Mac said, "So you paid Bellows to drive Kate to Indiana? You were from Illinois originally, from Chicago, right? Billington is north of there. You must have known what an inhospitable place it could be in January."

"I just knew it was a good long distance from here," Dr. Priestly said.

"Daniel told Bellows to keep Kate sedated all the way," Paula said. "I'm the one who thought of switching to street drugs so her condition wouldn't be traced back to a doctor. I told Bellows to take his time getting her there and to make sure he stripped her down to her underwear before he released her."

Kate chanced a quick glance at Mac. That underwear had led them right back to this present moment.

And perhaps to their deaths.

"The drugs were strong," Dr. Priestly said, "but I knew eventually Kate would recover her memory and make her way back home."

"But by then, you'd have compromised her reputation, taken control of the boys and their trust funds, shut Kate out of her own life. Is that about right?" Mac demanded.

"It was better than killing her outright like *she* wanted to do," Dr. Priestly said, using Mac's gun to point at his wife.

"But why didn't you just explain away the fall as an accident?" Kate asked, curious as well as anxious to keep everyone talking instead of shooting.

"Because sooner or later you would have remembered it wasn't an accident. Then you'd have made accusations and involved the police."

"Before he had the chance to imperil your right to your kids," Mac added, his hand brushing hers.

"I have a reputation in this community to protect," Dr. Priestly said, recovering a little of his bravado. "The people of Boward Key need me."

"But no one would have believed me," Kate insisted. It was stunning to realize that two people were dead and she and Mac stood poised on the brink of extinction all because, basically, of this man's ego. "It would have been your word against mine."

"That's not the point," Paula said, "If we'd done it that way, you would eventually have taken the twins away. That was unacceptable. My son is dead. I will not let you have his sons as well, or control even one penny of my father's money. Unthinkable! If we'd just killed you, it would have all been over, but Daniel got cold feet and hired that man to take you away. And that would have worked, too, if Mr. MacBeth hadn't found you."

"I want it made perfectly clear that I never ordered Casey Bellows to kill anyone," Dr. Priestly said anxiously.

And his vehemence on this point gave Kate a spark of hope. Dr. Priestly was trying hard to blame everything on his wife. His wife was trying hard to blame the lion's share on her husband. Maybe she and Mac were going to walk away after all…

"A doctor saves lives, he doesn't take them," Dr. Priestly repeated. It was, apparently, his mantra. Did he really believe it absolved him of complicity?

"Which means *you* ordered the murder of Dr. Michael Wardman," Mac said, glaring at Paula Priestly.

"I never heard of the man."

"Maybe you know him better as the bum whose clothes wound up on Kate."

"Oh, him. Well, once Kate found *you* and *you* started asking questions, that bum became a liability."

"So, you see, that was Paula's idea," Dr. Priestly pointed out to Mac. "She just admitted it. You're witnesses. After you came into the picture, Paula took over with Bellows. All I did was have him take Kate to safety."

Paula Priestly tossed her perfectly coifed head. "Stop trying to blame all of this on me, Daniel," she said crossly. "Now, shoot these two. I've set the groundwork, we'll stage it like a break-in. They came here to kidnap our grandchildren and we had to defend those poor little hapless babies. By using Mr. MacBeth's gun, it'll look as though you overpowered him in a struggle. Heroic stuff. Go on…"

"I'll do no such thing. I'm not guilty of anything but compassion."

"We're both into this up to our eyeballs," Paula said. "Don't kid yourself."

"But a doctor saves lives, he—"

"Give it a rest," Paula spat.

Dr. Priestly looked about the foyer as though searching for a misplaced resolution to his current predicament. He finally said, "Then we'll find Bellows. He'll know what to do—"

"Bellows," Paula scoffed, coming the rest of the way down the stairs. "He was supposed to make sure Kate never got back to Florida. He screwed that up. Then he was supposed to make sure she never stepped foot in this house. He screwed that up, too. The only one Bellows has managed to kill since he got rid of that bum up in Billington is Nellie and I bet he only killed her because she was in the wrong place at the wrong time. The man is hopeless. I don't plan on paying him another penny."

"Well now, I'm real sorry to hear that," a deep voice announced.

MAC HAD BEEN SO caught up in the present that he'd all but forgotten about Nellie's killer.

The wake-up call came in the form of the man himself, entering from the direction of the kitchen, holding in his good hand what appeared to be the same gun he'd fired at Mac just a few minutes before. The dark hilt of a knife jutted above the scabbard tied around his right thigh. Despite his cavalier tone of voice, the man looked to be teetering on the verge of an eruption.

Paula Priestly didn't miss a beat. "Oh, good, you're here, Bellows," she said. "Take Mr. MacBeth's gun from Dr. Priestly, won't you?" Gesturing at Kate and Mac, she added, "Shoot them."

Bellows said, "I've got my own gun. And then there's my knife." Leering at Kate, he added, "You like knives, don't you, sweetheart?"

A small cry escaped Kate's lips and Mac felt a tidal wave of fury aimed solely at the man in front of him. In that moment, he knew this bastard better kill him first because the second he tried to hurt Kate, Mac would take him out. He wasn't sure how, but he would.

The vengeance pinching Bellows's narrow features was proof positive of the trouble he felt Kate had caused him. That undoubtedly had been the reason he'd given up trying to kill her with a knife and switched to a more dependable long-distance weapon like a gun. Given half a chance, Bellows would carve Kate into small pieces and enjoy doing it.

Just let him try.

Bellows glanced at Paula and added, "Besides, you just fired me."

"And now I'm rehiring you. I'll pay you double what I told you before."

Bellows's eyes lit up with greed. "Triple," he said.

"Whatever. Just get it over with. Oh, and try to make it look like you struggled. Just be sure to use Mr. MacBeth's gun. Give it to him, Daniel."

Doctor Priestly blew his last chance for redemption as he handed Mac's gun to Nellie's killer. Bellows had to tuck the weapon into his waistband before he could accept Mac's revolver. He aimed Mac's gun at Kate and smiled.

And Mac suddenly understood Paula Priestly's ploy. You had to hand it to the woman—she thought fast on her feet.

When the law arrived in a few minutes, summoned by a distraught call from the mistress of the house, they would find Mac and Kate dead, killed by the same man who carried a knife stained with Nellie's blood. Paula would tell the cops that Bellows had broken into her house and that while Bellows took Mac's gun from him, she'd managed to sneak off and get her own gun, which she then used to shoot Bellows. Tragically, she would be too late to save Mac and Kate.

Ultimately, Paula would shift all blame and any unanswered questions onto Bellows, who would be way too dead to argue the fine points.

Couldn't Bellows see what was coming?

Was he consumed with revenge, or was he just stupid?

Kate closed her eyes.

Mac waited until he heard the click of the hammer. In the instant it took Bellows to register that the chamber of Mac's gun was as empty as Paula Priestly's heart, Mac sprang at the woman, gripped her hand, and swung her arm. By the time he took aim at Bellows, the killer had instinctively reverted to his knife, launching it in the same instant that Mac pressed down on Paula's trigger finger with a force born of cold hatred.

Bellows took a bullet in the forehead just as his knife tore through tender flesh.

Kate screamed and fell to the floor.

THE AMBULANCE left without sirens. The knife, intended for Mac, had instead pierced Paula Priestly's carotid artery, and despite the administrations of her frantic husband, she'd bled to death in seconds.

There was no need for sirens.

Dr. Priestly sat in the back of the squad car, head bent. As police combed the crime scene, Mac and Kate found a bench in the front yard on which to sit. Harry, whom Kate held, spoke gobbedlygook to his mother. Charlie was sound asleep in Mac's arms.

Not that he could yet tell the difference between the boys. All he knew was that this was the first time in his life he'd held a slumbering baby, and that it felt—dare he even think it?—good. Really good. Comfortable and fulfilling, somehow, very satisfying.

He glanced at Kate who had her arms wrapped tightly around Harry. He was relieved to see that she appeared to be almost completely recovered from the dead faint that had protected her from watching Paula Priestly die. Only the pale cast to her lightly tanned skin remained, and as the sunlight hit her face, Mac knew even that would soon change.

Officer Dryer ambled over, surrounded by a cloud of smoke. While Mac couldn't read the policeman's expression, he felt one thing was certain: Boward Key would be buzzing about what happened here for weeks, months, even years to come.

"I'll need you both to drop by headquarters tomorrow to go over your statements again," Dryer said, stamping out his cigarette with the toe of his shoe. When he caught sight of Mac's pointed glare, he picked up the butt and turned back to look toward the police car. "I never would have dreamed that a man like the doc would get involved in something like this."

"He's a proud man with a huge ego," Mac said. "In my experience, they're the worst kind."

"And Paula Priestly. I can't hardly believe any of it. If the doc hadn't started blabbing, I might have hauled you two off to jail."

"I hope you aren't waiting for us to be grateful to him," Mac said.

Dryer shook his head. "Nah. I can't believe you went in there with an empty gun. That could have backfired on you."

Mac shrugged. "My ammunition was back in the motel. I figured an empty gun was better than nothing. Besides, Kate was in there, I wasn't really thinking straight."

"Well, it all worked out. Sort of."

Mac got the feeling Officer Dryer would have found a scene that included Mac and Kate slain by a mad killer who had then been shot by the wife of the most prestigious doctor in town more to his liking.

Tough.

"Did you get the message I left this morning asking you to fingerprint my motel room?" Mac asked. "There should be a good set on the chair."

"I just got a call from the lab. The prints belong to a two-bit legman, name of Seymor Boyd, works for a Vegas high roller everyone calls the Boston Olive for reasons unknown," Dryer said.

Mac smiled. "Seymor, huh? No wonder he preferred Elvis."

Dryer grunted. "We've got an APB out on Seymor and Nevada police are looking for Olive. We'll get 'em." He tipped his hat at Kate and plodded back to the house as the squad car holding Dr. Priestly pulled out of the driveway. Mac watched

Kate's gaze follow the receding red lights until they were no longer in view. As tears spilled over her cheeks, Harry reached up and patted her face.

She kissed his pudgy fingers and, casting Mac an under-the-eyelash look, said, "I want to load my kids into a car and run away from here." Her grasp on her son was so tight it might take the jaws of life to save the poor kid from his mother's love.

"I don't blame you," Mac said, but his heart seized. What would he do if she ran away? Return to Billington, assuming Confit won his election, take a job he'd never have the heart to do without her at his side, go on as if he'd never met her? Die inside?

"I have an alternative," he whispered.

She waited.

"Come back to Billington with me."

She looked at him, her lips curved into a beautiful smile. "Oh, Mac, wouldn't that be wonderful?"

"I've been offered the job of chief of police," he added. "Of course, it's kind of an iffy offer at this point, but who knows?"

"You should take it."

"I'm considering it," he told her. "I just thought that maybe you should have some input into where you spend the rest of your life."

As her smile wilted, he realized she wasn't going to come home with him.

"Kate—"

"Hush," she told him.

"No. I can't hush." He looked so deep in her eyes that he could see her soul and added, "I love you."

She smiled faintly. "You've only known me a week and a half."

"I knew how I felt about you in a day and a half," he said.

"We've both acted rashly in our pasts. We've both thought we were in love before."

"Not like this," he protested.

"No, not like this," she said, nodding. Almost shyly, she added, "I love you, too, Mac. How could I not love you?"

Thank heavens he'd read her wrong. He started to gather her and Harry into what would have to pass for a hug, seeing as Charlie took up most of his lap and all of one arm, but she held him off.

"All my life I've been running," she said as Harry squirmed and she relaxed her hold on him. She cast Mac a quick glance and added, "It's time for me to stop."

He furrowed his brow. "Loving me isn't running—"

"Well, you see, how do I know that for sure? Running off with you is what I want desperately to do. Desperately."

"Then—"

"But the boys need to stay right here in the only home they've ever known, at least for a little while, Mac. There have been so many shattering changes in their lives. They need stability. The three of us need time."

"Then I'll stay with you," he said.

She touched his cheek and smiled. "It's too soon for that," she whispered.

He started to protest and then he remembered what she'd said before they found Nellie's body, that he didn't trust her in the important ways. It hadn't made sense then, but now he thought he understood. He had to trust her to love him. Trust her to want him. Ultimately, he had to trust the fact that he deserved this from her, that being loved was his right, just as loving others was his privilege.

"Will you give me this time?" she said.

"Can I fly down here every few days? Will you teach me to swim? Can I teach the boys how to fish?"

She laughed as tears filled her eyes. As she buried her head against his shoulder, he put his arm around her and closed his eyes. For a moment, he was floating in a paradise, and somehow, Kate was both anchor and magic carpet.

When their lips met, he forgot everything else. They had survived; it was a miracle. All he wanted, all it seemed he had ever wanted, was to kiss her, to make her his. He didn't care about her past or his own, either. They would help each other come to grips with remembered pain, they would help each other find joy in forever.

No doubt half the police force of Boward Key was watching, but he didn't care. He needed this kiss more than any kiss he'd ever needed in his whole life and he could feel that Kate needed it, too. It lasted until Harry's babble distracted them both.

As the tiny boy pointed at a nearby tree and chattered like a squirrel about something or other, Mac looked down at the sleeping child in his lap and felt a sense of belonging he'd never experienced before. And a sense of excitement. The next few months would be full of discoveries for all of them.

Kate caught him gazing at her. "Did I thank you for saving me?" she whispered.

But he wondered this: *Who had saved whom?*

Epilogue

Ten months later

Kate took a deep breath.

The past few months had been a maelstrom. While the legalities of the disasters Daniel and Paula Priestly had set in motion might take years to settle, Kate felt her part was just about over. All that remained of her first marriage was her boys' trusts, and those were being taken care of by a nice, impartial law firm. She, herself, wanted nothing from her late husband's estate or from her former father-in-law.

What she wanted was now in her grasp. It didn't escape her knowledge that everything that had happened to her had led to the present moment. There was no denying that not all paths to the future were landscaped thoroughfares. Hers had been unpaved, bumpy, painful, but she had survived.

She heard the music start and her pulse raced.

This was the beginning.

Billington in November was chilly, but the inside of Aunt Beatrice's house was warm and comforting, just as it had been the first time she stepped foot in it so many months before. She smoothed the silk skirt of her wedding gown and took a step.

Kate walked alone between the rows of chairs set up in the large living room, even though her father and brother had flown in from Oregon for the ceremony. She didn't want anyone giving her away. She'd belonged to the man she was about to marry since the first moment he caught her in his arms. The last few months had cemented their feelings for each other. She was already his; this was a formality.

And there he was, Billington's new chief of police, gazing at her, the smile on his face reflected in his eyes. Her Mac. Strong, vulnerable, hers. She felt her heart flutter as she looked at him. His big hands rested on the top of two blonde heads. Harry and Charlie, adorable in little black tuxedoes, leaned back against Mac's legs, totally at ease though their wide eyes hinted at an underlying excitement.

After all, they'd been promised cake.

"Mommy!"

Harry broke free and ran down the aisle toward Kate. She caught his hand just as Charlie joined them, so in the end, she didn't walk down the aisle alone, instead she was escorted by her two small sons.

Mac's smile grew even broader as Kate reached his side, and she felt her love for him consume her heart.

This was the beginning.

HARLEQUIN®
INTRIGUE®

Opens the case files on:

Unwrap the mystery!

January 2005
UNDERCOVER BABIES
by ALICE SHARPE

February 2005
MOMMY UNDER COVER
by DELORES FOSSEN

March 2005
NOT-SO-SECRET BABY
by JO LEIGH

April 2005
PATERNITY UNKNOWN
by JEAN BARRETT

Follow the clues to your favorite retail outlet!

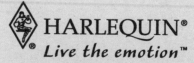

HARLEQUIN®
Live the emotion™

www.eHarlequin.com

Like a phantom in the night
comes an exciting promotion from

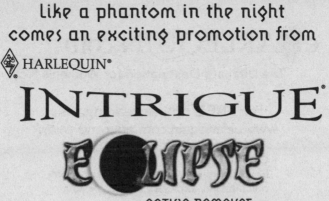

HARLEQUIN®

INTRIGUE®

ECLIPSE

GOTHIC ROMANCE

Look for a provocative
gothic-themed thriller each month
by your favorite Intrigue authors!
Once you surrender to the classic
blend of chilling suspense and
electrifying romance in these
gripping page-turners, there will
be no turning back....

Available wherever Harlequin books are sold.

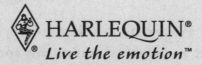

HARLEQUIN®
Live the emotion™

www.eHarlequin.com

HIE3

eHARLEQUIN.com

The Ultimate Destination for Women's Fiction

For **FREE online reading,** visit
www.eHarlequin.com now and enjoy:

Online Reads
Read **Daily** and **Weekly** chapters from
our Internet-exclusive stories by your
favorite authors.

Interactive Novels
Cast your vote to help decide how these
stories unfold...then stay tuned!

Quick Reads
For shorter romantic reads, try our
collection of Poems, Toasts, & More!

Online Read Library
Miss one of our online reads?
Come here to catch up!

Reading Groups
Discuss, share and rave with other
community members!

For great reading online,
visit www.eHarlequin.com today!

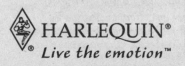

If you enjoyed what you just read,
then we've got an offer you can't resist!

Take 2 bestselling
love stories FREE!
Plus get a FREE surprise gift!

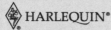

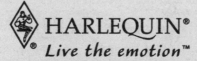

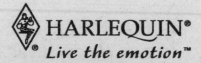